Praise for Frost Bite

"Fast-paced, clever, and nostalgic, *Frost Bite* single-handedly proves that Angela Sylvaine is a major rising star in the horror genre. This book's even got its own fabulous '90s playlist. Be still, my horror heart."

—Gwendolyn Kiste, Lambda Literary and Bram Stoker Award-winning author of *Reluctant Immortals* and *The Rust Maidens*

"*Frost Bite* is propulsive, wonderfully weird and joyously nostalgic. Loved this coming of age, speculative novel!"

—Erika T. Wurth, author of *White Horse*

"Sylvaine unleashes a horde of little horrors on the prairie in this infectiously fun creature feature, oozing with '90s nostalgia and heartland heart."

—Brian McAuley, author of *Curse of the Reaper*

"A gleeful romp through blood-drenched snow. Sylvaine's debut is both bone-chilling and heart-warming at once, equal parts nostalgia and fresh spins on classic tropes—a coming-of-age horror perfect for readers of any age."

—Lindy Ryan, Bram Stoker Award-nominated editor of *Into the Forest* and author of *Bless Your Heart*

"Fun as hell! *Frost Bite* is a campy, wild blend of *Gremlins* and *Invasion of the Body Snatchers*. As always, Angela Sylvaine delivers endless gore and laughs."

—Drew Huff, author of *Free Burn*

"The best books are the ones that offer big concepts without letting them get in the way of the story's heart: its characters. Angela Sylvaine's *Frost Bite* does exactly that. Sure, there's a crashed meteor and alien-infested prairie dogs causing chaos and memory loss into a North Dakota town's residents, but more importantly, there's Realene struggling to care for her mother with dementia, and Nate reeling from an abusive relationship. Sylvaine pairs these heavy moments with absurd '90s horror pulp to wicked effect. You think you know what you're going to get with *Frost Bite*? Trust me, it's all that and a bag of chips."

—Alex Ebenstein, author of *Melon Head Mayhem*

"Funny, terrifying, nostalgic, and full of heart, one bite will have you up all night! *Frost Bite* blends horror and sci-fi with '90s nostalgia to produce a truly unique reading adventure that's both horrifying and fun! This is my most anticipated fall release!"

—Meagen Dallner, Books Are Awesome, Parker, Colorado

FrostBite

Content Warnings

Death, Animal Death (Non-Domestic), Graphic Imagery, Violence, Addiction, Dementia, References to Domestic Violence, Implied Child Death, Death of a Parent, References to Child Abuse, and Profanity

Reader discretion is advised.

Edited by Rob Carroll
Book Design and Layout by Rob Carroll
Cover Art by Eric Hibbeler
Cover Design by Rob Carroll

ISBN 978-1-958598-03-0 (paperback)
ISBN 978-1-958598-39-9 (eBook)
ISBN 978-1-958598-40-5 (audiobook)

darkmatter-ink.com

FrostBite

Angela Sylvaine

DARK
MATTER
INK

For Zach, My Sweetie

One

COLD SEEPED INTO Realene's bedroom through the cracked bay window, frost spreading in bursts along both sides of the glass. She perched on the window seat, a thick, maroon knit cap stitched with 'Class of '97' pulled over her head, and one of her Oma's colorful hand-made Afghans wrapped around her shoulders. She dangled one denim clad leg over the narrow perch to thump against the headboard of her bed.

Their lot was on the outermost ring of Plainview Trailer Park, the backyard separated from an open field by a two-lane road that turned to gravel beyond the perimeter of the park. She drove that dead-end gravel road sometimes, her only company the billow of dust and ping of tiny pebbles on the car's undercarriage.

Her bedroom took up the back end of the trailer, and she stared out at the snow-packed landscape, the stark, endless whiteness of it glowing beneath the moonlit sky. In summer, she listened to the chatter of the prairie dogs that made their burrows in the field, but tonight they were burrowed deep underground in hibernation, and would be for the rest of winter.

"Another gorgeous North Dakota night," she said, holding the cordless phone to her ear. The wind picked up outside, cutting through the corrugated steel shell and wood-paneled walls to drop the temperature inside.

"You'll be mackin' on all those super tan coeds by next fall, yeah?" Nate said in that irritatingly positive way of his.

"Not likely. Found the milk in the cabinet and the detergent in the fridge today. Ma's getting worse." Her scholarship to Arizona State seemed like a cruelty now, a glimpse into a future she'd never achieve.

"She's lucky to have you, Rea, and you're lucky to have her, too."

"I know." She figured he was thinking of his own mom, who'd stopped talking to him after his asshole dad had kicked him out. "And stop trying to distract me. I'm clearly trying to wallow in self-pity."

"It's been five months of wallowing, though."

Her fingers tightened on the handset, the plastic creaking in her grip. "I wasted years studying, taking AP classes, doing that shit intern gig at the hospital, all for nothing. I think I'm entitled to a few months."

"They're holding your scholarship for a year. Plenty could change by then."

"Sure, sure," she said. "Too bad Lutherans don't do that laying on of hands stuff. I could sign Ma up for a healing on Sunday before the potluck. A quick cure from JC himself, followed by a healthy portion of Mrs. Felton's famous tater tot hotdish."

"Don't joke, that hotdish is truly sent from heaven. And you don't have to go evangelist-style, I saw an infomercial where you can send away for a miracle."

Realene laughed. "For the low, low price of nineteen ninety-five, I bet."

"Well, to start. As Reverend Zebediah would say, miracles aren't cheap, ya know?"

"He did not actually say that."

"Oh, he sure did. Has my mom believing salvation is only worth what you pay for it."

"Her and half the town. Irene's been tryin' to convert me and Ma ever since Dad died." Realene sighed. "Seriously, though, I can see how they get people. If I really thought saying some prayers and writing a check would help me get outta here, I'd sell off Oma's China and get down on my knees."

"Come on, it's not that bad here. And you still have me, right?"

Something flashed outside, drawing her gaze to the darkened sky, to a sizzling trail racing through the stars. She used one hand to wipe away the fog of her breath on the glass. "You see that? Outside?"

"Course not." The basement apartment he rented only had those emergency access window wells, and this time of year, they'd be piled nearly to the top with snow. "What's to see?"

"Shooting star." She watched the light cross the sky in a golden arc before closing her eyes and silently repeating the rhyme. *Star light, star bright, first star I see tonight. I wish I may, I wish I might, have this wish I wish tonight.*

"What'd you wish for?"

"Can't tell or it won't—" She gasped. The star crashed into the field across the street, with an explosive bang that sent a rumble through the ground, shaking the trailer. "Hey, I'll call ya back."

She slipped from the window seat and dropped the phone into its charging cradle, throwing the Afghan on the same twin bed she'd had since she was a kid. Her wood-paneled walls were still plastered with anatomy diagrams and Nirvana posters. But Kurt killed himself three years ago, and her pre-med scholarship came a week before Ma's diagnosis of early onset Alzheimer's. It was the room of a kid who'd looked ahead to a future of possibilities, not an adult faced with the harsh realities of life. But redecorating would mean admitting she was there to stay.

Her knee-length, hooded, navy-blue parka hung from the bedpost, and she threw it on over her sweatshirt and jeans. Already, she began to doubt what she'd seen. But she'd felt the rumble of the ground as the star slammed into the field, could still see the blaze of the fiery light across the sky. Skin tingling with anticipation of what she might discover, she walked down the narrow hallway past her bathroom and the back door. She stopped in the cramped kitchen, gripping the back of one of the vinyl chairs that sat at the Formica table, brutal reality sapping her excitement.

The lingering scent of their depressing supper—turkey TV dinners—filled the kitchen, whose cracked and yellowing linoleum transitioned to the thread-bare orange carpet of the living room, where their box TV strobed in the darkness from the far wall, playing an old episode of *Laverne and Shirley*. In the adjacent corner, their small Christmas tree twinkled with multi-colored lights. Canned laughter mingled with Ma's soft snores, and Realene prayed she wouldn't wake up.

Ma had fallen asleep in her recliner again, the footrest extended and their tabby cat, Pumpkin, snuggled at her side, his head sticking out from beneath the blanket on Ma's lap. The lumpy chair was once her dad's favorite spot, leaving the sofa for Realene and Ma. Since the dementia had worsened, she preferred the chair, insistent on keeping it warm for the husband she thought would walk through the door at any moment.

The need to escape gripped Realene tight, and she hurried past.

"Louie? Is that you?" Ma asked, her voice groggy with sleep.

He'd been dead two years now, but maybe it wasn't so bad Ma still lived in a world where he was alive. Their wedding picture hung on the wall behind the recliner, Ma in a simple white dress made in a rush after dad had proposed before being deployed to Vietnam, and he in his green dress uniform and cap. They were so young and happy, their whole lives ahead of them.

Realene felt that way once too. Clearing her throat, she said, "It's me, Ma. I'm goin' outside to check on something."

"You better not be sneaking cigarettes again, Realene Marie."

In junior high, Ma had caught Realene puffing on a stolen butt from her dad's ashtray. Realene had been convinced that smoking would make her cool, but she later realized that it just makes you dead from lung cancer.

"*I Dream of Jeannie* is starting," Realene said with a silent thank you for *Nick at Nite*. Old things, familiar things, were what tethered Ma to reality.

"Oh, I love that Larry Hagman. He's so handsome," Ma said, giggling. "Don't tell your father I said that." She raised one hand to fiddle with the jeweled earring that hung from one sagging earlobe. Even when she forgot to shower or brush her hair or change her clothes, she never went without earrings, one of dozens gifted from Realene's dad. At least once a month, he'd fish a gift from his pocket with a sly smile, and Ma would act surprised every single time.

"It'll be our secret, Ma." Realene swallowed past the lump in her throat.

She walked through a doorway into the entry room, an add-on her dad built. Metal shelves stacked with tools, camping supplies, ice melt, and other crap lined the back wall. Her childhood bike was leaned against a side wall, behind an assortment of shovels. Already shivering at the prospect of the sub-zero temperature outside, she slipped on the insulated duck boots she'd left to dry in the plastic boot tray near the door, wrapped a scarf around her neck and the lower half of her face, zipped her coat to her chin, and tugged the hood over her hat before putting on her gloves. She closed her eyes, picturing that blazing light crossing the sky.

A gust of icy wind hit her when she opened the door, but she pressed forward, stepping onto the worn wooden porch. Directly ahead in the field, a billow of white smoke rose into the sky from the impact of the shooting star. Her pulse skipped in anticipation.

A door banged open, and their neighbor, Calvin, peered out at her from the back door of his trailer, clad in a red flannel and long johns. "What's all that racket?" he called, the long, white whisper of his comb-over flapping in the wind.

Prickling with irritation at another delay, she said, "Something crashed. Goin' to check it out."

"Should I come with ya?" A plump, stuffed squirrel was tucked beneath one arm, its tail extending in an exaggerated curl. She'd dropped off a pie for him on Thanksgiving and discovered his obsession with taxidermy.

"I'll be fine."

"It's colder than a penguin's pecker out here. Sure you don't need help?"

She couldn't help but snort a laugh at the charming mental picture that conjured. "I'm sure. You go on in." She didn't stay long enough for him to protest, descending the porch steps and trudging through their backyard and past the small shed she'd helped her dad build at least a decade ago. They were halfway through December, and the snow was the hard, crunchy kind that wouldn't melt for months.

The wind bit at her exposed skin, and she lowered her chin as she crossed the seldom traveled road that ran behind the trailer park. Her boots sunk into the drifts that blanketed the field. By the time she reached the spot where the shooting star collided with the earth, sweat dotted her face beneath her scarf.

A bowl-shaped crater at least twelve feet in diameter had been blasted into the ground, revealing the dirt beneath the packed layers of ice and snow. In the center of the crater sat a boulder-sized rock, faint wisps of smoke still rising from its surface.

"Whoa." Sitting down, she let her feet dangle over the rim of the crater. A faint heat seeped through her jeans. The projectile must have been blazing hot to burrow such a deep hole in the frigid ground. She slid down the slope and approached the rock. The mottled surface reflected the sheen of the full moon, its color seeming to shift between gunmetal silver and deep purple.

A hissing sounded from inside the object and Realene moved closer, reaching out with one, trembling gloved hand. Tightness filled her chest as she considered the immenseness of the universe, a universe where she was no more than an insignificant blip of life. Not exactly a cheerful thought, but a thrill of excitement filled her at being the first person to witness this celestial object up close, to bask in its enormous power.

The hiss from inside the object rose in pitch, like a blazing hot kettle reaching a boil, and she froze, her fingers hovering inches away. Her eyes watered from the bite of the bitter wind, and she blinked away the ice crystals forming on her lashes, gaze fixed on the rock. A thunder-crack sounded, and the thing ruptured, splitting into two neat halves. With a yelp, she stumbled backward and fell, landing painfully on the hard ground.

The inside of the object looked much like the outside, that same mottled, metallic rock. Realene climbed to her feet, eager to touch the thing, to claim it somehow, though her brain argued that may not be the best idea. She stopped when thick, black liquid welled from the pores inside the rock, filling the air with the scent of burned motor oil. The stuff moved slowly, not dripping or pooling like a normal liquid; rather creeping along the cleaved surface. The cold air is freezing the stuff, she told herself, until the rivulets hit the exposed dirt and skittered across the ground in a web-like pattern. Realene gasped and backed up before the sludge hit her boots, slipping but managing to stay upright. She watched as the gunk stopped and seeped into the frozen soil to disappear.

The wheeze of her rapid breathing echoed in her ears as she crept backwards, eyes locked on the fallen star. The scent of burnt oil singed her nose as the last of the black sludge slithered from the rock and sunk into the earth. No evidence of the stuff remained. Beneath her feet, the ground rumbled, and she extended her arms to keep her balance. An aftershock from the impact, she thought. A high-pitched shriek, like that of a wounded animal, swelled from beneath the ground, mixing with the whistle of bitter wind, and she cringed.

"Well, shit," she said, trying to convince herself this whole situation was more funny than terrifying. "Can't imagine I'm getting my wish now."

Two

AFTER A RESTLESS night's sleep, Realene woke excited for the first time in months. The meteor, or whatever it was, waited a few hundred feet from her trailer. She'd called the police the night before to report the crash landing, and everyone would be clamoring to hear about her discovery.

Media, police, scientists, and curious townspeople blocked the view of the crater, but she managed to shoulder her way through the crowd. The meteor's landing area was roped off with caution tape, a task that required chipping away at the winter-hardened soil to insert a ring of metal posts, and a police officer manned the perimeter.

Clad in a balaclava and black coat marked with a starred patch signifying his authority, he raised one hand as she approached. "This is a restricted area, ma'am."

"I called last night. I live right over there. I'm the one who reported the landing." Her smile wilted at his serious expression.

"We received a number of calls, ma'am, and this area is for authorized personnel only."

"But I—"

"Return to your home, ma'am." He fixed Realene with glare.

"Fine," she replied, and wove her way back through the crowd and into the road.

A cameraman filmed a woman with perfectly styled hair and puffy white earmuffs who spoke into a handheld microphone. "Reporting live from the Demise, North Dakota, this is Shelley Schraeder. Stay tuned throughout the day for breaking news from WDIZ."

"All clear," the cameraman said, and Shelley lowered the microphone.

Realene recognized Shelley from the local news and angled toward her.

"Miss, hi, I saw the landing last night." She wished she'd taken the time to do her makeup, but she'd assumed she'd be talking to the police. Being on television, though, that was even better. "I live just over there, was the first one over to the crater."

Shelley smirked. "You and half the trailer park."

"But I really did discover it," Realene said. "Like, I almost touched the thing."

"Listen, hon, this is the biggest story of my career. If I handle it right, *20/20* will be beating down my door, but that's not going to happen with a bunch of b-roll of small town hicks."

Realene clenched her fists at her sides. "Listen, if you don't want to hear what I have to say, then I'll just go talk to someone else. You'll be sorry when—"

"Chief Andersen, can I get statement?" Shelley shoved Realene aside, causing her to slip and fall on the icy asphalt, pain blooming through her bruised tailbone. The cameraman and other media nearby eyed her, some holding back snickers.

Heat flaming up her neck and face, she got up and trudged through her backyard, not looking back. Once inside her trailer, she tore off her gloves and coat, leaving them in a pile on the floor, and kicked off her boots. Of course, no one would care what she had to say.

She stomped into the living room and stopped at the sight of Ma sitting on the carpet, wrapping paper, tape, and a small white box beside her.

"Oh, you're back," Ma said. She grabbed the box and clutched it to her chest. "Don't peek."

Realene's mood thawed. "You didn't get me another gift, did ya?" Ma had taken to wrapping items from around the house the last few weeks, everything from her own clothes to food from the cupboards.

Ma giggled. "You're really going to love this one. Your dad gave it to me before you were born." She winced when she tried to stand, and Realene took her elbow to help her up.

"Ma, you don't have to do that. I already have a dozen gifts under the tree."

"Oh, I know, but you deserve it, sweetie." Her eyes shone as she pushed the little white box into Realene's hands. "Here, open it now, I can't wait."

"Okay, okay." She removed the lid to find a heavy, silver ring with a large oval stone nestled on the cotton pad. "It's beautiful."

"It's a mood ring. Irene said they're getting popular again with you kids."

Realene didn't normally wear jewelry—the closest thing was the hairband she kept around her wrist for when she needed to tie her hair back—but she slipped the ring onto her middle finger and thought she might never take it off. The stone's color shifted to a bright green. "I love it."

"Wait 'til your dad sees how nice it looks on you." Ma's face crinkled with a wide smile. "You'll have to wait for the rest of your gifts though. No more until Christmas."

Realene pulled Ma into a hug, squeezing her tight, and wondering how many good days she had left.

The ring's stone turned black.

STANDING IN THE driveway beside her beat up Ford Escort and staring at the crowd of people that clogged the road between her yard and the field, Realene was forced to admit nothing had changed. The meteor was the most exciting thing to happen in Demise, maybe ever, and even though she had discovered it, no one cared. She was nothing more than a small town trailer park hick, and no wish would change that.

Since everything was the same, Friday meant breakfast and the Bingo Palace.

She finished scraping the frost from her windshield and climbed into her car, thankful it hadn't died since the battery needed replacing—the cables detached from the corroded terminals on a semi-daily basis. She tossed the combination brush-and-ice-scraper into the backseat.

"Got your dauber?" she asked, her previously wet hair now frozen in curly icicles that crinkled when she glanced at Ma in the passenger seat, where she sat bundled up in her tan, wool coat and blue knit scarf.

Ma reached for her souvenir canvas Mount Rushmore bag and managed to spill the contents on the floor. "Here it is," she said, holding up a plastic tube with a bright pink cap, her signature dauber. All the ladies in her Friday morning bingo group had their preferred color of ink, and pink was Ma's. The tradition was at least a decade old, and Realene always made sure to keep Ma well stocked with supplies, taking over the responsibility after her dad passed.

"It's my lucky day, today, I can feel it. Might have to take your father out for a steak dinner with my winnings." She grinned, her cheeks and nose rosy from the cold.

"Oh, yeah?" Realene said. "Where you gonna go?"

"Ponderosa, I think. They have an unlimited salad bar, and you can make your own ice cream sundaes," she said.

Realene smiled in spite of her mood. "He's going to be so excited."

Ma giggled, reaching up in an unconscious gesture to check her earrings. Today she'd chosen one of her favorite pairs, glossy rose buds with a clear gem dangling from one petal like a drop of spring rain. Fridays were often Ma's best day. The breakfast-and-bingo tradition was familiar, and it offered her an easy comfort.

"Ready, Lizzy?" Realene said, patting the dash. Her dad taught her to always name your vehicles, insisting they performed better that way, so she'd dubbed the Escort Elizabeth Blackwell, after the first woman in the U.S. to earn her medical degree. At the time, Realene believed she'd be an M.D. too, someday.

She exited Plainview, the scene of the meteor landing shrinking in her rearview mirror. On the same side of the road as the trailer park, she passed a neighborhood of older homes, including the one where Nate's parents, Dick and Sophia, still lived. She knew he preferred to be called Mr. Haugen or

Richard, because he told her as much every time she had the displeasure of meeting him. That's why she made sure to call him Dick. Sometimes she even shouted obscenities toward his house as she drove by, but she resisted with Ma in the car.

The landscape to the right consisted of field after field that had been surrendered to the prairie dog colonies. Without fail, each summer some local asshole would write into the community column for the *Demise Daily*, suggesting the farmland-ruining, disease-spreading vermin be eradicated. Luckily, the animal rights people managed to stop that from happening. Realene grew up with the prairie dogs in her backyard, and their frolicking and chatter only ever brought her happiness. She glanced in her rearview mirror at the crash site, hoping the shooting star hadn't done any damage to the colonies that populated the field.

Ma bent forward, humming "On the Road Again," as she piled her spilled belongings back into her bag. She glanced out the window. "Such a nice day out today."

"Yeah, heard on the news it's supposed to get up to ten degrees this afternoon."

"Oh, wonderful," she said, not picking up on the sarcasm in Realene's voice. Ma sat back and continued with her humming. Willie Nelson was Dad's favorite.

They approached the overpass that rose over the railroad tracks, and a green and white sign announced they were now entering the Demise city limits, population 4,944. The first white settlers to the area in the 1800s had apparently not been prepared for the severe weather and lack of drinkable water, and dozens perished that winter, earning the town its name. Every so often, some local politician would suggest they change the name to something more appealing, but it never went anywhere. North Dakotans wore the harsh conditions of their environment as a badge of honor, so why not be totally up front and name your town after literal death.

REALENE PULLED INTO one of the spaces along the front side of Gramma Butterwicks, a squat, tan building with faded red trim. The large windows that wrapped the building were decorated with white Christmas lights and offered a glimpse at the customers, mostly Ma's age, crowding the vinyl booths. Tacky plastic ferns hung from the ceiling between each table, and Realene wondered, not for the first time, who thought dust-collecting plastic plants were a good idea.

Ma's best friend, Irene, stood next to her rusted baby-blue Ford Bug, her perfectly curled brown hair unmoving in the breeze. She raised a mittened hand to wave, and it struck Realene how much younger she seemed than Ma, though they were the same age. Alzheimer's and the trauma of losing Dad aged Ma more than Realene realized.

Ma opened her door and stepped carefully from the car.

"Have fun," Realene called after her.

Ma crouched to peer through the open door. "Wish me luck."

"Luck and a steak dinner," Realene said, sending Ma into a fit of giggles as she closed the door.

Irene met Ma and ushered her into the restaurant, but didn't follow, instead rushing back to Realene's driver's-side door.

Realene rolled down the window. "Hey, Irene. How are ya?"

"Oh, you know, pretty good." Irene poked her head partially inside the vehicle.

Realene's nostrils were assaulted by the copious amounts of Aqua Net it took to keep Irene's hair helmet in place. "Cold out there. You don't have a hat?"

"Oh, I'll only be out a minute. Just got my hair done, so."

"Ah. What can I do for you, Irene?" Cold air gusted in through the open window, and Realene wished the woman would get to the point.

Irene lowered her voice. "We're havin' a special service today over at the church, what with it raining brimstone and all. I was hopin' you and your ma could make it."

"Brimstone? Do you mean the meteor?"

Irene stuck her whole head through the window. "Reverend Zebediah says the end times are here. There isn't much time left to repent, to show you're part of the worthy—"

Realene leaned farther away from Irene, from the menthol-cigarette breath now overtaking the hairspray for most offensive smell. "I saw it land, Irene. Definitely just a meteor, no fire or brimstone."

"Oh. Well, there've been other signs too. False prophets, and wars, and natural disasters. Not to mention loose morals. The reverend has been preaching about the signs the past few years, and wouldn't ya know, here they are. You and your ma, you're good people, and I wouldn't want to see you all burned up with the heathens."

"Loose morals and heathens, huh?" Realene's mouth twitched, but she managed not to laugh. "I appreciate the thought, Irene, but Ma likes Bethel Lutheran, been goin' there for years."

"Well, I'm sure they're very nice, but Reverend Zebediah says the seven plagues—"

Realene pasted a polite smile on her face. "Listen, I gotta get goin'. And don't you be talking about this judgment day conspiracy stuff in front of Ma."

Irene stood, her mouth agape. "Listen, now, I'm not one of those conspiracy nuts. There's a big difference between—"

"Okay, well, you have fun at bingo, and make sure to get her home by noon. No stoppin' by your church either, or I'll have to come in and make a big fuss to get her. I'm sure your reverend wouldn't like that very much." Realene rolled up the window and pulled out, leaving Irene standing in the parking lot, staring after the car.

"What a nut," Realene said, with a tolerant shake of her head. Irene could be a bit much, but she was good with Ma, and at least her theories about judgment day were better than an alien landing conspiracy. Heaven's Gate happened earlier that year, and Realene still remembered the images of those poor people lying on their cots in their matching outfits, convinced a Hale-Bopp-riding UFO would rescue them from Earth and deliver them to some alien paradise.

Realene drove down Dahl Street, one of four roads that ran east-west across town. All four were named for one of the settlers who'd perished that harsh winter more than a hundred years prior, which she'd always found a bit morbid. Dahl held many of the town's businesses, and she saw sign after sign capitalizing on the meteor. Leon's Auto Repair boasted 25% off body damage repairs for a 'Crash Landing Sale," HobbyShop advertised a Christmas special on binoculars and telescopes to watch the skies, Waldenbooks boasted of sales on books about space, and the Piggly Wiggly advertised "Everything You Need for your Meteor Party." Even the new Blockbuster video on Dahl and Main got in on the action, with posters for *Independence Day* and *Mars Attacks* featured in the brightly lit front windows.

Glancing at her dashboard clock, she decided she had enough time to stop in and grab a video for later, after Ma went to bed. Pulling up in front of the store, she left her car running with the heat on full blast, making sure her spare key was in her pocket before locking the car door. While there was an unspoken rule that one did not steal running cars in the middle of the North Dakota winter, you could never be too safe.

A bell dinged as she entered, and she gave a cursory smile to the girl behind the counter who chirped, "Welcome to Blockbuster Video." Realene strode past the full-sized cardboard cutout of Arnold Schwarzenegger from *Jingle All the Way*, shivering partially from the cold, partially from the thought of having to sit through an Arnold and Sinbad Christmas comedy.

A display labeled "Space Movies" had been set up on the side wall next to the new releases, and she scanned the shelves. The new releases advertised in the front window were all rented, their empty VHS display boxes left behind to mock her. She managed, however, to snag a copy of *Total Recall*, a much better Schwarzenegger option.

Snagging a box of Jujyfruits from one of the end-cap candy displays, she approached the checkout desk between the enter and exit doors. Pulling her Blockbuster card from her wallet, she set her items on the counter next to a little sign that said, "Be Kind, Rewind." The guy working glanced up from the computer.

"Realene, hi, wow. You look great." A pink flush crept up his neck, and he tugged at the bottom of his blue polo with yellow cuffs and collar.

She sucked in a breath. "Hey, Tony. How are ya?"

"Oh, good, good. You know, been here a couple months now, and it's pretty chill. They're making me a lead soon, I think. And there are Blockbusters everywhere, so when I finally get outta this hellhole, I'll be guaranteed a job."

"That's cool," Realene said. She slid her plastic-boxed video and candy across the counter and handed Tony her card. "Just this."

He scanned each item with the small hand-held scanner before returning it to its cradle. "I'll take care of the movie for ya. I get a free rental every day, so."

"Oh, you don't have to do that."

"You'll have to owe me one." He gave her a wink.

"So, how much then?" she asked.

"Oh, uh, ninety-nine cents for the candy." He gestured toward the parking lot at a motorcycle with the Misfits logo painted on the tank. "Been working on my bike, too, fixing her up with parts from my uncle's junkyard. She handles like a dream."

"Kinda cold for riding, isn't it?" She dug a dollar from her wallet and handed it to him, her eyes straying to the front door as if focusing on it would get her out of there faster.

"Nah, not if you're dressed right. Gotta be careful on the ice, but I know how to control her." He handed her a penny in change, and she threw it in the 'find a penny, leave a penny, need a penny, take a penny' tray. "So, crazy about the meteor, huh? Too bad it didn't blow the whole town off the map. That would have been something."

"It landed by my house, so pretty glad that didn't happen."

"Oh, sorry. I didn't mean you, you know. You're cool. I mean, you know, I wouldn't want you to die or anything." He cleared his throat. "Anyway, so you saw it. That's awesome."

"Yeah, yeah. It was pretty cool." She shrugged. "Blasted a hole in the ground at least six feet deep. I was actually the first one out there after the crash."

"Whoa, that's sick. I bet the reporters are like beating down your door, huh?"

She blushed this time, because wasn't that exactly what she'd been hoping for? "Nah, no one wants to hear from me."

"Tony, can you work returns?" It was the girl who'd welcomed Realene when she'd first walked into the store. She was just staring at the two of them now, annoyed hands on hips.

"Just a minute, Julie," Tony said.

"I better get goin' anyway," Realene said. "I'm meeting Nate for breakfast."

"Still hangin' out with him, huh? You guys like, a couple or something?"

"Just friends," she said, her words clipped. Why did everyone assume a guy and a girl had to be romantically involved?

"Oh, good—I mean, he's a cool guy." He picked up her video and candy and set them on the other side of the counter, past the alarm that would sound if anyone tried to leave with a video. "So, uh, I want to hear more about this whole meteor crash. Want to like, meet up at the lake later? A group of us are headin' out there to hang out, have some drinks, you know. We got a portable space heater for the back of the truck and everything."

She cringed, remembering the one time she'd gone out to Sauer Lake with him in high school. He was pretty cute, and he hated Demise as much as she did, which was a plus, but that date had been a huge mistake. "Uh, thanks anyway, but I have to work."

"Oh, okay, well, what're you doing—"

"Tony. Returns," Julie snapped.

Realene wanted to kiss the girl for interrupting and took the opportunity to grab the video and candy. "See you around."

Rushing outside, she fumbled with her key to unlock her door before making it inside and tossing her purchases on the passenger seat. She'd have to find somewhere else to rent videos. Not that Tony was the worst, but he couldn't seem to get it through his skull that she didn't like him, not like that. His interest in her meteor story had been nice, though.

Pulling onto Main Street, which started at Sauer Lake and continued all the way across town to the trailer park, she glanced in the rearview mirror toward the lake. Despite being a couple blocks behind her, she could still see the eerie mist that rose from the water's surface, hovering in the air. So salinated it didn't freeze, even in subzero temperatures, the lake was totally inhospitable to marine life.

Come to think of it, that was probably why she didn't have fond memories of her date with Tony. Mayor Opdahl had convinced the city council to stock the lake with some specially bred catfish, certain they would be a boon for fishing touristry, but the water was too salty for them. The night of Realene's date with Tony, they'd been sitting on the beach, getting drunk on Zima, when she made the terrible decision to kiss him. Right at that moment, hundreds of dead catfish washed up on shore, which promptly caused Realene to puke Zima onto their creepy little whiskered faces, and a bit onto Tony as well. After that incident, she gave up two things: Tony and seafood (even lutefisk, which for a Norwegian was sacrilege).

REALENE HEADED TOWARD McDonald's, glancing at her watch to make sure she still had time. She'd be cutting it close to grab food and get home in time to catch up with Nate, but Walt was usually cool if she rolled into work a few minutes late.

She passed Irene's church, Revelation Evangelical, previously known as Faith Evangelical. The large, windowless building was three-stories high, with a steepled roof. A large cross overlain with the number "7" was bolted to the brick exterior just above the main door. A one-story section of the building jutted out to one side, and half a dozen large, metal shipping containers sat behind the church. Even on Friday, cars packed the parking lot that sat before the building and directly off the road. The sign at the curb read "If I am a man of God, let fire come down from heaven and consume you and your fifty—2 Kings 1:10."

Realene thanked God her folks never got sucked into that church like Nate's parents had. The previous leader, Reverend Miller, had been a stand-up guy, often volunteering to call bingo on Fridays and always showing up at the Bethel's charity car wash to chip in a few bucks. He'd died several years back of a heart attack, despite being in his early forties and healthy. Zebediah, who'd been the assistant reverend, took over and changed the church's name to Revelation.

A white van with a speaker mounted on the roof, and that same cross-plus-seven symbol painted on the side, pulled out from the church parking lot, cutting in front of her.

She laid on her horn, shouting, "Watch it, asshole!"

Ahead of her, a deep voice, probably Zebediah, boomed from the speaker. "Witness the fire reigning down from the heavens. The end times are upon us. Repent, sinners. Repent or perish."

"Oh, for Christ sakes," she mumbled, slowing down to put space between her and the Revelation van.

The roads were pretty busy, typical for a weekday morning, and she ended up stopped at the light by Skateway, a metal warehouse-style building painted in rainbow stripes. Even they'd gotten into the meteor mania, their front sign advertising "Space Skate 4pm-8pm." For a second, she thought of going, even though Space Skate probably only meant they'd be running the disco ball. She and Nate loved hanging out at the rink in junior high, scrounging quarters from the coin returns of the arcade games when they didn't have enough money to rent skates. Two speakers mounted to the outside of the building belted out "The New Pollution" by Beck.

Humming the song long after she'd pulled away from the stop light, she continued to McDonald's and pulled into the drive-thru lane. The building was recently remodeled to add what they called a 'PlayPlace' to the front of the store, which consisted of a giant kid's area that featured a jungle gym and ball pit, visible behind floor-to-ceiling windows. It was still very early in the morning, but sugar-fueled children had already swarmed inside. The person in the van ahead of her, which thankfully had no speaker mounted on the roof, took a ridiculous amount of time ordering, and she tapped her fingers impatiently on the steering wheel. Maybe it hadn't been such a good idea to stop for a video. Finally, the van pulled ahead.

A teenaged voice squawked over the speaker, "It's going to be a while, dude."

Realene examined the van ahead of her and realized it boasted a Carpet Emporium logo.

"Damn it."

Vickie, the owner of Carpet Emporium, was notorious for keeping a real live tiger name Murray as a pet. In the summertime, she would load him into the bed of her pickup,—which had been outfitted with a cartoonishly large loop and chain to restrain the animal—and take him for spins around town.

Nate had spent a summer working at McDonald's and shared that Vickie liked to bring Murray through the drive thru, where she would order several dozen burger patties at a time.

The van rocked in place, and Realene doubted it was because of frisky teens. Murray growled from inside the vehicle, confirming her fears. Her watch told her she didn't have time to wait, so she pulled out of the lane to snake around the van. She made sure to give Vickie—whose teased, bleach-blonde hair made her look like an aging Poison groupie—a glare as she passed. Why the hell did a carpet store owner need a tiger? Why did anyone need a tiger? They belonged in the jungle, or at worst a zoo. And didn't Vickie realize lunch started after 10:30 a.m.? At least wait until then to request burgers. But Realene figured crazy, rich people who owned tigers could do whatever they wanted.

Pulling back into traffic, Realene headed for home. The town cemetery sat on one side of the road, and their largest park, adjacent to both the elementary and junior high schools, sat on the other. The playground was vacant, but a hockey rink had been erected at the edge of the park, defined by an oval of shoddy plywood that served as the rink's boards. The ground inside the rink had been flooded with water that would stay frozen all winter due to the frigid temperatures. A group of kids clad in winter coats and hats zoomed around the ice, shouting and slamming one another into the boards.

The rinks were set up by the city at all three of the town's parks, hockey being the sport of choice, for boys at least. Girls were expected to figure skate, but Realene never had an interest in either, couldn't understand the appeal of winter sports. Another reason why Arizona was so perfect for her.

Movement at the edge of the park caught her eye, and she slowed, peering out her passenger side window at a group of prairie dogs scampering across the snow. They moved as a unit, tiny brown bodies romping through the drifts. She never saw them act like that before, and the sight drew a surprised laugh from her throat. "Go back to bed," she called, knowing the weather was much too cold for them to be above ground. Silly things. Were they jostled awake by the meteor crashing?

A honk from behind made her jump in her seat, and she tore her gaze from the animals. An impatient driver tailgated her, but she was careful not to go too fast as she continued through the intersection and crested the icy overpass above the railroad tracks that divided her rundown edge of town from the rest of Demise. She glanced in her rearview mirror, searching for the prairie dogs, but saw only the hockey players and large expanses of snow-covered grass.

Three

WHEN REALENE ARRIVED home, she found that security around the landing site had multiplied, and most of the gawking townspeople were gone. A chain link fence topped with barbed wire formed a wide perimeter around the crater, which was still marked with caution tape. Spotlights on tall metal tripods ringed the inside of the fence, probably for use in darkness, and police officers dotted the outside of the fence every ten feet or so. Inside the fence, a group of people in white hazmat suits—scientists and professors with nearby NDSU's aerospace program, she'd learned—clustered near the crater.

She stood in her backyard, eating her Jujyfruits and glaring at the cars still lining the rarely traveled road that led nowhere, including four news vans, a couple civilian vehicles, half a dozen police cruisers, and several military jeeps. Steele Air Force Base, where her dad worked as a mechanic after his tour, was fifteen miles outside town, and she wondered what they'd made of the object falling from the sky.

The area had been the site of many missile silos, thanks to the Cold War and Ronald Reagan, her dad's personal hero. She'd always thought Reagan a jellybean-eating idiot but never said that out loud. The last active missile silo, the Echo-One Minuteman Missile Alert site, was decommissioned a few months prior. She bet the assigned soldiers remembered their days spent waiting to launch a nuke at a moment's notice. How many of them went for their red buttons when the meteor crashed, intent on defending God and country, only to find those buttons disconnected?

Several police officers, all dressed to match the one who'd been so rude to her earlier, stood at the edge of the field near the fence's gate, keeping reporters and looky-loos at a reasonable distance.

Realene watched as the pair of military personnel in heavy, olive-colored parkas shook hands with one of the scientists, then exited the fenced-in area to head toward their jeep. They'd likely realized this was not the hostile action of a foreign enemy, and therefore not their problem. As the men reached their vehicle, she recognized one of them as Colonel Harmon, her dad's former boss at the Air Force base.

"Colonel," she called out, stuffing the empty candy box in her coat pocket as she trudged through the snow toward him.

He turned at the sound of her voice and raised one hand in a wave. After saying something to the other man, he continued across the road, meeting her at the curb and drawing her in for a crushing hug. She squeezed him back as hard as she could, imagining for a moment he was her dad.

"Pretty casual today, colonel." She angled her chin toward the black, Air Force logo'd baseball cap sticking out from his fur-lined hood.

"Expected me out here in my dress blues, did you?" He winked, drawing focus to the old scar that ran from beneath his eye to his earlobe. She'd asked him about it once, and he'd said, "You should see the other guy."

"Haven't talked to you in a few weeks."

"Sorry I haven't checked in." She resisted the urge to look away. "Just busy."

"Uh-huh. And how's your ma?"

"Today's a good day. She's off playing bingo, hoping to win big and take Dad for a steak dinner."

He crossed his arms. "You sure you're okay? She's not getting to be too much for you?"

"Nah. We're doing alright. Really." She forced a smile, not wanting to worry him when there wasn't anything he could do.

"You start returning my calls, and I'll believe that. Told your dad I'd look out for you, and I don't take that lightly."

She squirmed under his stare. "Okay, okay. I get it." She wouldn't want to be one of the soldiers under his command.

"So how you dealing with all this hubbub? Nobody's harass-ing you or anything, are they?"

"I wish. Might be able to earn a few bucks telling my story to the *National Enquirer.*"

"Very funny. Seriously, though, if the reporters get too aggressive, if they're bothering you, let me know."

"Yes, sir." She gave a mock salute, and he shook his head indulgently. "What can you tell me? About the meteor?"

He shrugged. "Egg heads from the university say it's just that, a meteor. Not an attack, so it's in their hands now."

She considered mentioning the gunk she'd seen leak out of the rock the night before, but abandoned the thought. He'd only scoff at her overreaction to some space mud.

Footsteps crunched through the snow behind her, and Nate joined them.

"Colonel." He shook the man's hand.

"Son." The colonel smacked Nate on the shoulder with his free hand. "You takin' good care of our girl, here?"

"She can take care of herself," Nate replied.

"Damn straight," Realene said.

The colonel gave a disapproving grunt at her language. The man waiting at the jeep called out, and the colonel said, "Duty calls. I'll talk to you later in the week." He gave her a pointed stare before heading to his vehicle.

Shelley Schraeder rushed up to the colonel, trailed by her cameraman, and peppered him with questions. He ignored her completely and left her staring after his vehicle as it drove away, which Realene found extremely satisfying.

"What a circus, huh?" Nate said, surveying the scene. The temperature warmed a bit from the previous night, but not enough to justify his unzipped lime-green ski jacket flapping in the stiff wind. Unlike her, he seemed built for the wretched North Dakota cold. He'd even delivered the local paper each morning for years, starting in third grade and stopping when they hit high school.

"I think you missed your chance for an up-close of the meteor." When she'd called him back the night before with the news, he wanted to drive straight over, but she talked him into waiting. Though the object had given her the creeps, she'd felt like it belonged to her, somehow, and didn't want to share it with anyone quite yet.

"Meteorite. Everyone calls them meteors, but that only applies when they're in the sky. Once they've landed, they're meteorites," Nate said. "How big did you say it was?"

She held up her gloved hands about three feet apart.

"Amazing. Most debris burns to dust before it ever reaches the ground." He stared wistfully at the group of scientists. He'd talked throughout sophomore and junior year about going into astronomy at NDSU, but by the time they were seniors, he'd stopped bringing it up, deciding college wasn't for him.

"What's the big deal about these *meteorites*, anyway?"

"They allow us to study space." he bounced on his heels like an excited kid at his first science fair. "Some say they can even contain Martian life."

"Martian life? Like some of those creepy gray aliens could come crawling out of the rock or something?"

He laughed. "No, more like bacteria or fossils."

"Oh, yeah, of course." She scrubbed her gloved hand over her face, the image of that black sludge skittering across the ground flashing through her mind. The more she considered it, the more certain she became that the dark had been playing tricks on her cold-addled brain.

"You okay?"

"Yeah, just slept like crap." She'd been too excited and anxious to sleep much, thoughts of the meteor consuming her. And the wind was especially bad the night before, swelling again and again in that same pitch that sounded like screams.

A figure tromped toward them through the snow, and she recognized Calvin's weathered face beneath a fur trapper hat with ear flaps he'd likely made using the pelt of some animal he'd caught and skinned. Yuck. He stooped to inspect a hole in the snow, circular and smaller than a footprint. Other, similar holes dotted the yard, along with tiny paw prints peppering the top layer, probably left by the rabbits that liked to winter beneath her porch.

"Hey, Calvin," Nate said.

Calvin stopped beside them and pulled a joint from his pocket, placing it between his lips.

"Dude, you do see those cops, right?" Realene asked.

He frowned. "Yeah, so?"

"It's a hand-rolled cigarette, nerd." Nate socked her in the arm.

"Shut up," she shot back. Heat flooded her cheeks. "Not everyone's an expert like you."

Nate's brow furrowed at the mention of the cause of his criminal record and subsequent stint in juvie, but he didn't say anything.

"What're you two talkin' about?"

"Never mind. And you shouldn't smoke." She glared at him.

"You think I don't know that?" Calvin pulled out a pack of matches.

"What's that hat made of?" Nate asked, as if picking up Realene's earlier thought.

"Prairie dog." Calvin grinned, displaying tobacco-stained teeth. "Caught and skinned it myself."

"You're proud of that?" she asked. "Killing those harmless little guys?"

"Not harmless. Them and the gophers build their burrows in the grazing fields, cows step in the holes and break their ankles. Then guess what happens to the cows. Hafta' be shot."

"And shooting the prairie dogs is better?"

"Not shooting, poisoning. And I don't know about better, but they pay me to do it. Gotta keep the farms runnin.'"

"You poison prairie dogs for a living?" Nate asked, eyebrows raised.

"Not just them. I can take out any kind of vermin. Got a knack for it." Calvin raised his chin, proud of the macabre skill.

"I gotta get ready for work," Realene said, ready to be done with the conversation. She'd recently switched to day shifts at the gas station to be home in the evenings. Ma got worse after dark.

"Hey, no Egg McMuffin?" Nate asked.

"Oh, yeah, sorry. Vickie and Murray were jammin' up the drive thru. You want a Pop Tart?" Realene gestured toward the trailer. "I got some of those new Wild Berry."

"Well, I can't turn that down. How often do they come out with a new Pop Tart flavor?"

"What about me?" Calvin asked.

"I'm still pissed at you for killing those harmless little prairie dogs." She refused to reward such behavior with processed pastries.

"They're not harmless," he called after her, but she didn't engage. Knowing he killed helpless animals for a living tempted her to never talk to him again, though she knew she would. Ignoring one's neighbors might fly in the big city, but not in North Dakota, where politeness reigned supreme.

"ONE OR TWO?" Realene asked, pulling the box of Wild Berry Pop Tarts from the cupboard above the canary yellow stove that matched the fridge.

"One's good, as long as that's enough for you." Nate wandered into the living room and flipped on the TV.

"I already had some Jujyfruits." She opened the foil package and placed the purple and teal frosted pastries in the toaster. She hadn't tried the new flavor yet and looked forward to it, the bright colors a sure sign they would be tooth-achingly sweet.

"Seriously? I swear, you have the metabolism of a hummingbird."

"What can I say, my body craves sugar." Most kids grew out of their candy addictions, but hers only intensified. And she didn't discriminate, loving every candy equally.

She leaned one shoulder against the side of the fridge and watched as he flipped the channels.

He stopped on MTV and cranked up the volume. The MTV News logo of a satellite dish spinning and a typewriter ball spelling out "news" filled the screen.

"I'm Kurt Loder with an *MTV News Brief.*" He wore a T-shirt and blazer, and sat in front of a graphic of a spinning globe. "Late last night a meteor hit in Demise, North Dakota, a town of about five thousand residents."

Several photos of the meteor landing site, including one with Realene's trailer in the background, appeared beside Kurt on the screen.

"Holy shit," Nate mumbled.

"The collision measured a three on the Richter scale, equivalent to a minor earthquake, but no damage to nearby structures has been detected. Scientists with the North Dakota State University astrophysics program shared that initial samples from the meteor appear to contain water and certain amino acids crucial to the existence of life. Early reports demonstrate this may be one of the most important scientific artifacts of the century. That's the news for now, stay tuned for more throughout the day on MTV."

The toaster popped, but Realene ignored it, staring at the TV, which switched to a commercial for the *Real World*. Evidence of life, no wonder they'd beefed up security.

"Can you believe that? Incredible." Nate's eyes sparkled with excitement.

"I don't know why you never applied to NDSU. You could study that nerdy stuff all day long."

He turned away, so she could only see the back of his head. "I guess I've just accepted my fate, you know?"

"Screw that." Realene hated the thought of fate, the idea that no matter what you did, your future was predetermined, and you could do nothing to change that. "You should do whatever it takes to get out of here. Hell, apply for *Real World*. You'd be the only normal person in the house."

"That's why I'd never make it," Nate replied. "Not crazy enough." He shrugged, then walked past her into the kitchen to grab his Pop Tart.

"Speaking of crazy, you should've heard Irene this morning. The reverend's got her believing that God's raining down fire and brimstone. He was even driving around earlier in a weird van with a speaker spouting off about end times."

"That guy is seriously dangerous."

"Not to mention fashion blind. I think all he owns is denim. And I bet he irons his jeans."

"I guarantee it." Nate snickered. "Well, if we're all going to die, I'm gonna go try again, see if I can get up close to this God-sent meteor."

"Don't you mean meteorite?" Realene grabbed her own Pop Tart from the toaster and raised it in a toasting motion.

"Eh, if Kurt Loder calls it a meteor, guess I will too. Wish me luck."

"Luck. Call you later?"

"I'll be around. Unless the storm hits early." Nate gave a wave, munching on his breakfast as he left.

Realene watched from the kitchen window above the sink, which offered a view of the front door, deck, and Calvin's place.

Nate thumped down the steps and crossed the yard. No way would he get anywhere near the crater.

Leaning back against the stained, yellow countertop, she surveyed the kitchen. Dishes filled the sink, and she wished for the thousandth time they'd invested in a dishwasher, but Ma considered it a waste of money.

Stacks of junk mail and church programs collected from months of Bethel Lutheran Sunday services piled the table and countertops. Realene periodically tried to clean up the mess, but Ma panicked every time something was thrown away, as if one of the nondescript envelopes addressed to 'Resident' or the announcement of the church's annual chili cook-off might be the vital piece that would illuminate a past that was receding further and further into the shadows of her mind.

Her despair from the night before came flooding back, even sharper than before. While glad for the short break from Ma, being alone only intensified the depression she had to hide when Ma was home. Realene ate her toaster pastry in a few large bites, hardly tasting the preservative-packed breakfast she'd normally savor. It struck her that she used to love Pop Tarts, used to think of them as a treat when she and Nate would eat them as kids. But setting mattered, didn't it? If she were splayed out on a twin bed in her ASU dorm room, absorbed in an anatomy textbook, her pastry would taste totally different.

Her eyes burned, and she blinked rapidly as she swallowed her last bite and brushed the crumbs from her hands. Pumpkin wandered up and rubbed against her legs before giving a little "meow."

"Hungry, Punky?" She grabbed the Whiskas from the pantry and filled his bowl, placing it on the floor. He trotted over to munch on his dry bits of kibble.

The *Daria* theme song began to play, signaling the start of an episode, and she considered ditching work altogether to veg on the couch. But they needed the money. With a sigh, she flipped the TV to Turner Classic Movies for Ma before clicking it off, then donned her winter gear, heavy boots and all, and stepped back out into the cold North Dakota winter.

Realene glanced toward the police perimeter and saw Nate talking with one of the officers, maybe the same one who denied her entry. She should have let Nate come over the night before. The meteor landing was a big deal to him, to everyone, but she'd been too focused on wanting to keep it for herself. Even now, she briefly considered marching back out to the reporters and trying to tell her story, but she couldn't risk a repeat of her earlier embarrassment.

She slogged through the snow to the driveway, where she'd parked next to Ma's minivan, whose block heater plug extended from beneath the closed hood and connected to the extension cord plugged in to an outlet on the side of the trailer. Realene hadn't been home for long, so she didn't bother to plug her own car back in, and it started up on the first try since the engine was still warm. Nate's dirty work truck was parked at the curb. It had chains on the tires, a plow blade attached to the grill, and a two-hundred-gallon plastic deicing tank with sprayer strapped to the truck bed. She navigated around it as she backed out of the driveway.

Realene couldn't resist another look at the gathered crowd as she pulled from the trailer park, and she noticed a man standing back from the others, on the fringe. Reverend Zebediah. His creepy van sat parked at the curb, the speaker blessedly silent.

He turned slightly as she drove by, wearing his signature Canadian Tuxedo beneath a wool coat. She couldn't comprehend how anyone thought head-to-toe denim was a good idea. Irene's comments came back to her, a reminder that he'd convinced his parishioners the meteor landing signaled some kind of final reckoning.

After flicking the guy off and feeling quite good about it, she continued down Main, away from the landing site. Her car's old tape deck didn't work, and she couldn't afford a CD player, so she flipped on the radio to the local alternative rock station. "It's another beautiful day in Demise, with temperatures above zero. We've even got fiery meteors falling from the sky. In honor of the event, here's 'Firestarter' by The Prodigy."

Realene cranked up the volume. As much as the meteor ended up being a disappointment, she had to admit it was nice to have some excitement for a change. And while no one would ever recognize her for it, she was the first one to actually see the landing site. That counted for something.

Four

REALENE CRANKED HER steering wheel to pull into the parking lot of the Snack Station, situated on the other side of the overpass on Main and Olson, and advertising unleaded for $1.20 per gallon, diesel for $1.12. The squat building and two gas pumps were positioned in the center of the lot, a plowed oasis walled-in by dirt-marred snowbanks that wouldn't fully melt until spring. Rich Hall laughingly called it *snirt*—a mixture of snow and dirt—but the stuff was more depressing than funny, signifying a bitter, never-ending winter in which even the pure, white snow was tainted with grime.

Further down the block stood Toppers, a '50s-themed diner with killer milkshakes and an antique jukebox, and beyond that lay the Cinema Twin Theater. Nate had worked at the theater for a few months before getting the plowing job, and he still had the key to the place. He and Realene had talked about sneaking in late at night to watch movies, but she doubted they would ever do it, not now that they were both responsible adults…and chickens afraid of getting caught.

She claimed the farthest parking spot in front of the station and shut off her engine, staring ahead at the neon signs advertising propane, cigarettes, and hot coffee. Red and green Christmas lights lined the roof of the building, hardly visible under a dusting of snow. Clerking was supposed to have been a part-time summer job, a way to earn some money before leaving for school. Now she worked full-time, and there was talk of making her a manager.

Walt, another full-timer, walked out the front doors and zipped-up his coat. Apparently, he'd seen Realene drive up and decided not to wait for her to clock in. She didn't blame him.

Realene stepped from her car and approached his truck. "Hey, Walt. How was your shift?"

"Been pretty busy, what with all the traffic out to the crash site. Made the morning go quick, though, so that's good." Walt had been at Snack Station for going on twenty years and seemed perfectly happy with the job, which earned him enough money to shower his dog, Trout, in toys and treats, and to finance his annual fishing trip to Manitoba each summer.

"Thanks again for switching," she said. "I really appreciate it." Walt used to work the day shift, but took over nights when Realene needed to be home for Ma.

"Oh, it's no trouble." He gave a genuine smile that creased his face. "How's your Ma? You need help with anything up at the house?"

Her throat tightened, and she got the sudden urge to hug him, but didn't. It'd just embarrass him. "She's having a good day. I dropped her off this morning for bingo."

He kicked at a chunk of ice lodged in his wheel well, the tip of his steel-toed boot glinting silver, the leather almost completely worn away. "Never did understand the appeal, myself. To each their own, I guess."

"I hear ya." She thought of Walt sitting alone in his house, only his dog to keep him company. "Hey, you're off on Monday, right? Would you ever want to bring Trout over? Ma would love to meet him, and I bet I could talk her into making her world-famous lefsa."

"Oh, yeah. That'd be great. And you could introduce me to Pumpkin. I know cats can be stand-offish, but I'm pretty good with animals."

"Cool, let's plan on it." She eyed the door, stamping her feet to keep her toes from freezing. "S'pose I better get inside. See ya."

"See ya." He gave a wave and climbed into to his truck as she headed into the warmth of the store.

A four-foot-tall, rosy-cheeked, cardboard Santa waited by the front door and issued a "Ho-Ho-Ho" when Realene passed. She groped behind the head and flipped the off-switch of the motion-detecting device that triggered the greeting, knowing that if she didn't, Santa would be snapped in two by the end of her shift.

Fluorescent lights beamed down on the coolers of chilled drinks that lined the side wall and the aisles of candy, snacks, motor oil, and other gas station staples that filled the store. The back wall held a fountain soda machine, a coffee station, and a rolling display of hot dogs and sausages. The smell of cooking meat, gasoline, and bleach tinged the air.

She pushed through the little swinging door to the cashier's station, hanging her coat on the back of the chair that sat behind the counter. A plastic Crystal Clear Pepsi bottle half full of soupy brown liquid—the remnant of Walt's chewing tobacco habit—sat on the counter by the register, and she cringed. Acting like it was a container of toxic waste, she pinched the bottle by the neck, with forefinger and thumb, and carefully dropped it into the trash can at her feet. She made a mental note to remind him not to leave behind his disgusting spit bottles.

Perching on the chair, she glanced down the candy aisle and remembered how much she loved the place as a kid. Nate lived with his mom and prick dad back then, in their house near the trailer park. Now he lived a block past the movie theater, in a basement apartment that smelled permanently of urine due the previous renter's incontinent ferret.

As a kid, he would sneak out to walk the distance to the Snack Station with Realene, whose pockets held whatever change she could beg, scrounge, or earn. Over the years, they'd spent hours perusing the selection of candy, carefully choosing their purchases and savoring them on the long trek home. Back then, she didn't have enough money for full-sized candy bars, and more often subsisted on Fire Jolly Rancher sticks and Candy Cigarettes.

The childhood version of Realene would have thought it a dream come true to work at the gas station, when it actually meant her future was going nowhere. Would she end up like Walt in twenty years, still living in the trailer park, only a cat to keep her company? She didn't like to fish, but maybe she could take up crocheting to pass the time.

The radio next to the cash register blared Garth Brooks, and she flipped the dial to the same station she had on in the car. "I'm Just a Girl" by No Doubt played, and she cranked the volume up a notch. She pushed away thoughts of her future, knowing they'd be waiting close by, and jumped from the chair.

She grabbed the broom propped in the corner and did a spin, holding it like a mic stand and serenading the now-silent cardboard Santa. Realene knew she couldn't hold a tune, but there was no one around to hear her, so she figured she might as well try to infuse some fun into this weird day.

The overhead lights flickered, and the radio cut off, leaving her listening to her own off-key voice. She fiddled with the radio dial, but no sound came from the speakers, so she crouched to examine the cord and outlet. Finding no problem, she got back up when the lights flickered again, and the radio blared back to life.

They did occasionally have power outages during winter due to ice-caked power lines breaking. The local council tried to put in a city tax increase to pay for installing underground power lines, but Mayor Opdahl vetoed the resolution, quoting George Bush's campaign slogan, "Read my lips: No new taxes." So, they were left with eyesore power lines criss-crossing the town, and several power outages every winter.

Throwing on her coat, she went outside, broom still in hand, in case she needed to knock loose the accumulated snow. The parking lot was deserted aside from her car, and she made her way around the far side of the building.

Rounding the corner, she stopped short. The gray utility box sat attached to the brick exterior at shoulder height, and a cluster of cords ran from the bottom of the box down to the ground and through the wall into the building. Two prairie dogs stood on hind legs, clasping the cords with tiny, clawed hands, and chewing on the wires.

"Hey, shoo." Her demand elicited no response from the critters.

She stepped forward and swatted at the prairie dogs with the broom. "What are you doing, guys? It's too cold for you out here." *Too damn cold for me, too,* she thought, her teeth already chattering.

The creatures peered at her with beady eyes, lips curling to bare tiny teeth in an expression more suited to a rabid dog.

"Jesus," she said, chucking the broom in their direction. It missed and clattered to the ground, but the sound still sent them scampering off behind the building.

She glanced behind her to make sure no one saw her embarrassingly uncoordinated throwing skills—one of many reasons she'd consistently been picked last in dodge ball—but the lot remained empty. After retrieving the broom, she grabbed a couple of bundles of firewood from the pile beside the propane cage and stacked them in front of the power cables, hoping to deter any more munching.

Beginning to numb from the cold, she ran back into the store, rubbing her hands together and blowing hot air on her fingers to warm them. The power and radio were still on, so at least the electricity problem was solved, but the prairie dogs definitely weren't acting normal. She picked up the phone affixed to the wall behind the counter.

Thankfully, a dial tone sounded, so at least the little troublemakers hadn't chewed through the phone line. Flipping through the yellow pages, she found the number for animal control and dialed.

"Animal Control. How can I help you?" a woman asked.

"Yeah, hi. I need to report some prairie dogs."

"Prairie dogs? Ma'am, it's the middle of winter."

"Well, that explains all this white stuff everywhere," Realene said, beginning to wish she hadn't called. "Seriously, though, I'm over at the Snack Station and there were two of them chomping on the electrical cords out here."

"Prairie dogs hibernate in winter."

"Yeah, I know that, but I saw a bunch of them in the field earlier, and now they're chewing on the cords over here and messing with the power. They looked weird, too, like, not right."

"Ma'am, I don't have time for jokes."

"I'm not joking," Realene said, her voice raised. "Can you please send someone over here?"

"Fine, I'll put in a report."

"Great, thank—"

The dial tone sounded, and Realene stared at the receiver, realizing the woman hung up on her. Sure, the image of prairie dogs running amok in the freezing cold did sound far-fetched, but that didn't make it any less true.

The memory of the little creatures baring their teeth flashed through her brain, and she shivered, though her body was warming. She'd spent years watching the ones that lived behind the trailer, even trying to feed them a few times before her dad lectured her about rabies. Never had she seen a prairie dog out of hibernation in winter, and she'd *certainly* never seen one that looked like the ones chewing the cords. Pulling her coat tighter around her, she hung up the phone and sat down to wait for animal control.

THREE HOURS, TWO Mello Yello, a pack of Hostess Cupcakes, and a whole roll of Bubble Tape later, Realene had run out of cleaning and straightening to do in the store. She scratched at the jagged scar on her palm, which was irritated and raised from the harsh cleaning products. The scar usually brought a smile to her face, surfacing the memory of the day she and Nate found a pocketknife abandoned in the gutter. After cleaning it up, they'd used the blade to slice open their hands and shake on the pact that they would remain best friends forever. Now, the sight of the scar made her sad for that naïve little girl who once believed you could conquer anything with your BFF by your side.

The door dinged, and a man in a ski mask entered, only a tiny area of skin around his eyes and mouth visible.

"Gettin' colder out there?" Realene asked.

"Yeah, guess a blizzard's comin' in tonight too." The man slid a ten-dollar bill across the counter. "Eight dollars on pump two, and a bottle a Heet."

She rang in the man's purchase and handed him back thirty-two cents in change and the bottle of Heet, a crucial ingredient for stopping gas lines from freezing in winter. "You stay warm now."

"Yeah, okay. You too." He headed back outside toward the pumps.

Motion in the parking lot caught her eye, and she squinted at the small shapes running across the snow-packed pavement that now glistened under the midday sun. It was a group of prairie dogs—at least half a dozen—scampering across the back corner of the lot. They climbed the snowbank and disappeared behind it. Clearly, the woman she had spoken to at Animal Control had blown off her report.

"Let's hope Miss Friendly's on her lunch," she said to herself as she turned down the radio and picked up the phone to hit redial. All she got was a busy signal.

The door dinged, signaling another customer, and Realene plastered a polite expression on her face as she hung up the handset.

Her expression melted when she saw Brooke, looking like she waltzed off the pages of a ski magazine in her lavender puffer pants and jacket with the white fur-lined hood.

"Realene? Is that you?"

"Sure is." She had to admit it: Brooke, who was her very first girl-crush, and the one who made her realize she liked guys *and* girls, was still smokin' hot. Too bad people's insides didn't always match their outsides.

"Well, this doesn't look much like Arizona." Brooke's sapphire-blue eyes widened in mock confusion.

"No shit," Realene mumbled.

"Seriously, though, weren't you like valedictorian, supposed to be going med school or something?"

"Salutatorian, actually." She had no desire to share the tragic details of her life with Brooke the Bitch. "What're you doing home? Flunk out already?"

"Uh, no, it's Christmas break, and you know how much my mother, like, loves the holidays." They'd been friends once, and Realene thought there was a chance for more there. Then Brooke outed her to everyone as a lesbian—not exactly true, but close enough—and mocked her mercilessly through all of junior and senior year. "I'll be heading back to Minneapolis in a couple weeks. The city's like, totally amazing, you know?"

Back to school and her bright and shining future. And now that Brooke knew Realene worked at Snack Station, Realene could look forward to being taunted for years to come. "Can I get you something?"

"Yeah, give me ten worth of gas on pump three." Brooke dropped a ten-dollar bill on the counter, and Realene smelled the citrus and floral of Brooke's Guess perfume, the same scent she'd worn since high school.

She rang in the sale and set the pump. "That it?"

"There's another five in it for you if you pump the gas for me. That smell. Ew." Brooke scrunched her button nose in a way that she likely knew was adorable. "I hate getting it anywhere near my clothes, you know? But you're probably, like, used to it by now."

"We're self-service."

Brooke gave an exaggerated bat of her eyelashes. "I'm just trying to help you out. You're always so tight on money, and I can't imagine this job pays that well."

"I'm fine," Realene said, though the job did not pay well, except for the unlimited snacks her boss offered as a perk.

"Alright, well, I guess there's, like, no helping some people. See you next time." Brooke sneered, and the implication was clear: Realene would never make it out of this town.

She strutted out the door in her wedge-heeled snow boots. "Barbie Girl" by Aqua played softly on the radio in the background, almost as if the lavender-clad ski bunny had summoned the song with her evil powers.

Realene barely waited for the door to shut before muttering, "Bitch."

She grabbed the phone and dialed Nate at home.

"Yellow," he answered.

"Hey, it's me."

"Sick of work already?"

She groaned. "Brooke came in. She's home for the holidays."

"Uh-oh. How'd that go?"

"About how you'd expect. She loved me still being here. How much do you want to bet she finds a reason to stop in every single day of her vacation?"

"Don't give her any of your energy. That only increases her power," he said in a haughty voice.

"You might be thinking of Freddy Krueger. Brooke's much more dangerous."

He snickered. "Yeah, her claws are all natural."

Realene stared out the front windows, watching as Brooke gassed up the red Mustang she'd driven since sophomore year. "I'm going to be stuck here, working at this gas station forever, and it's my own fault."

She hadn't applied for scholarships to any local colleges, though there were a few less than an hour away in Fargo. She never considered staying near Demise, there was no way would she'd make her deadline for Arizona State next year, and she had no way to pay for school anyway. Even if she did manage to get student loans for next year, working and going to school full-time while also caring for Ma would be impossible.

"I dare you to go one day without the pity party," Nate said. "I swear you'll—"

Realene lowered the phone from her ear as several prairie dogs scurried across the parking lot, running one way, then stopping to change direction. A pair of them wandered over to Brooke and she waved her arms, trying to shoo them away. The creatures only moved closer, then stood on hind legs at Brooke's feet.

Realene grinned at the expression on Brooke's face, savoring the crack in little miss perfection's facade. Brooke was scared, something Realene never thought she'd witness, and for a moment, she was glad Animal Control hadn't arrived yet. She hoped the security cameras were capturing the action so she could re-watch it later. Maybe she'd nuke some Jiffy Pop in the gas station microwave and invite Nate for a little viewing party.

Brooke backed up into her car, then lashed out and kicked the closest prairie dog, sending the animal skittering across the icy pavement.

"Hey!" Realene put the phone back to her ear and said, "Brooke just punted a prairie dog. I mean, they are attacking her, but whatever, I gotta go."

"What the f—" Nate started, but she hung up on him.

The other prairie dog threw itself at Brooke, latching onto her leg, and she screamed. She clawed at the animal, finally grasping its furry body and flinging it off her. The creature pinwheeled through the air like a furry Frisbee, reminding Realene why Brooke had always been picked first in dodgeball, and every other team sport.

She threw on her coat and grabbed the bat they kept hidden beneath the counter before rushing out the doors. A dozen or so prairie dogs surrounded their fallen pack-mate, and Brooke weaved past them, clutching her leg. A blood stain widened on the thigh of her designer ski pants.

Realene met Brooke halfway across the parking lot, grabbing her shoulder. "Hey, are you okay?"

"What?" She shook her head. For a moment, her expression was blank, then her mouth twisted in a sneer. "Wait a minute. Do not tell me you're working here."

"Uh, yeah. Still here five minutes later."

"You're, like, a gas jockey now, or whatever? I knew you were making up that Florence Nightingale crap, like they would let you work at the hospital. Everyone at school is going to die when I tell them."

"At school? Why would your college friends care where I'm working?"

"College friends? Have you been huffing gas? We go to the same high school."

Realene reached out to steady Brooke, wondering if she hit her head too. "You're not making sense. I think you're really hurt."

"Get away from me, you lezzie trailer trash." Brooke stumbled closer, reeking of spilled gasoline. A wisp of black, like a tiny worm, flitted across the white of her eye, and she shoved Realene.

Realene slipped on the icy asphalt and fell on her ass, which reignited the pain in her tailbone. Brooke had always been a bully, but she never physically attacked anyone. She preferred to decimate people with gossip and name-calling.

What the hell was wrong with her eye?

Brooke shook her head, as if confused. The blood stain on her thigh had stopped spreading, and she glanced down at the dark spot.

"Come inside with me, okay?" Realene urged. "We'll call 9-1-1 and get you help." She was already trying to figure out what she'd say to the dispatcher.

Hello, yes, this girl I really hate got attacked by rabid prairie dogs that are impossibly awake in the middle of winter.

That conversation would go about as well as the one with Animal Control.

"Dad," Brooke whimpered. "I need my dad." Lips quivering, she limped toward her car.

"Wait! Stop!" Realene shouted. Brooke's dad had died the year prior of a heart attack, while in bed with his mistress. It was front-page news in the Demise Daily.

She climbed to her feet, but the Mustang peeled out of the parking lot before she could say any more, the car spraying her with muddy slush that splattered her coat and jeans.

The yipping of prairie dogs filled the air. The creatures that had been huddled around their injured friend were now staring right at Realene.

Five

THE PACK OF prairie dogs waited in the middle of the ice-slicked parking lot, the gas pumps behind them. They watched Realene with bulging, black eyes, completely focused on her as if she were prey.

These were not the creatures who amused her with their summer antics, chasing and calling to one another through the tall grass and wildflowers. Her dad's lectures played through her mind, and she knew these animals were sick. As an intern at the hospital, she'd seen the effects of rabies after an infected dog bit a person. In addition to physical symptoms, victims could experience confusion and agitation. Like Brooke.

"It's okay, little guys. I'm not going to hurt you." Brandishing the bat, Realene backed up until she reached the gas station's front doors. She raced inside, clicking the lock behind her before realizing how ridiculous that was. Prairie dogs couldn't open doors, even when rabid.

The shrill ring of the phone split the quiet, and she jumped. It only lasted half a ring before going silent. Overhead, the lights flickered and went dark. Bat still clutched in her hand, she grabbed the phone to call 9-1-1 and heard no dial tone or static, just dead air. The handset slipped from her grip, the plastic cracking on impact with the tile floor to display the phone's wire guts. Though sunny outside, the light barely penetrated the store, leaving most of it in shadow. She half expected one of the tiny animals to come creeping out of the darkness of the candy aisle, its tiny muzzle foaming.

"Well, shit." Realene watched as the prairie dogs stood on their hind legs a few feet from the doors, peering through the glass. She started to worry maybe they could open doors, or even pick locks with their sharp, little claws. The one in the front gave a few short, sharp barks, and Realene wished—not for the first time—that she could understand their complicated language. The pack dropped to the ground and ran toward the corner of the building, disappearing from sight.

She returned to the door and flipped back the lock. Opening the door a crack, she stuck her head out and looked both directions. No sign of the prairie dogs. The prospect of being stuck in the store with no power or phone urged her to make her escape while she had the chance. She didn't want to go out unprotected, so she grabbed the cardboard Santa by a handle on its back, located just below the battery pack and on-switch.

Careful to be quiet, she slipped through the doors, frigid air stinging her bare fingers that held the bat in one hand and Santa in the other. She braced the cardboard cutout against her chest like the shield of some medieval knight, but instead of a coat of arms, her shield wore a ridiculous red suit, a wide grin with several teeth blacked out by mischievous kids, and sported a speech bubble that said, 'Thank you for shopping at Snack Station.'

Her beat-up Escort was an island oasis in the icy expanse of the parking lot, and she quick-stepped toward it, careful not to slip, her unzipped coat flapping around her. Wrenching open the door, she tried to shove Santa inside, but only succeeded in bashing him into the doorframe and snapping off the fluffy white ball atop his hat.

"Fine, stay here," she said, before throwing him to the ground.

The impact flipped the on-switch, and he called out 'Ho, ho, ho,' his pink-cheeked face staring up at her.

"Shut. Up," she whispered, then plopped into the driver's seat, closed the door, and pressed down the lock. Santa called out another 'Ho, ho, ho,' and a panicked giggle bubbled from her throat.

Shivering, she took a moment to zip up her coat before fishing her key from her pocket and jamming it into the ignition. The engine cranked but didn't start. She slammed her hands on the steering wheel. "Dammit!" Of course her battery cable would pick now to come loose. Eyeing the door to the Snack Station, she wondered if she might be better off holing up until someone came to her rescue. Animal control, a customer, anyone.

She noticed the mood ring on her finger, which was a bright yellow, and she cursed her own stupidity. Ma was home alone in the trailer a few hundred feet away from the rabid prairie dog colony. Realene needed to get home. *Now.*

Trembling, she tugged her gloves from her pocket and put them on, her skin already starting to itch from exposure. The car windows were frosted at the edges, but she could still see outside. There were no prairie dogs in sight, but she'd seen *Cujo* plenty of times and knew a rabid animal could be sneaky. Sure, that had been a Saint Bernard attacking a Pinto, but the parallel was close enough.

Hoping she could prove to be half as brave as Donna from the movie, Realene forced herself to grab the handle and push the door open, cringing at the creak of rusty hinges. She popped the hood, grabbed her bat, and rushed around to the front of the car. 'Ho, ho, ho,' Santa said, and she pressed her lips together to avoid releasing a tirade of cursing.

Her breath coming in fast pants, she forced herself to wedge her gloved hand in the crack to release the latch, sure one of the creatures would be waiting there to bite her. But the pain she expected never came, and when she raised the hood she saw only her car's inner workings, free of vermin. She set the bat against the bumper and bent over the engine. Working quickly, she tightened the cable and lowered the hood with a quiet click.

A bark sounded behind her, and she whirled around, knocking over the bat, which rolled beneath her car. A single prairie dog rose on its hind legs and barked. Answering barks sounded from behind the gas station, out of sight. Realene lunged beneath the car, her chin scraping the asphalt and head banging into the undercarriage. Her fingertips brushed the handle of the bat for an instant before it rolled again, out of her reach.

Something scratched at the denim cuff of her jeans, and she screamed, kicking her legs as she crawled further beneath the car. Her fingers finally grasped the bat. 'Ho, ho, ho,' Santa said again.

She scrabbled backward, extracting herself from beneath the car. A prairie dog managed to latch onto her jeans at the ankle, but she smacked it with the bat, sending it skittering across the ground. She got up and rounded the car, jumping inside and slamming the door behind her. Safe for the moment, she pressed a hand to her racing heart.

More prairie dogs followed their friend, at least a dozen of them now, and they began to howl high and shrill, the sound raising every hair on her arms. In all the years she'd listened to them from her bedroom window, she'd only heard this cry once—when owls had targeted the colony and snatched up several baby prairie dogs. Realene ran into the backyard, screaming at the birds to stop, but they ignored her in favor of an easy meal.

Shaking away the memory, she tried the engine again. It sputtered and coughed, failed to turn over.

"Come on, Lizzy." She twisted the key again and said a silent prayer.

The engine caught, revving to life.

"Yes! Good girl." Realene patted the dashboard.

A prairie dog leapt up on the hood of the car with a thump and crept toward the windshield, its claws scraping against the metal.

She threw the shifter into Reverse and stepped on the gas, sending the *Total Recall* VHS to the floor to mingle with the remaining items from Ma's spilled bag. Shifting into Drive, she hit the gas again and shot forward. Santa gave a single 'Ho' before being crushed beneath the Escort's tires as Realene sped past the gas pumps toward Main. A glance in her rearview mirror showed a smear of blood on the asphalt near the now dismembered Santa and several furry creatures scampering after her.

The back end of the vehicle fishtailed as she whipped out of the parking lot, and she struggled to regain control on the slick road. She forced herself to tap the breaks, reminding herself she couldn't help Ma if she wrecked.

She crested the overpass and made it safely to the other side, passing only one car speeding in the opposite direction. Light traffic was typical for her end of town, with no businesses on that side of the railroad tracks. She hoped that meant fewer people out and about amongst the diseased prairie dogs.

Halfway home, Realene sped past a sedan that had jumped the curb, both doors thrown open and the emergency lights flashing. Several homes lined the road on that side, but she saw no sign of anyone.

Black tire marks looped ahead of her, leading to a blue truck that dove nose-first into the ditch that ran parallel to the fields, leaving only the rear end visible. She slowed, recognizing the bumper sticker that proclaimed, 'A Bad Day Fishing Is Better Than a Good Day Working,' and pulled over.

"Goddammit, Walt."

She shifted into Park, but left the car running.

Expecting to see a pack of prairie dogs chasing her down the road, she glanced in the rearview mirror, but the strip of asphalt trailing behind her remained empty. She grabbed her bat.

"Walt? Are you okay?" she asked, walking toward the truck. The wind whistled around her, chilling her exposed earlobes and dampening any other sound.

Stepping over the curb on the driver's side of the vehicle, her boots sunk deep into the bank as she ascended the slight incline. The driver's-side door hung open, and the faint sound of 'Achy Breaky Heart' played from the car's speakers.

"Hey, Walt? Are you here?"

Snow crunched beneath her feet as she made her way up the small hill that tapered down into a ditch.

"Hello?" a man's voice said.

"Walt? Is that you?"

Walt appeared from around the front of the truck, gripping the open door. The hood of his parka was down, and blood marred his forehead. "How do you know my name?" He half-hid behind the door, as if to protect himself from her.

"It's me, Realene. Did you hit your head, buddy?"

He raised one hand to his forehead, and his glove came away smeared red. "I'm bleeding."

"Come on up here." She inched down the hill, holding on to the truck bed with her free hand. "I'll get you some help, okay?"

His brow furrowed as if he didn't trust her, but after a moment, he pulled himself past the open car door. He cried out after taking a big step and bent to grasp his ankle, where his work pants were stained dark and torn.

"What happened to your leg?"

"I don't know." His face crumbled, as if he might start crying.

"Shit." He must have been bitten too. She stretched the baseball bat toward him. "Grab on. We need to hurry, okay?"

He groped for the bat, but wasn't close enough to reach. Wincing, he struggled up the truck's cab to get closer.

A bark sounded, and Realene straightened. She backed away from Walt to check out the road. Brown specks galloped across the field in the distance, coming toward them from the direction of the Snack Station.

"Walt," she whispered, as if the prairie dogs might hear her otherwise. "Get up here now." She held onto the truck bed with one hand and reached out with the bat as far as she possibly could without falling.

Blinking rapidly, he stumbled closer, swiping at the bat with his fingertips before finally getting close enough to grasp it.

Realene grit her teeth and took a careful step backward, then another, drawing him up the steep side of the embankment.

Walt made it to the truck bed and hooked his free arm over it, then inched the rest of the way himself. By the time he reached the top of the rise, his chest was rapidly rising and falling from the exertion. "I gotta get home and let my puppy out. He can't make it more than a few hours, being so young."

The confusion from the bite had already affected him. Trout was at least three now, and Walt had installed a doggie door for him to go out anytime he wanted.

"We'll get you home soon," she said. "I promise. Just need someone to check you out first."

Walt let her lead him down the gentle slope of the ditch closest to the road and over the curb, before stopping and tugging his elbow from her grip. "What's going on here? Did you run me off the road?"

"I stopped to help when I saw you'd crashed, remember?"

She left Walt standing there and jogged to the other side of the street, where her car sat idling, and opened the back door. "Get in. We'll get you some help."

He shook his head and took a step backward, crying out when his injured ankle slipped out from beneath him on the icy pavement.

Realene could only watch as Walt careened backward, his windmilling arms doing nothing to slow this descent. His head hit the curb with a crack, and the air left his lungs in a soft puff from his open mouth.

Realene screamed, sprinted back to her injured friend, and fell to her knees beside him. She angrily discarded the bat. Blood pooled beneath Walt's head, ice crystals forming at the edge of the crimson liquid. She tugged one of her gloves off and pressed it to the back of Walt's head to stop the bleeding, but the section of his skull there had caved in.

"Oh, no. No, no, no." He'd been such a nice guy. She imagined Trout, waiting expectantly by the front door for his best friend to come home, and her eyes stung.

"I'm so sorry, Walt."

He stared up at her, unseeing. A pair of little black worms wiggled across the whites of his eyes.

She scrambled away, letting the man's head drop back down to the pavement with a thump.

Brooke had that same worm in her eye.

Realene knew eye worms weren't a symptom of rabies. Rabies was a viral disease. Worms were a parasite.

Cackling yips filled the air, and she glanced behind her to see that the wave of prairie dogs had arrived. Several were now perched on her car's hood and roof, and more had climbed inside through the open doors.

She stood, wiped her bloody hand on her coat, and walked a few steps to grab her bat. She gripped the handle with both hands and widened her stance, holding the barrel out in front of her.

"You little fuckers! Why did you have to get Walt?"

She no longer cared that the animals were diseased, that it wasn't their fault. She wanted to smash every one of them to pulp.

The animals continued to cry out in sharp barks, the unnaturalness of which made her cringe. A few more jumped into her car, then up onto the dash. They watched her from the hood, the roof, and all over the interior.

Keeping her eyes on the evil critters, she backed away in the direction she'd been driving, sparing a last look of farewell for Walt, cold and dead on the ground. She was still a quarter mile from home—too far to walk while demonic prairie dogs roamed free, but what other choice did she have?

Her car sat running and ready to go, exhaust billowing from the tailpipe, but totally useless to her. A prairie dog leapt from the hood and raced toward her, baring its teeth. She swung as it reached her, and the bat made solid contact with the little fur ball. This time, she savored the crack of tiny bones breaking and the hollow thump of its limp body hitting the asphalt. *For Walt.*

"Ha! I gotcha!"

She took several more steps back, careful to keep her footing on the slick road. The wind nipped at her face and bare hand, but she ignored the cold. If she made it home with just frostbite, she'd consider herself lucky.

Another prairie dog lunged, and she swiped it away with the bat. But then a third one jumped, springing higher than she'd thought possible, and chomped down with razor teeth onto her coat sleeve. Her stomach twisted at the prospect of getting bit, of getting whatever disease or parasite these things were spreading.

Screaming, she flung the thing off her sleeve and sent it flying in a tumbling arc into the ditch, where it disappeared behind

Walt's truck. The advancing prairie dogs ignored their injured friends and continued toward her, several still inside and on top of her car. The engine began to chug and whine in protest.

There was no point in trying to circle back to Lizzy, not when so many of the animals seemed set on guarding the vehicle. The pack slowed and fanned out, as if trying to surround her. Realene considered running away as fast as she could, but she couldn't risk them jumping on her, latching on to her back. At least by facing them, she could fight back.

Her boots hit a patch of black ice, and she went down hard on her butt. A panicked cry spilled out her mouth. She channeled Wendy Torrance from *The Shining* and swung the bat from her seated position as the prairie dogs closed in around her. She knocked back the first few, but she knew she had no chance against so many. Eventually, one of the creatures would sink its fangs into her flesh. Then the others would swarm her, cover her in a mass of furry, biting, clawing bodies. Would she even live long enough to be infected?

A horn sounded behind her, and the prairie dogs stopped their advance to stand alert on hind legs. She risked a glance over her shoulder and saw Nate speed past her in his work truck, the shining silver blade of his plow glinting in the afternoon sun. The truck's tires screeched on the pavement as Nate whipped a donut around Realene and lowered the plow blade to the ground so as to shovel the bloodthirsty horde of prairie dogs away from his one and only best friend. The creatures were shoved, crushed, and thrown from curved surface of the blade, their little bodies sailing effortlessly through the frosty air.

The truck slid to a halt, and Nate pushed open the passenger door from the inside, yelling, "Get in!"

Realene scrambled inside and slammed the door behind her. Panting, she sat rigid, the bat still clutched tight in her aching hands.

"So, how was work?" he asked.

She licked her chapped lips and swallowed to wet her throat. "Got off early, which is nice."

"That is nice."he eyed the rearview mirror. "Is that... Walt?"

"Yeah." she exhaled through her nose. "How did you know I was in trouble?"

"After you hung up, I called the store, and the line cut out. Called again, and it wouldn't even ring. Tried calling 9-1-1, but I couldn't get through to them either. Saw all the carnage at Snack Station and figured you might've taken off for home."

She squeezed his hand. "Thanks. I thought I was prairie dog food."

"Nah. You might've gotten chewed on a little, but not eaten. They're herbivores."

"That's comforting." Her shoulders slumped. Exhaustion weighed on her overexerted muscles.

"I do have a question though. What the hell did that cardboard Santa do to you?"

She shook her head. "Can you take me to check on Ma? I want to make sure she made it home okay."

"It's a little out of my way," he joked, "but I guess."

She watched as several of the wounded prairie dogs got up.

Nate mashed his foot on the gas and whipped another donut to plow through the remaining rodents, then straightened out the vehicle in the direction of Plainview.

Realene bonked her head on the side window during the maneuver, then put the bat on the floor and clicked on her seatbelt. She rubbed the bump on her head and looked back to the road behind them. Motionless lumps of blood and fur dotted the pavement. About half the prairie dogs had survived, but they didn't appear to be pursuing them...yet.

Six

REALENE STARED OUT the window as they passed the neighborhood Walt had lived in, and caught a glimpse of his cul-de-sac. She'd been to his house a few times, a ranch built in the '60s that still looked nice because he kept it that way. He painted the outside every few years and even built a matching doghouse that sat in the fenced backyard. She knew Trout would be okay for a while, but eventually he'd realize that it had been too long since his best friend came home.

"You okay?" Nate asked.

"We need to check on Trout," she said softly. She swiped at her eyes with her gloved hand. "I mean, once we're safe."

"Yeah." He went silent for a moment, then glanced at her. "What the hell is going on here?"

She shrugged. "Not sure, but it seemed funny at first. Seeing them attack Brooke like that… I was totally planning for us to watch the security footage later." She gave a bitter laugh.

"Yeah, about that. What exactly happened?"

She recounted Brooke's attack at the gas station, and how she escaped and found Walt. She started to get emotional at that part, so Nate held her hand and squeezed it tight. By the time she finished the story, they were parked in front of her house. Her chest felt hollow, like someone had dug out her insides with an ice cream scoop.

"They must be sick. Rabies or something," Nate said.

"Or something," she replied. The prairie dogs certainly acted rabid, and the symptoms from Brooke and Walt fit too. But that didn't explain the worms, if that's even what they were.

"We'll try Animal Control again after we call an ambulance for Walt. Come on." He turned off the truck and hopped out.

She shuffled after him up the path, her mind still replaying the events of the last hour. The whole thing seemed unreal, like something from a movie. Nate had insisted the prairie dogs were herbivores, but they had looked ready to eat her one tiny bite at a time—*would have,* if Nate hadn't shown up at that exact moment.

And to think, Irene would've driven that same route to drop Ma back home. Sucking in a deep breath of frigid air and blowing it out, she followed Nate into her trailer, bracing herself for the sight of an empty recliner.

But Ma made it home fine and was seated in the chair with her favorite Afghan slung over her lap.

"Ma! You're okay." Realene rushed over to wrap Ma in a hug.

"Okay?" Ma asked.

Realene leaned against the back of the recliner and placed one hand on Ma's shoulder to confirm the woman was really there. "How'd you do at bingo? Is there a steak dinner in your future?"

"Dinner? No, no. We ate a wonderful breakfast though. Their pancakes are something else, so much fluffier than my Bisquick ones. I should ask them for the recipe.

She gave Ma a weak smile, knowing she had already forgotten their conversation from only a few hours ago.

Ma noticed Nate standing in the doorway. "Nathan." Her face creased in a grin that quickly fell into a frown. "I know your mother didn't let you out with no hat or gloves. You'll catch your death of cold."

A pained expression crossed his face, but he quickly recovered, then leaned down to plant a kiss on Ma's cheek. "I'm okay, but I appreciate you lookin' out for me, Mrs. Gustafson."

"We need to use the phone real quick, okay?" Realene said. "Don't let us distract you from your show."

Ma looked to the TV. "*Cat Ballou* is on. You know, with Jane Fonda. Such a talented young lady."

"Uh-huh," Realene said, grabbing the phone from the wall behind the recliner. The long cord trailed over a plywood bookshelf that housed an old set of encyclopedias Dad had bought from a door-to-door salesman at a discount, because it was missing the letter "D." She stretched the cord across the kitchen table, which threatened to send a pile of bills tumbling to the floor.

Nate grabbed the phone book that sat next to a junk collection bowl on the bookshelf and joined her in the narrow hallway by the back door.

She dialed 9-1-1, then turned her back to keep Ma from hearing. The operator answered and asked for their emergency. Nate pressed his ear to the backside of the phone so their heads were touching.

"My friend Walt needs help. Well, I mean, he's not breathing. I think—"

"Slow down and tell me what happened, ma'am."

"His car ran off the road, and I tried to help him, but he slipped and hit his head. There was a lot of blood." She pressed her eyes closed, knowing she would never forget the image of Walt lying on the ground, staring up at her—blindly, accusingly.

"Where was this?"

Realene described the location and gave her contact information, then said, "There's something else. A prairie dog bit him before he fell. I think they're rabid or something, and they're attacking people."

"Ma'am, abusing the 9-1-1 system is crime. If this is a joke—"

"No, no. Please, help Walt. I just wanted to let you know about the prairie dogs. They could be dangerous."

"I sincerely doubt there are prairie dogs awake in the middle of winter," the operator snapped. "I need to clear the line. We'll send an ambulance for your friend."

There was a click and a dial tone.

"Shit," Nate said.

"Nathan Haugen, you watch your language, young man," Ma said.

"Sorry, Mrs. Gustafson."

Realene took the phone book from him and flipped to the number for Animal Control. "Hang up the phone," she whispered.

He crept back across the kitchen and pressed the button to hang up the call.

Ma glanced back, and he froze, then casually leaned against the bookshelf.

"Hey."

She looked from him to Realene, her brow furrowing, then shook her head and returned her focus to the TV. Apparently, she'd decided that whatever they were up to wasn't worth interrupting *Cat Ballou*.

Nate rejoined Realene.

She dialed and held the phone to her ear. "Busy. Now what? Should we drive to the police station, you think?"

He snapped his fingers. "The cops are already here. In the field. Let's go tell them."

"Brilliant. I mean, assuming they haven't all been bitten already." The joke soured on her tongue. She nearly went back to the truck for her bat, but she thought twice of it. She had no desire to be arrested for threatening a police officer.

THE AFTERNOON SUN peaked out from behind the clouds and shone down on the snow that blanketed Realene's back-yard; the temperature still hovered barely above zero. The crowds had thinned out even more, only one news van left and no sign of any onlookers. A crane had been pulled up to the fence, the arm and hook hanging out over the crater. Police still ringed the barbed wire fence, and military personnel mingled with the scientists inside the perimeter, but Realene couldn't tell if any of them were Colonel Harmon.

Near the fence's gate, several people in hazmat suits stood sentry around a small pull-behind trailer parked at the curb that was little more than a flatbed of wood slats on two wheels. The two halves of the meteor had been hauled from the crater and were tied flat-side down on the bed with two straps that wrapped around the curved surfaces. She hoped they'd fastened the straps tight, because there were no sides on the flatbed to prevent the precious space rocks from sliding free.

Three officers stood in a cluster in the road. One pulled his balaclava beneath his chin and sipped from a thermos that wafted steam into the frigid air, while the other two joked about something. They were decidedly uninfected, and Realene commended herself for not bringing her bat.

She pulled on an old pair of gloves she'd fished from the winter clothing bin in the trailer's entryway as she and Nate ran up to the group, all of whom straightened.

"This is a restricted area," the middle and shortest officer said, screwing the cap back on his thermos and replacing his balaclava while he fixed them with a glare that exuded authority.

"We're not trying to get into the crash site," she said.

Nate craned his neck in the direction of the trailer that held the meteor. "I mean, I wouldn't mind seeing it—"

She smacked him in the arm, and he winced. "Sorry."

"We need help," she said. "Something is wrong with the prairie dogs. They're being super aggressive and attacking people."

One of the other officers, a woman, snickered, and the short one said, "That's a matter for animal control."

"I already talked to them They thought I was joking or something and never came." She shot her own glare at the officer who'd laughed. "We tried calling them again, but we can't get through."

"I'll radio it into the station and let them know to check in with animal control on your report."

"No." She moved closer, and all three officers placed their hands on their holsters. She stopped and raised her hands. "Please, listen. They bit my friend, Walt."

"Does he need medical attention?"

"No, I mean, we already called 9-1-1. But they wouldn't listen either. I think prairie dogs ran his truck off the road and then bit him. He acted confused, like the same as this other girl I know, Brooke. She was bitten, too." Realene heard her voice rise in pitch and her words speed up, but couldn't stop herself. "Then I found Walt, he crashed, and I tried to get him to come with me, to get him help, but he slipped and fell and hit his head on the curb, and he died."

The officer narrowed his eyes. "He slipped and fell and died."

"Yeah. Then they tried to attack me, too, but my friend"—she gestured toward Nate—"came and picked me up, and now I'm not sure where they are, but they're dangerous." Her rapid breaths formed plumes in the frigid air.

"They're seriously rabid or something," Nate said. "I saw them too."

"What's your full name and address, ma'am." The officer pulled a small notebook from his pocket and flipped it open.

She told him, then asked, "So, what are you going to do?"

He walked away to talk with the third officer, leaving the woman officer to watch Nate and Realene.

Cheeks stinging from the cold, Realene surveyed the road, not for cars, but for prairie dogs. Tiny tracks crisscrossed the snow, but there was no sign of any furry attackers. Perhaps they'd headed in the other direction, knowing there were more victims farther into town than there were on the outskirts. She shrugged off the thought, knowing that prairie dogs, even diseased ones, weren't capable of such logic.

The third officer jogged off, heading toward his squad car, and the first officer returned.

"Officer Hendricks is going to call dispatch, check your story. If we find inconsistencies—"

"She didn't do anything wrong." Nate moved closer to Realene, as if to protect her.

The officer cocked his head to the side and eyed Nate. "Don't I know you, son?"

Nate's jaw twitched as if he were clenching his teeth. "No."

"I do know you. I remember now." He slipped the notebook back in his pocket. "I busted you a couple years ago. Nathan, right?"

Realene looped her arm through Nate's. Despite the cold, a hot flush swept up her chest and neck. "That has nothing to do with this."

"You were dealing drugs, weren't ya? Got any on you now?" The officer eyed Nate from head to toe.

"I don't do that stuff anymore," he said, his voice quiet.

"Sure you don't."

Nate scoffed. "You're all a joke, you know that? If you spent as much time trying to actually protect people as you do busting kids who smoke weed—"

"You don't look much like a kid anymore, son." The officer rested his hand on his holstered gun. "If I did find something on you, you'd be tried as an adult this time."

Realene tugged on Nate's arm. "Let's go. They're not going to help us." She felt the tension in his arm and pulled harder. "Come on."

Nate pressed his lips together, as if holding back the words that wanted to spill from his mouth, and let Realene drag him away. She wanted to run but forced herself to walk at a normal pace.

They made it off the road and into her yard, when the officer called, "Got my eye you, Nathan. You too, Realene. Anything seems out of the ordinary with that friend of yours, I'll be seeing you."

Nate stopped in front of the shed, the structure hiding them from view.

"He may not remember, but I met him once before I got arrested. He came to the house after my dad busted my mom up real bad, responding to a call from the neighbors." His Adam's apple bobbed in his throat.

"What happened?" She knew his dad was an abusive asshole, but he never talked much about specifics.

"Dad convinced him she fell. She went along with the story, and the guy never even asked me what happened." He kicked a chunk of crusted snow. "By the time he left, him and dad were joking like old friends, even shook hands and apologized for the inconvenience."

"I'm sorry." She squeezed his arm tighter, laying her head on his shoulder for a moment.

"Yeah. Me too."

They were silent as they trudged toward the porch, then Nate said, "Can we go check on her? My mom? Make sure she's at least safe from these things."

"Yeah, of course."

The back door of Calvin's trailer burst open, and he came out, his gun slung over his shoulder.

"Careful, Calvin. Those cops are itching for fight." Nate angled his chin toward the gun.

"Ah. They can't do shit. I'm allowed to hunt outside city limits." He tromped down the back steps. "Worthless pigs, the whole bunch of them."

"You got that right. Tried telling them something's wrong with the prairie dogs, but they won't listen."

Calvin stopped, pointed one bony finger in their direction. "Damn right something's wrong. One of those little buggers came right at me, tried to take my damn finger off. Never seen anything like it."

"Did you get bit?" Realene asked.

"Nah. I might be old, but I'm still too fast for those little buggers. Shot him in the head. And the couple of others that were with him."

"They've got rabies or something," she said. "They're attacking people in packs, and we can't get through to animal control. Tried telling the cops, but they won't listen."

"Rabies, huh?" Calvin said. "That's bad news. Only way to stop it from spreading is to kill 'em."

"But it's not their fault they're sick. Isn't there any other way?" She knew, deep down, they were still those sweet, frolicking animals who'd entertained her during summer. She also knew rabies was incurable.

"I don't like it either," Nate said. "But they tried to kill you. We gotta do something, right?"

"Us?" she asked.

"Well, yeah. We tried Animal Control and the cops. Who else is there?"

"I don't know. But why is it up to us?"

"Because there is no one else. And if we don't stop them, they'll keep attacking people. Could be us next, or your mom, or mine. We can't let that happen." Nate fixed her with a determined stare.

She knew he was right. "Even if we wanted to, we've got no way to stop them."

"Sure we do." Calvin pulled a cigarette from his pocket, placed it between his lips, and lit it with a match.

"Which is?" she asked.

He took a long drag and exhaled several impressive smoke rings into the air. "We can poison the little buggers."

Seven

CALVIN'S EYES LIT up at the mention of poison, and Realene took an involuntary step back. Far too excited about the prospect, she knew survival wasn't his only priority. "Oh, yeah, that's perfect. Because we all have vats of poison in our pantries next to the Fruit Loops."

"You don't, do you? Have a vat of poison?" Nate brow furrowed.

"Hey now, you kids quit lookin' at me like that," Calvin said. "I don't have it in my house, but I can get it from work."

"Where do you work again? Prairie Dog Assassins 'R' Us?" Her earlobes started to burn, a sure sign of impending frostbite, and she pulled her fur-lined hood over her head.

"Demise Extermination. Make fun all you want, but next time you get a cockroach infestation, see who you call about it."

"Creepy crawlies getting in your house is one thing, but those prairie dogs are building their homes, just trying to live." Realene pressed two fingers to her temple, massaging at the thumping pain building there.

"They're vermin, a menace. Their *homes* can spiderweb out for miles underground, popping up in every field from here to Fargo if we let them. *I* help those farmers stay in business, make sure they can feed their families and all of us."

"You're the one writing into the paper, aren't you?" She jabbed her finger in his chest. "Those frickin' letters to the editor trying to convince everyone to kill all the colonies?"

"And we wouldn't be having this conversation if anyone actually listened."

"Maybe that's true, but you clearly *like* killing those poor animals. For Christ's sake, you even make them into hats." She flicked one of the ear flaps on the fur hat topping his head.

"I don't waste none of the little buggers, use every part. And I'm not takin' sass from someone who sits behind a cash register all day, nice and sheltered, never havin' to get her hands dirty."

"Listen, you little—"

"Okay, now, let's all calm down." Nate wedged himself between her and Calvin and pushed them apart. "This isn't helping anything, and we don't have time for it."

"You said you have poison? Where is it?," Nate asked Calvin.

Calvin threw Realene a satisfied smirk before answering. "Warehouse up off Highway 2, where we store all the pesticides and equipment. I can be there and back in thirty minutes."

"And you can get enough to kill all these prairie dogs?"

"This is nothin'. Last summer, I took out a den of over a hundred on the Walker farm. Dropped the poison right down into the burrows and was able to till 'em over by the next week."

"You do know the ground is frozen, right?" she gave him a smirk of her own.

"We put the poison in treats, stuff they want to eat," he replied. "These things might be rabid, but I'll bet my shriveled left nut they're still hungry. Especially with no grass or anything around to munch on."

"Great. Head over there now, okay? We're gonna go check on my mom, but we'll be back to help after that," Nate said.

Calvin hitched the strap of his gun over his shoulder. "Who said I needed your help."

Nate raised his hands palms out. "Hey, man, we're not trying to step on your toes, we've just seen how dangerous these things can be when they travel in packs. Right, Rea?"

While she wanted to snip at Calvin again, she also knew he wouldn't be able to fight the things on his own. As much as his whole job creeped her out, the prairie dogs were dangerous, and she didn't actually want Calvin to get hurt. "They got ahold of my friend. He didn't make it. And I wouldn't have made it either if Nate hadn't shown up."

"Alright. But don't be too long with your folks. I'm not gonna wait for ya." He high-knee'd it through the snow and around the front of his trailer. A moment later, the engine of his truck roared to life.

"So, we're really gonna do this? Poison the little guys?" she asked.

Nate started toward his plow truck. "I don't like it either, but we don't have a choice."

She glanced over her shoulder at the field again. The prairie dogs were hibernating peacefully less than a day ago. She really wished they'd stayed asleep.

NATE TURNED ONTO Main, his body rigid and tense. Outside, the wind gusted, shaking the bare branches of the trees that lined the road.

"How long has it been since you saw your folks?" Realene asked.

"Other than secretly driving by to see if I can catch my mom alone? My birthday." He kept his focus straight ahead.

She curled her gloved hand into a fist at the mention of his birthday. They'd planned to gorge themselves on burgers and shakes at Toppers, and see a double feature at the Cinema Twin. Instead, Nate had been woken by a suitcase hitting him in the face. His dad demanded he pack his stuff and get out. That was almost a year ago.

"Still no luck getting ahold of your mom?"

"Nah. Every time I call, he's the one who answers. I'm not even sure he lets her talk on the phone anymore." His fingers flexed on the steering wheel, and she worried for a moment that he might snap it off. "Tried writing too. All my letters are returned unopened."

"I'm sorry. I'm sure she misses you." She'd seen the two of them together, seen how much she loved her son.

"Maybe." He cleared his throat. "But I don't really care about that, you know. I mean, I do, but mostly I just want her out of there. Even if it means she never talks to me again, at least she'd be safe."

"Yeah." She knew he'd done everything he could, even called the police himself a couple times, but that only made his dad angrier. One time, Nate and his mom actually left, though only for a couple days, then she took his dad back. He'd been so satisfied, gloating to Nate as if it was a contest to be won.

Realene blinked back the sting in her eyes and looked out the passenger window. A deer—a doe, judging by the lack of horns—ran across the snowy field. Though rare, they did occasionally see deer in the area.

A trio of prairie dogs pursued the deer, as if they were an apex predator.

"You don't see that every day," she said.

"Deer are faster than prairie dogs," he said, but not with confidence.

They turned into Nate's old neighborhood, a cul-de-sac of a dozen ranch-style homes, and parked across the street from his parent's house. The garage door was open, and Dick stood inside with his back to them.

Nate grabbed the baseball bat from the floor of the truck.

"Hey," Realene said. "You're an adult now, like, legally."

"Yeah, so?"

"Meaning if something happens, if he comes at you or eggs you on or whatever, you could be charged with assault. You heard that cop, with your record and everything, they're going to assume the worst."

He rubbed one hand over the back of his neck. "So, you're telling me I shouldn't use this to bash his brains in?"

She grinned. "That bat is for bashin' prairie dogs only."

"Check." He wrenched open his door and got out, striding toward his childhood home and the man who'd made his life hell. Realene jogged around the truck to catch up.

The next-door neighbor buffed a purple and teal snow-mobile parked on an ATV hauler out front of his house. The guy, who wore a purple and teal jacket and snow pants to match the snowmobile, was clearly preparing for exactly the kind of winter adventure Realene tried to avoid.

"Hey, Fred," Nate said.

"Nice weather we're having, huh?"

"Oh, yeah. Real nice."

Realene held back a laugh. What was nice about zero flippin' degrees?

"Well, good to see ya." Fred headed back into his house, leaving the back hauler gate down and the key in the snow-mobile's ignition.

Realene almost yelled after the guy to come back, figuring the discussion with Nate's dad might go better with a witness. Then she realized Fred probably went inside for just that reason. He had to have heard fights at the Haugan's before and, apparently, had decided to mind his own business. What an asshole.

Nate's childhood home boasted sidewalks cleanly shoveled all the way to the edges of the lawn—no half-assed, barely wide enough path for Dick. A waist-high plastic nativity display complete with a camel and two sheep sat on the porch beside the front door. She tried to picture the inside of the house and couldn't, any mental image long gone. Embarrassed about his home life and not wanting to expose her to his dad any more than he had to, Nate rarely invited her over. Realene's house was smaller and more run down, but he'd always been welcome there, always been loved.

They proceeded up the driveway shoulder to shoulder and stopped before they reached the open garage door, standing for a moment in silence. A path was shoveled through the grass beside the house, creating a walkway to a small structure in the backyard that was constructed of cinder blocks and boasted a riveted, metal door that faced the backyard. While she hadn't been there often, she felt sure the odd shed was new.

The inside of the detached garage resembled the stockroom of an Army surplus store. Hooks on the wall held a variety of sheathed knives and tools, and multiple pairs of boots and stacks of winter gear filled a long worktable along the back wall. Beneath the worktable were boxes filled with canned goods.

Stocky and muscular, but with a pronounced beer belly, Dick wore Carhartt overalls, a matching work coat, and a skullcap. He rifled through an Army-green duffel bag that sat atop the workbench. Several gun stocks stuck out from the top of the duffel bag, and they watched as he lifted an axe off the wall and held it up to inspect the blade.

"Since when is your dad a prepper?" Realene whispered, wishing she were anywhere but there.

Dick ran one finger along the edge of the blade, as if testing the sharpness, his breath pluming in the air like a cloud of sulfur. She imagined the smell of rot emanating from his nose and mouth.

"He's always liked hunting, guns, big on defending his home, but the bomb shelter is definitely new," Nate said.

"Is that what that is?" She peeked past the garage at the cinder block structure.

Dick noticed them, his mouth twisting in a snarl. "What're you doin' here, boy?"

Nate squared his shoulders. "Wanted to check on mom, make sure she's okay."

"Why wouldn't she be?" His eyes jumped from Nate to Realene. "You aren't welcome here. Neither is your little girlfriend."

"There's something wrong with the prairie dogs," Realene said, not bothering to correct him about her and Nate. "We wanted to warn you."

Dick threw his head back and laughed, a sharp barking sound that made her flinch. "Scared of a few prairie dogs, princess?"

"It's not funny." Nate took a step toward his dad. "People have been attacked, even killed. Something's wrong."

Dick's face changed in an instant, all good humor draining away. "It's time, that's all. For all you sinners to pay what you owe."

"Sinners? What the hell are you talking about?" Nate asked.

"The fire's come down from heaven to punish the sinners and free the righteous."

"Guess you've been drinking Reverend Zebediah's Kool-Aid, huh, *Dick*," Realene said.

"Richard." He glowered at her. "The faithful have been preparing for this day, and it has finally come, as he predicted it would."

"The meteor landing isn't some sign from God," Nate said. "It's a rock that's crashed to Earth. That's all."

"Think you're so smart, don't you?" Dick pointed at Nate with the axe. "Judgment's comin' for you, boy. I only hope I'm there to see it."

Nate's grip tightened on the bat, and Realene placed a hand on his arm.

"Where's mom?" he asked. "I want to see her. Now"

Dick shook his head. "Big man, huh? Well, you're not bigger than me."

"Maybe we should go." Realene's chest tightened at the sight of Nate's proximity to his dad, at how Dick wielded the axe like he would be happy to use it.

"I'd listen to your girlfriend." He moved closer, and the sharp, acetone scent of gun cleaner hit her.

"Mom!" Nate yelled, his voice echoing through the empty street. "Mom, are you in there?"

"Shut your mouth, boy." Dick half-raised the axe.

A metallic creaking noise sounded from the backyard, and Realene and Nate moved away from Dick and his axe to check around the side of the garage. The metal door set in the bunker swung wide, and Nate's mom walked out carrying another box of canned goods. Sophia wore heavy-duty coveralls that were too big for her, the sleeves bunching at the wrists, and the legs bunching at the ankles.

"Nathan?" A smile lit up her face, which appeared a decade older than the last time Realene had seen her, just over a year ago.

"Mom." Nate exhaled the word, the relief in his voice palpable, and he jogged down the grass path toward her.\

Realene watched the reunion from the driveway, not wanting to interfere.

Nate and his mother stood staring at one another for a moment, as if neither knew what to say or do.

"Here, let me take that," he said, grabbing the box.

She closed the heavy metal door with a thump, slid the metal latch in place, and secured it with a combination lock.

Dick didn't come out of the garage, just went perfectly still, as if listening through the wall.

Realene wanted to yell at Nate, tell him to say what he wanted, quickly and quietly.

Nate's mom placed her hands on either side of his face and whispered something to him.

"Sophia!" Dick yelled, staring at Realene as if he could see the scene with Nate through her eyes, and he didn't like it.

Sophia nudged Nate ahead of her down the path, but didn't touch him after that. He rounded the corner with the box and dropped it on the cement floor inside the garage. Sophia paused when she saw Realene and asked, "How's your mom doing?"

"Good," Realene said, because it wasn't the time for truth.

Sophia continued into the garage, looking skinnier than Realene remembered. *Skin and bones,* Ma would say.

"What took you so long?" Dick asked.

"Just packing up more food." She dropped her gaze to the ground.

"Is that a bomb shelter?" Realene asked, eyeing the strange building.

No one answered.

Nate looked around the interior of the garage, walking a small circuit that placed him closer to his mom. "Why are you emptying it?"

She opened her mouth to answer, then glanced at Dick and clamped her lips closed.

"Not even letting her talk now, huh?" Nate asked.

Dick threw the axe, sent it slicing through the air between Nate and Sophia. The blade landed with a thunk in the garage wall. Sophia didn't even flinch.

He sauntered across the garage, as if preening for all the eyes on him, and gripped the handle of the axe, pulled it from the wall.

Bile tinged Realene's tongue. She was tempted to spit at him, but her sense of self-preservation prevailed.

"You're not welcome here, boy."

Nate ignored him and offered a hand to Sophia. "Mom, it's not safe here. Come with us."

"You should go," she said.

"You heard her. Go and don't come back." Dick flipped the axe, letting it spin once in the air before catching it by the handle. "Next time I won't be so nice."

Sophia bit her lip. "Just go."

Nate sighed heavily. "At least stay inside. It's not safe out here." He strode from the garage toward Realene.

As if to prove his point, a chorus of chirps sounded down the street from the direction of Main.

Realene turned toward the sound, and her stomach threatened to send back the hostess cupcakes she'd eaten for lunch.

A pack of prairie dogs were scampering down the street, heading straight for them.

Eight

"THEY'RE HERE," REALENE said, watching the pack of prairie dogs approach and thinking she'd much rather be fighting poltergeists like little Carol Anne. She grabbed the closest objects that could be used as a weapon—several cans of Campbell's Cream of Mushroom from the top of the box Nate had dropped inside the garage.

"Stay inside and close the door," Nate said to his mom, raising his bat to ready for the attackers. She rushed to the worktable instead, rummaging through one of the duffel bags.

Dick strode outside, axe in hand, and stopped beside Realene. "Told ya I'm not afraid of some little rodents."

"Good for you. Just try not to let them bite you," she said, very much not in the mood for Dick's tough-guy routine.

The pack, which numbered about ten, reached the edge of the driveway. They were scragglier than the ones that had previously attacked Realene, their fur matted and bloody.

Nate stepped forward and swung the bat toward the ground in a wide arc, golfing the lead rodent and sending it flying.

Dick grunted, almost approvingly.

Realene chucked a can of soup at one of them and missed.

The prairie dogs leapt over the rolling can one by one in a choreographed display to rival the most well-trained horses. She tried again, drawing back her arm as she focused on one specific animal and mentally calculating its speed as she released the projectile. This time the can hit the critter in the head with a thunk, knocking it to the ground. The prairie dog writhed where it fell, clearly injured, and gave a whining cry. "Yes!"

Realene, Nate, and Dick lined up in a row midway up the driveway, with her in the middle. Another prairie dog ran at them, and Nate took it out with another swing of the bat, this time sending it sailing so high in the air that it landed on the roof with a thump. Realene waited for the thing to come sliding down, but it didn't, destined to mummify in snow and ice. On her other side, Dick swiped at an attacker that was mid-leap, slicing the animal across the belly and splattering Realene's coat with blood. The prairie dog dropped to the ground, its guts leaking out. He gave it one more chop, cutting it in two.

"Jesus." Realene cringed.

"Blasphemer," Dick said, still focused on their attackers.

The rest of the prairie dog group split in two, half falling back to the sidewalk across the street while the others took cover behind the snowmobile hauler. Nate watched the first group, that appeared to be circling around on the left, and Realene and Dick tracked the group near the hauler, one of which scampered up the back end of the snowmobile and onto the seat. The little creature looked about ready to take the handles and drive.

She glanced behind her to see Nate bash another of the animals with his bat. There were still two more watching him from further up the street, but they seemed to be hanging back to calculate their best plan of attack. She refocused on the snowmobile just as that prairie dog jumped from the seat to the small windshield. The critter bared its blood-stained teeth as it launched itself toward them. Dick released his axe, sending it spinning through the air, end over end. The blade caught the creature in mid leap, slicing its tiny head from its body.

Realene only had a second of relief before she realized the others in the group had run beneath the hauler. One emerged from the end closest to them. "Watch out," she called to Dick, who was bent over his kill.

One of the prairie dogs ran up his leg and clung to his back, claws and teeth lodged in the heavy fabric of his coat. Realene threw one of her last two cans as hard as she could, and it nailed Dick in the middle of the back, right above where the creature hung, and it let go, scampering back beneath the trailer.

Dick spun around, eyes narrowed and cheeks flaming red, and punched Realene in the face. Pain bloomed across her jaw as she stumbled backward and fell on her ass, the air leaving her lungs in a whoosh. Her last can slipped from her grip and rolled down the driveway.

Nate witnessed the blow and raised his weapon before Realene had hit the ground. He swung the bat into Dick's outstretched hand—the one that hit Realene in the face—and connected flush with the man's wrist. The sound of the bones snapping echoed through the cold air, and Dick screamed.

"Keep your hands off her." Nate extended the bat to barely touch Dick's chest, as if holding him at a distance.

"You broke my fuckin' wrist." He grabbed the bat with his good hand and chucked it to the side, where it lodged in a snowbank. The axe still lay on the ground by the decapitated prairie dog, and Dick's eyes cut to it, as if he meant to grab the blade.

Something moved in her peripheral, and Realene looked across the street to where the prairie dogs had grown tired of waiting. They galloped toward the driveway, uttering a series of chirps.

"Behind you," she yelled to Nate, getting up. The creatures that hid beneath the hauler ran out at the same time.

Dick managed to grab his axe in time to fight off the two nearest him, but Nate and Realene were left with no weapons thanks to that asshole. She figured kicking the creatures had the least likelihood of getting her bit, given the thick rubber of her duck boots. Easing out a breath that filled the air with a cold mist, she readied herself to deliver the kick of her life and tried not to think about the fact she'd whiffed every kickball at-bat she'd ever attempted.

Realene slipped a little on the ice, pinwheeling her arms to keep from falling, and time slowed. Both prairie dogs leapt, clawed paws extended and mouths wrenched wide. She screamed and raised her arms to cover her face, when two gunshots rang out in rapid succession from behind her.

The creatures exploded in a spray of blood and fur, one after the other, and bits of guts splattered Realene, Nate, and the driveway like the world's worst piñatas.

Ears ringing from the crack of the gunshots, she turned to see Nate's mom holding a rifle, finger still resting on the trigger.

"Thanks." Realene panted. "Nice shot."

Dick screamed, drawing their attention back to him. He dropped to his knees and clutched his injured wrist with his good hand.

Two prairie dogs, the last of their would-be attackers, lay dead beside him, but he didn't take a moment to thank his wife for her dramatic intervention. "Can't you see I'm hurt!" he screamed. "Get the fuckin' kit!"

Sophia ran into the garage, putting the rifle down next to the duffel bag, and grabbed a rusted metal box from the workbench. She rushed out to the driveway and set the box beside her husband, then crouched to open it. "Is it broken?" she asked.

"Your son smashed it with a bat. What the fuck do you think?"

"You shouldn't have hit her," Nate said, his voice sounding years younger.

"I'm okay, really," Realene said.

Sophia uncapped a small syringe. "Ready?" Her face paled despite the sting of the cold air.

"Get on with it," Dick said.

She stabbed the needle through his work pants and into his leg, and pressed down on the plunger.

Dick's eyes clenched shut. After several seconds, he slumped in relief and opened them again. "Come on. Splint."

She dropped the tube on the ground before pulling two sticks and an ace bandage from the box.

Nate bent to pick up the tube and held it out for Realene to read. *Morphine.*

She caught sight of motion next door, the curtains rustling as Fred peered out the front window. He met her gaze with wide eyes, then his face disappeared, and the curtains closed. She didn't really blame him for not wanting any part of the shit show.

Dick slipped off his coat, wincing as the sleeve scraped his injury, and dropped it beside him in a heap. He wore only a short sleeve T-shirt, and visibly trembled from the cold. Sophia placed the two sticks on the front and back of his wrist, which was already swelling and turning purple. He held the splints in place as she expertly wrapped the bandage around and secured it.

"Mom. Since when do you shoot?" Nate asked. Sophia never liked guns because her dad died from a self-inflicted gunshot wound when she was pretty young.

She dropped her chin to her chest, shrinking into herself. "We've been practicing at church, getting ready. We all have to do our part."

"Huh. Us Lutheran's mostly make Chili," Realene said.

Dick stood, shoving Sophia away when she tried to help him up. "Don't think I'm gonna forget this," he said to Nate. "I owe you, boy."

"Guess I owe you too then, huh, Dick," Realene said.

He huffed a half laugh. "You brought this evil to our doorstep. It followed *you*."

"The prairie dogs are sick. There's nothing evil about it." Nate grabbed the bat from the snowbank, as if he felt safer around his dad with a weapon in his hands.

"You're the ones who're sick, corrupted by the devil. Every one of you is gonna pay." Dick swiped the axe from the ground with his good hand, leaving the coat and medical kit for Sophia to grab.

"Every one of who?" Realene asked.

"All you wretched sinners. For the wages of sin is death."

Sirens sounded, drawing their attention to the main road. Several police cruisers sped past, lights flashing, headed toward town.

"That can't be good," Realene said, imagining prairie dogs swarming downtown Main Street.

Dick shuffled toward the garage. "Now, get the fuck off my property before I exterminate you myself."

"Go ahead and try it." Nate raised the bat to rest on his shoulder.

Realene caught his eye. "Not helpful, dude."

Sophia screamed, dropping the kit, which hit the concrete with a metallic bang. She covered her mouth and pointed where the cruisers had just passed.

A deer galloped toward them, hooves clopping on the asphalt, muzzle snorting plumes of frost in the air. Spots of blood marred its tawny coat.

"Run!" Nate pushed Realene and Sophia toward the garage. Dick followed close behind. Once they were inside, he hit the button on the side wall to lower the door. The chains on either side of the opening cranked and clanged, moving slower than any garage door in the history of the world. The garage was detached, so it provided no escape into the house.

Realene crouched to watch the approach of the infected animal as it neared the driveway. She turned and surveyed the worktable, started to reach for a hunting knife but stopped. Thinking it would be better to maintain some distance, she grabbed the snow shovel from the wall, figuring the heavy metal scoop would be perfect for bashing.

Nate held his bat in front of him, focused on the lowering garage door. "Come on, come on."

A foot of daylight remained when the deer hit, smashing into the door at full speed, denting the metal and pushing the door partially off the tracks. The motor whirred, stalled, then stopped.

"You did this." Dick took a step toward Nate, the axe gripped in his good hand.

"Please." Sophia put a hand on his chest. "Don't hurt him."

"*Don't hurt him,*" Dick mocked, his voice high and whiny. He knocked her hand away, and she shrank back. Nate moved in front of her, blocking her with his body.

Dick sneered and raised the axe.

Realene grabbed his injured wrist and squeezed. He yowled in pain and dropped the axe, which pinged against the concrete floor.

"Killer deer, remember?" she said.

The creature rammed the door again, wrenching it

completely off the track. It grunted and battered at the door with its hooves, the metal shuddering beneath the onslaught. One more big hit, and the deer would be inside with them.

"Come on." Nate grabbed Sophia's hand and tugged her toward the garage's side door, but she pulled out of his grip to pick up the axe and hand it to Dick, and then grab her gun.

The four of them rushed out the door into the side yard, Realene the last one out. She closed the door behind her an instant before the deer crashed inside.

"The bunker," Sophia said, leading the way.

Behind them, the beast smashed around the garage, but Realene resisted the urge to look back. She knew they needed to get somewhere safe before it busted through the door.

They ran down the shoveled path and stopped at the shelter door. Sophia set her gun down and started twisting the combination lock.

Cracking wood sounded, and Realene turned to see the deer crash through the side door. It stumbled outside, shaking its head as if dazed. Blood oozed from the bite marks on its side, and she felt a stab of pity for the creature.

The lock opened with a snap, and the deer swung its head to stare at them.

"Open it," Dick said, helpful as ever.

Realene backed up to stand beside Nate, keeping one eye on the deer. It opened its mouth and uttered a bleating scream that curdled her stomach. She grabbed Nate and pulled him to the side, intending to dodge behind the cinder block structure for cover.

Sophia slid the lock from the latch and wrenched the handle to open the door.

The deer charged, frothing at the mouth.

Dick ran straight at the animal, meeting it a few feet from the bunker and burying the axe in its side. The deer stumbled and fell against the side of the garage, its legs crumpling. He pulled the axe free, releasing a spray of blood that slashed across the snow. Dick brought the axe down again and again, chopping at the creature until it finally lay limp and dead, its brown eyes wide and sightless. Realene wondered if those little worms wiggled around in there, invisible against the dark iris.

Dick strode toward the bunker and swung the door wide with his good arm. "Go on," he said to Sophia.

"Not you," Dick said to Nate, before sneering at Realene. "Or you, princess."

"We can't leave them." Sophia stepped toward Nate, but Dick grabbed her arm, stopping her.

"It's okay." Nate gave his mom a small smile. "We have a date with some poison. To stop this."

Realene nodded, no more doubt in her mind about what needed to be done and who needed to do it.

Nate gave Sophia a kiss on the cheek. "It was good to see you, Mom."

She grasped his face in both hands, then drew him into a hug.

Realene started up the path, giving them their privacy. She stabbed her shovel into the snowbank on the side closest to Fred's house.

A grunt sounded, and Realene glanced at the deer on the ground, but it hadn't moved. Another grunt drew her attention to the street, where another deer, this one a huge buck boasting a ten-point rack, waited. The animal raised its head, as if scenting the air, then rotated its head to stare right at her.

With a guttural groan, it reared on hind legs, then galloped toward them.

Realene dove to the side, landing in the snowbank beside her abandoned shovel.

She looked up just in time to see the buck barrel past her, giving her an up-close view of the bloody gouge in its side.

Dick grabbed the gun and raised it to his eye, struggled to steady the weapon one-handed. Behind him, Nate wrapped Sophia in a tight embrace, as if to cocoon her from any blows.

The creature lowered its head and barreled into Dick. Horns skewering him at the waist, the buck raised its head to lift the man into the air. He flailed and dropped the gun. The animal flung him free of its horns and into the side of the cinder block structure, his head smacking hard against the concrete. Dick sunk to the ground, limp, and the buck lunged forward to chomp down on his neck.

Sophia screamed.

Dick's body had been sitting upright against the structure, but after the buck's bite, it slid to its side to lay limp in the snow.

"Dad?" Nate croaked, and Sophia squirmed from his grip, drawing the buck's attention. The animal raised its head, blood dripping from its muzzle.

"Hey! Over here!" Realene yelled, rising to her knees and grabbing the shovel. The beast gave a deep growl and ran straight toward her. A moment before it was upon her, she fell back against the snow and stabbed upward with the shovel, scoop end first, catching the buck in the throat. The sharp metal blade meant for scraping ice from driveways and sidewalks sliced through the animal's hide and into the muscle of its neck.

The buck faltered, then fell forward, hooves sinking into the snow on either side of her body. The animal brayed and spit blood, its horned head looming dangerously above her.

Realene let go of the shovel before the weight of the animal drove it downward into the snow, and she rolled to the side between its front and hind legs, barely clearing the animal before its body landed where she had just been, the momentum driving the blade end of the shovel deeper into its neck.

The buck grunted, eyes rolling to meet hers, before its head slumped, and it crashed to the side, dead.

Nate ran up behind Realene, dropping the bat to pull her to her feet. "You okay?"

She gave a thumbs up, unable to speak, her pulse pounding so hard in her throat she thought she might choke.

A wail drew their attention back to Sophia, who knelt by Dick's body. His eyes were closed, as if he could have been sleeping or unconscious, but a jagged bite mark marred his neck and bloody antler holes punctured his torso.

"Mom, I'm so sorry." Nate reached out to put a hand on her back, but she shrugged him off.

"Leave." She didn't look at them.

"Mom," Nate said, his voice strangled.

"Get out of here!" she shouted, glaring at them before hunching forward to wrap her arms around her husband.

Nate's shoulders slumped. He gave his mom one last forlorn look, then walked past Realene down the path.

Weariness weighing down Realene's limbs, she trudged past the buck to follow him, her boots leaving blood-laced tracks in the snow.

Nine

THEY PULLED ONTO the main road, leaving the carnage behind them. Realene removed her gloves and held her frozen fingers up to the vent in an attempt to unthaw. She surveyed the field and surrounding area but saw no sign of any animals. She hoped that meant Sophia would have time to get inside, get somewhere safe.

Nate had said nothing since they got in the truck.

"So, that didn't go great," she said.

"No, it did not." He gave a humorless laugh. "I'd imagined all kinds of scenarios for how badly that reunion could have gone, and none of them involved killer deer."

"If this disease—or whatever it is—is spreading to other animals, do you think it can infect people in the same way? Turn them violent? I mean, Brooke and Walt were acting more confused when they got bit, but maybe that's how it starts."

"Maybe." Nate's voice was monotone, devoid of emotion.

Realene cleared her throat. "How're you doing? I mean, with your dad…"

"You mean, how was it seeing him gored by a deer?"

"That, yes. But more how are you doing with him, like, dying? I mean, I'm assuming he couldn't have survived that."

"No, I wouldn't think so." He sniffed, wiping a hand across his face. "I've wished for him to die lots of times. Dreamed about it."

"Of course you did. That's totally normal considering everything he did to you and your mom." Others might judge him for saying such a thing, but not Realene. Hell, she'd fantasized a number of times about killing Dick herself.

"Now that it's happened, I don't know. I just, I don't know."
Nate sighed. "You think my mom... You think she'll be okay?
Maybe we shouldn't have left her."

"She'll be fine, dude. Did you see her with that gun? She's
stronger than she looks, plus she has that bunker. And we're
about to go back into battle. You don't want her there for that."

"Yeah, I guess you're right."

The whoop of a siren sounded, and another police car sped
past them, away from the landing site. A military vehicle
followed close behind.

"Crap. I know they were jerks, but I was hoping to talk to
them again, see if they'd finally believe us. There've got to be
other people seeing what's going on and reporting it by now,
right?"

Nate slowed as he approached the trailer park entrance,
and Realene surveyed the road ahead. All that remained
were two civilian vehicles, a Jeep, and the pull-behind trailer
that held the two halves of the meteor. A soldier stood near
the trailer, and there were a handful of people in hazmat suits
within the fence, but all the police officers appeared to have
left.

"The whole situation with the meteor crash is kind of creepy,
right? Like it's weird that all the animals started freaking out
around the same time, don't you think?"

He turned onto Plainview. "Don't tell me you buy all that
crap about the end days."

She scoffed. "No. I don't think the meteor is an act of God's
vengeance. That's some cult shit, like thinking an alien ship is
hitching a ride with Hale-Bopp."

He pulled up in front of her trailer and stopped. "You don't
think they'd do something like that, do you? Like some kind of
suicide pact. My mom—"

"No way," she said, regretting making the comparison.
"Reverend Zebediah has convinced them all the sinners are
being judged. She's going to be okay."

"I hope so." The corner of his lips ticked up. "Can we talk
about that shovel move you pulled? Fuckin' rad."

She grinned, glad to see him joking again. "Yeah, I totally nailed that, huh? I guess all that training shoveling this goddamn driveway finally paid off."

He turned off the car and angled his chin toward the field. "How you feeling about killing those little guys now?"

"Sucks we have to." Despite everything, she still felt bad for the infected animals. "But I guess it's kill or be killed."

Next door, Calvin stood in his driveway, messing with something in the back of his little Ford pickup truck. He stared at them, arms crossed. "You two necking in there, or what?"

"Did he seriously just say *necking*?" she asked. "I can't believe we're putting our faith in an old taxidermy-loving weirdo."

Nate shrugged. "He's all we've got."

She put her gloves back on, promising herself a giant mug of piping hot cocoa with extra mini marshmallows and a splash of her dad's Wild Turkey as a reward for saving Demise.

They walked up to Calvin's driveway, passing the plastic reindeer in his front yard. The animal bore a buck tooth and cutesy Disney eyes, but it still gave her the creeps after their recent encounter with the killer deer. Realene glanced back at her own house, thankful Ma made it home before the attacks escalated. Hell, with how quickly Reverend Zebediah had escalated his preaching after the meteor crash, it was lucky Irene hadn't kidnapped Ma.

"Where the hell you been?" Calvin asked.

"We got held up," Nate said.

"Just didn't want to help out old Calvin, I bet. Too young and soft and all sad about killing the poor little prairie dogs."

"We were attacked by a pack of prairie dogs and barely avoided getting bit before a couple of infected deer showed up," Realene said. "One of them killed Nate's dad...probably."

"Oh." Calvin shuffled his feet. "Well, sorry 'bout your dad."

"Don't be," the two teens said in unison.

"Infected deer means it's spreadin.' We better get a move on."

"We've got to actually find the prairie dogs, first," Realene said.

"Um, I don't think that'll be a problem." Nate pointed toward the field. Prairie dogs were popping up from the ground, their little heads breaking the surface of the snow as they climbed from their burrows. They crept toward the fenced perimeter around the landing site.

"Alright, what's the plan?" Nate asked, turning back to Calvin.

Calvin hefted a cardboard box piled high with apples from his truck and stuck it in Nate's arms.

"Apples?"

"They love 'em. Cut a small hole, stick the poison in, and Bob's your uncle. "

"Neat," Realene said, resisting the urge to tell him off again. They did need to get rid of the animals before the disease spread. Calvin handed her a box, then took one himself.

"Basically, the same process to make a bong," Nate said.

Realene rolled her eyes and started the trek through his yard. Nate and Calvin kept pace beside her.

"Commence Operation Poisoned Apple," Calvin said.

Nate snickered, and Calvin said, "What? I thought you might like it better than Operation Prairie Dog Massacre."

"Definitely better," Realene agreed. Cold stung her cheeks, so she dipped her head, tucking her chin into the collar of her coat for warmth.

Someone screamed, and the soldier left his post, running through the gate and toward the far side of the crater. The white-suited scientists seemed to be struggling with something at the back of the fence.

Calvin, Nate, and Realene crossed the street and stopped at the edge of the field, setting their boxes down near the curb behind the meteor trailer.

Realene craned her neck to see what the scientists were fighting and caught sight of tawny fur and rearing hooves. "Is that another goddamn deer? Where the hell are they all coming from?"

The prairie dogs picked up speed, galloping toward the fence.

"Come on, let's get their attention." Calvin removed his fur hat, revealing his bald head, and waved the hat around. "Hey, ya little buggers, over here! We got some treats for ya."

Realene did the *smooch-smooch* sound she normally reserved for Pumpkin. "Come here, little guys, we've got something yummy for you."

A few of the prairie dogs closest to the trio stopped, stood on hind legs, and looked in their direction.

"Now, chuck 'em." Calvin picked up an apple and threw it as far as he could. Nate and Realene did the same, each lobbing half a dozen apples in quick succession before they paused to watch the curious prairie dogs.

The closest animals sniffed the apples, then gave a series of sharp barks. The rest of the creatures changed direction, veering from their path toward the fence to head back for the smattering of apples on the snow.

One prairie dog held an apple between its tiny paws and took a bite, its cheeks working and whiskers wiggling as it chewed. After a moment, it gave a high-pitched call. The others responded with a series of chirps, and several moved to pick up an apple of their own.

"I think they're taking the bait." Nate bounced on the balls of his feet.

The remaining animals were bounding toward their own apples when the first prairie dog began to howl and roll on the ground. The apple rolled from its paws as it spasmed and twitched. After a moment, the prairie dog went totally limp.

"It worked," Calvin said. "Hot damn."

"R.I.P. little guy," Realene said.

The rest of the creatures stopped to stare at their fallen friend. They chirped and barked, as if having a conversation.

"Come on, just eat them," Nate said.

The prairie dogs went silent and every single one dropped their apple.

"Uh-oh." Realene backed up. "I think they know there's something bad in those apples."

"Nah. They're not that smart," Calvin said.

Her stomach clenched. "Guys, I think we should go."

"Just gotta tempt 'em." Calvin threw several more apples, which all landed with a crunch of snow.

The animals stood once more on hind legs and turned as a group to stare with beady black eyes at their human adversaries, like a scene from the *Children of the Damned*. They bared their tiny teeth in something like a snarl and began to growl, the collective sound seeming to travel through the ground and into Realene's bones.

"They know it was us," she said, her panicked breath fogging the air. "We gotta get outta here."

Calvin bent to pick up his box, and Nate said, "Leave it. If they eat them, great."

The prairie dogs, at least twenty of them, dropped to all fours and set off in a gallop toward the trio, their angry cries filling the air.

"Run," Nate said, taking off toward Realene's trailer.

Realene ran as fast as she could across the street and through her snow-covered yard, huffing from the effort as she struggled through the crusted snow.

Behind them, Calvin yelled, "Come get me, you little fuckers! See this hat? It's your cousin. I killed and skinned him just like I'm gonna do to you!"

Realene looked back to see him grab the rifle from his shoulder and aim it at the approaching pack.

"Calvin! Come on!" she cried, but he didn't respond.

Gunshots cracked through the air, each pop making her muscles tense, and by the time she and Nate reached the porch of her trailer, several dead prairie dogs littered the ground around Calvin.

But many more remained and were headed straight for him.

"Calvin!" she yelled, but he laughed and continued taunting the infected animals.

A few of the prairie dogs broke off at the sound of her voice and veered in the direction of her trailer.

"Go, hurry," Nate said, pushing her from behind. She opened the front door of the trailer, and they rushed inside, closing it behind them.

Though they were safe in the warmth of the trailer, Realene began to tremble, every muscle in her body shaking. She bent at the waist, bracing her hands on her thighs. "He's going to get himself killed, or at least bit. But we can't go back out there."

Nate leaned back against the wood-paneled wall, panting. "I'm starting to question the wisdom of this plan."

"No shit." Realene peeked through the doorway to the living room, where Ma sat dozing in the recliner.

"They knew we poisoned their friend, right?" Nate paced the small room, completing a circuit between her childhood dirt bike and her dad's old set of golf clubs. "How's that possible?"

She wiped the fog from the small window set in the front door and watched Calvin run away from the remaining prairie dogs, still waving that fur hat like a maniac.

Laughter bubbled up from inside her and came out in a crazy cackle. That morning, she'd thought her life might be changing for the better, but instead, things had gotten so much worse. "This is fucking perfect, you know?"

"What?"

"I shouldn't even be here. And now not only have I lost my chance at an actual life away from this shit hole, we're being hunted by diseased prairie dogs and psychotic deer. It's really just fucking perfect."

"Are you being serious right now?" Nate stopped his pacing to gape at her. "People have died today, you know."

"Yeah, I do know." She didn't want to think about Walt, not now.

"And you're *still* complaining about Arizona. As if we all don't have bigger problems right now."

"I know we have bigger problems, that's my point. If things had gone the way they should have, they wouldn't be *my* problems at all."

"So, screw the rest of us, huh? Me, your mom, everyone else in this town. Fuck us, as long as you get your dream life."

"You know that's not what I meant. I'd never want anything to happen to you or my mom, or even the assholes in this town." She rubbed the back of her neck. "I'm just venting. I worked hard to get that scholarship, and it's not fair."

"Fair? You think you're the only one who hasn't gotten a fair shot?"

"Of course not. People get screwed all the time, I just got my hopes up, ya know?" She crossed her arms. "Look, is this about your dad? I get that he was a major asshole today, well, every day, but that's not my fault."

"This is about *you* being an asshole."

Her jaw dropped open. "What did you call me?"

"You were so excited to get out of this town, to leave everything behind. Like I didn't matter to you at all, like we haven't been best friends for ten fucking years."

She scoffed. "I asked you to come with me to Arizona, and you said no."

"Yeah, because I knew I'd end up stuck in a town where I don't know anyone while you were off with your new college friends."

"What do you want me to say? I'm not going to apologize for wanting a better life." The trailer creaked on its foundation, shifting in the frigid wind.

"You don't get it," he said, throwing up his hands.

"Whatever. It doesn't matter now anyway." She yanked off her gloves and stuffed them in her coat pockets. "We need to get the hell out of here. Grab my mom, stop and get yours if you want, and then get as far from Demise as possible."

"What about everybody else?"

"We tried, we did the poison plan and failed. There's nothing else we can do. They won."

"Screw that." He strode past her and reached for the door handle.

"Where the hell are you going?" She grabbed his shoulder, and he smacked her hand away.

"Even now, all you want to do is run away."

"Yeah. Because, as if this town wasn't bad enough already, it's being overrun by diseased animals. And no way is this rabies. We need to leave. *Now*."

A pair of faint gunshots sounded outside, and Realene cringed.

"You can leave if you want," Nate said. "I'm going to the police station to make sure they know what's happening and see if I can help."

"Don't be stupid. You could get hurt. Or killed."

Nate always felt the need to save everyone.

"Now you suddenly care about me, huh?" he asked. "If only you were in Arizona, you wouldn't have to think about me at all. Go ahead and do it. Run away."

Realene clenched her teeth. "Even if I wanted to, I couldn't. My car has been overtaken by diseased prairie dogs, remember?"

"Your mom has a car. Take it and leave. That's what you've always wanted to do anyway, so here's your chance." He wrenched open the door, letting in a frigid gust, then stomped out and slammed the door behind him.

Ten

REALENE STARED AT the closed door, heat flushing her body despite the cold. She balled her hands into fists, wanted to punch something. Nate was supposed to be her best friend, and he'd driven off and left her like she was nothing to him.

"Louie? Is that you?" Ma asked.

Realene unzipped her coat and threw it on the floor before going into the living room. She didn't bother removing her boots. A dirty carpet was the least of her worries. Ma sat in the recliner with the footrest raised, clad in her dirty flannel pajamas instead of the clean clothes Realene helped her dress in that morning. Pumpkin sat on her lap, head peeking out from under the blanket.

"Why are you wearing those?" Realene asked.

"They're my favorite. What's wrong?"

"Nothing. Get changed into some warm clothes."

"Don't tell me nothing. Did something happen at school?"

She almost said she wasn't in school anymore and never would be. "No. Nate's being a jerk."

Ma's face crinkled with a grin. "He's a good boy. Whatever it is, I'm sure he'll apologize."

"Yeah, right," Realene said, though she certainly felt entitled to an apology. He'd acted like a toddler throwing a full-on temper tantrum.

"Your father and I fight sometimes, too, but we always make up."

"Nate's not my boyfriend." Ma always assumed she and Nate would end up together, couldn't comprehend having a close friend of the opposite sex. Realene never got around to telling either of her parents she was just as likely to date a woman, and for a second, she thought of saying it, right there, right then, but Ma would only get upset and forget anyway.

"Where is your father? Did he say he'd be late?" she asked.

If he were alive, he would have come home for lunch by then—a baloney and mustard on white bread with Old Dutch potato chips.

"Can you please get dressed? We're going to take a ride in the car."

"After lunch."

"He's not coming home for lunch today, okay?"

Ma pressed her lips together and upped the volume on the TV, the voice of Dick Van Dyke filling the room.

Realene resisted the urge to snatch the remote from Ma's hand, instead striding to the bookshelf to dig through the junk bowl, a chunky ceramic monstrosity she'd made in junior high art class. She rifled through the bowl, finding a handful of discarded change, assorted buttons, and some Halls cough drops, but no sign of Ma's keys.

"Where are your car keys?"

Ma turned up the volume. Realene had made the mistake of asking a direct question, and not in the most patient tone, a sure-fire way to make Ma shut down.

"Fine. Watch your show." Realene crossed the living room, briefly blocking the view of the TV.

"No shoes in the house," Ma said.

Biting back an acid response, Realene untied her boots and kicked them off before continuing down the short hallway that led to Ma's bedroom. She stopped in the doorway at the sight of the mess. Even though she'd just straightened up in there, clothes now covered the queen bed and stacks of books littered the floor. The top of the dresser to the right of the door was covered with jewelry, as if Ma had removed half the earrings from her jewelry box to display them in neat pairs.

Realene entered the room and promptly stepped on a stray earring that pierced the ball of her foot. "Fuck!" She bent and picked up the earring, a gaudy, jeweled butterfly, and chucked it across the room. It hit the wall and bounced into the pile of dirty clothes that had spilled from an overturned hamper.

She limped over to the jewelry box on the dresser, rifled through its now half-empty compartments, but found no keys. She searched the dresser itself, but found only clothes—both clean and dirty—crammed into the drawers. Random dishes and more jewelry and clothes hid beneath the bed, but there were no keys there either. She dumped out Ma's canvas bag, but found only Ma's wallet, several bingo daubers, Carmex, and a roll of Lifesavers, one of the few candies Realene did not like.

After checking every inch of the bedroom and bathroom with no success, she grabbed the clean jeans and sweatshirt she'd originally dressed Ma in that morning from the pile on the bed, and strode back into the living room.

Ma still sat in the recliner, staring at the TV.

"We're going soon," Realene announced, "and you can't wear those dirty pajamas. Change into these." She dropped the clothes in Ma's lap, earning a growl from Pumpkin. She'd need to find the cat carrier, too, so they could take him with them.

Ma pushed the clothes onto the floor, and Pumpkin jumped from his spot to skulk away. "You watch your tone, young lady."

Realene pressed her fingers to her temples, which began to throb. "We're going outside. Now, please, put on the clothes."

"When your father gets home, you can bet he's going to hear about your attitude problem."

"He's not coming home." She stalked up to Ma and gripped her by the shoulders. "He's not ever coming home."

"How dare you say something so hateful." She lashed out, slapping Realene across the face on the same side Dick had hit her.

Realene gasped and let go, placing one palm on her cheek to soothe the throbbing pain in her jaw. Ma had never hit her before.

"You go to your room right now, Realene Marie. You're grounded." Ma cranked the volume on the TV even higher, filling the trailer with laugh tracks.

Holding in a frustrated scream, she stomped past Ma and into the kitchen. She rifled through the cabinets, the pantry, and the refrigerator. She found many things where they didn't belong, but no car keys.

They had no way out, and the prairie dogs could already be surrounding them. Stalking over to the phone, she picked it up and dialed 9-1-1, but got a message saying, "All circuits are busy. Please try your call again later."

Her gaze landed on the picture of her dad in his uniform. "The Colonel, he'll help us," she mumbled, hanging up the phone and dialing his number.

It rang at least ten times, and she was about to hang up when someone picked up, and a voice said, "Hammond."

"Colonel. It's Realene. I need help, the prairie dogs—"

"We know. Rabies outbreak. You staying inside?"

"It's not safe here, we need to get out. Can't you come get us?"

"We're declaring a state of emergency, hole up and look after your ma. I'll check in when I can."

"Wait, no, I don't think it's rab—" The line went dead. She stared at the handset of the phone for a long moment, then hung up and dialed his number again.

The message said, "All circuits are busy. Please try your call again later."

Ma chuckled at something on the TV, their fight already fading into the darkness.

Realene squeezed the handset so hard the plastic creaked, but hung it up carefully so she wouldn't upset Ma again. They had no one to call for help. The police were gone from the field. Nate left her, and she couldn't find Ma's keys. Panic squeezed at her chest, but she shoved the feeling deep down into the pit of her stomach.

The colonel was wrong. They couldn't stay there, not with the strange disease spreading to other animals and even humans. Her only option was to reclaim Elizabeth Blackwell from a horde of bloodthirsty prairie dogs.

Injecting a false lightness into her voice as she grabbed her
boots, she said, "I'll be right back, okay Ma?"
She hoped that was true.

REALENE JOGGED THROUGH the trailer park, avoiding the
route closest to the landing site. She saw no sign of any prairie
dogs other than the dead critters scattered about Calvin's yard,
and his truck was gone. Hopefully, he'd gotten away without
being bitten.

She made it out of Plainview and continued down the center
of Main, cursing her hatred for physical activity and the result-
ing painful burning in her side. If she made it through this, she
pledged to take up Step Aerobics. Her mouth twitched, fought
back a smile, as she imagined making Nate go with her and
wear some ridiculous spandex outfit.

"Screw him, you don't need him," she mumbled to herself.
Sweat beaded on her forehead, turning icy in the bitter cold.
She passed his parents' street and glanced in the direction of
their house. The neighborhood appeared quiet, normal, no
sign of an epic battle. She hoped Sophia was somewhere safe,
wasn't still holding her dead husband's body in the snow.

Every breath now grated her burning lungs, so she slowed to
a walk. After another block, she glimpsed her car, still there,
just waiting in the road, both driver's-side doors hanging open.
A quick scan of her surroundings showed no sign of infected
animals. If she could get her car back home and pick up Ma,
they'd be able to get far enough away to find help.

She slowed as she approached the vehicle and went around
it in a wide circle, searching for any hiding prairie dogs. When
she saw no hint of them, she allowed herself to relax. Maybe
something would finally work out in her favor.

Walt's truck sat abandoned, back end sticking out of the
ditch, and a frozen halo of blood still marking the concrete
near the curb. His body was gone, likely picked up by the
paramedics, but someone had marked the area with caution

tape, stringing it around four orange cones. A police car was parked nearby, with its door open and its overhead lights still flashing.

There was no sign of an officer, and Realene couldn't help but picture that big buck chomping into their shoulder and hauling their body down into the ditch. Tearing through clothes, skin, and muscle, feeding on tender organs.

No. There was no sign of that, nothing in the snow but her and Walt's footprints.

Pushing thoughts of Walt from her mind, she closed the back door of her car and climbed into the driver's seat, tensing as she realized she hadn't done a thorough check inside. Shaking with the anticipation of claws latching into her ankle, she bent sideways to peer beneath the seat. Nothing lurked in the shadows except a handful of crusty McDonald's french fries.

She wondered if she'd ever have McDonald's again, if she'd missed her last chance because of Murray the tiger's burger habit. Straightening, she twisted the key in the ignition. Nothing happened, not even the typical struggling churn of the car's engine.

"Come on, Lizzy, come on." She patted the dashboard and tried the key again. Nothing.

After popping the hood, she got out, on guard for any movement in the fields. A pack of infected prairie dogs could come galloping along any minute. She opened the hood, and all the air left her lungs, leaving her deflated and hollow.

Every visible wire and hose was severed or mangled, chewed through by tiny teeth.

"Shit!" She slammed the hood closed, the metal-on-metal sound reverberating through her frozen bones.

Those animals were not infected with rabies. A rabid dog didn't stalk its prey, it bit whoever crossed its path. These creatures had cut power, chewed phone lines, and now disabled her vehicle. She felt like an animal being herded to slaughter.

Shivering and needing shelter for a least a few minutes, she climbed back in the car and closed the door. She mentally reviewed what she'd seen of the creatures and of the humans they'd infected, trying to make sense of it all:

- The worms in Brooke's and Walt's eyes were symptomatic of a parasite, not a virus.

- When the one prairie dog ate the poisoned apple, the rest of the pack seemed to know instantly what had happened, as if they were all telepathically linked.

Not that any of that mattered. She had no one to tell her theories to and no way to escape. Soon enough, she and Ma would get bitten too. Realene slumped forward to rest her head on the steering wheel, mentally shouting at herself to get the hell up and go home. Ma needed her. But Realene was so tired, so tempted to pass out right there in the car. They say when freezing to death, you get cold, then warm, then fall unconscious. It would be like falling asleep.

Her eyes landed on a few things still on the passenger side floor, including *Total Recall* and some junk Ma left behind after spilling her bag. The bright red corner of a Skittles bag poked from the pile, and Realene grabbed the candy, figuring the sugar might at least give her the energy to get up and go home, even if the pieces were frozen solid. When she snatched up the candy, the Blockbuster case slid aside and revealed something else hidden on the floor mat. A keyring with a monogrammed "M" holding several keys. Ma's keys. They were in her bag, after all. They'd just ended up on the floor when it spilled.

Realene grabbed the keys, squeezed them tight in her hand, and thanked God for finally helping her. She placed them in her inside coat pocket with the zipper, so she wouldn't lose them, then tore open the Skittles and threw a handful in her mouth.

Now she just had to make it home without getting bit, convince Ma to leave with her, and make it out of Demise while under attack by roaming packs of infected animals.

No sweat.

Eleven

REALENE HAD ALWAYS hated the minivan, which was a constant reminder of her unpopularity. Ma bought it cheap from a neighbor, with visions of hauling around Realene and her many friends, but she only ever drove Realene and Nate. They came close to selling it over the summer, would have if they'd been able to get more than a couple hundred bucks for it. Despite having been plugged in earlier, the van barely started and required a long warm up. It also required a spray of lock deicer on each door and a hefty amount of window scraping before being drivable.

"Got your dauber?" Realene asked as she pulled from the driveway.

Ma was again bundled up in the passenger seat with her Mount Rushmore bag at her feet. She craned her neck to look out the window at the sun high overhead. "It seems…late for bingo."

"Yeah, I uh, think they had a tournament or something this morning." Telling Ma they were going to bingo was the only way she could think of to get her dressed and into the car without a fight.

"Oh. Well at least it's not canceled. I'm feeling lucky today." She gave a half-hearted smile.

As much as Realene wanted to barricade herself and Ma inside the trailer and wait for help to come, she knew she couldn't. There was no help coming. The parasite was spreading fast, and the longer they stayed in Demise, the more likely they were to get bitten.

Realene pulled up to the stop sign at the trailer park entrance. There was no sign of any people remaining at the landing site, and the fence had been shoved over in several spots, probably by that deranged deer. Poisoned apples still dotted the field, and several bloody-faced prairie dogs appeared, scampering across the snow and moving to surround the pull-behind trailer that held the meteor. They stood on hind legs to watch the minivan.

Realene turned onto Main faster than she normally would and earned a glare from Ma.

"Sorry," Realene mumbled, glancing in the rearview mirror.

The meteor landing must be related to the sick animals, just not in the way Reverend Zebediah thought. Nate said meteors contained alien life, meaning that black goop she'd seen slither from the meteor could be more than plain old space mud. That stuff could have seeped into the ground and infected the prairie dogs while they slept.

Like the Krites from the movie *Critters*, who'd ridden into town on a meteor and began chomping away on unsuspecting earthlings. Not exactly the same, but close enough. If she was right and the prairie dogs were infected by some kind of alien life, how was anyone supposed to stop them? In the movie, the townsfolk were saved by shape-shifting alien bounty hunters, but there would be no saviors on spaceships arriving in Demise... Not that she knew of anyway.

They passed Realene's car, which Ma appeared to recognize. She pointed to comment, but Pumpkin yowled from his carrier in the backseat, and Ma lost the thought. The old cat sat amongst two duffel bags of clothes, a golf club for self-defense, a grocery bag of food, and a box of their most precious keepsakes—in case they didn't make it back home again.

"Pumpkin, my sweet boy, what are you doin' here?" Ma twisted in her seat to give air smooches to the cat.

"He's due for his shots." Realene hoped her flimsy lies would keep Ma calm for as long as possible, at least until they had settled into a motel a minimum of fifty miles from the alien invasion.

They passed cars in various states of abandon on both sides of the road. Some parked at the curb, some at angles with doors open, and others crashed into light poles or fences. A squad car crested the overpass, coming toward them with its lights flashing but siren silent.

A crumpled car and overturned red and white ambulance sat in the middle of the road ahead, one rear door open and the end of an empty gurney sticking out. Slowing further as she squeezed between the ambulance and the curb, she came within a few feet of the open back of the ambulance and glimpsed a pair of legs capped with black boots, the tips gleaming with a hint of steel toe. Walt.

"Is everyone okay?" Ma wrung her mittened hands in her lap.

Throat tight, Realene pulled forward a bit farther, so Walt's body wouldn't be visible to Ma, and shifted into park. She wondered if there was any part of Ma that still remembered the day Dad went into the hospital for the last time, the paramedics strapping him to a gurney and loading him into an identical ambulance.

The police car whipped to a stop on the other side of the accident.

Realene patted Ma's hand. "It's okay. The police are here. I'm going to go talk to them for a second. You stay here where it's warm."

Ma's face sagged with worry and exhaustion.

Realene got out of the van. She had to try talking to the officer, make sure he knew the animals were dangerous. Medical supplies littered the ground around the gurney, including several vials of medication, needles still in their sealed wrappers, and a portable defibrillator encased in plastic and red leather, like the one she'd trained on during her internship at the hospital. She squinted into the shadowed rear of the ambulance, guilt over Walt's death a rising bile in her throat that tainted her tongue. He'd been thrown off the gurney, and his face was smashed to a bloody pulp, unrecognizable.

She looked away. While it felt much longer, only an hour and a half had passed since she'd called for the ambulance. They must have crashed shortly after, but how had Walt's head gotten so damaged?

A cry came from the other side of the vehicle, and she rounded the back. The police officer struggled with two paramedics, a man and a woman clad in heavy black coats with reflective yellow trim at the wrists. The man grabbed the officer's arms from behind, and the woman launched herself at him, biting into his cheek.

"No!" Realene cried, distracting the paramedics and allowing the officer to break free.

The officer stumbled, slammed into the hood of his cruiser, then pulled his gun from its holster and aimed it at his attackers.

The paramedics paid no attention to the weapon. Instead, they turned to stare at Realene, black specks flitting through the whites of their eyes.

"What—what's happening here?" the officer asked, swiping at his face. He gave a cry when his hand brushed over the wound on his cheek. "Which one of you did this?"

Realene froze, flashing back to Brooke and Walt, to the confusion they both displayed after being bitten. The officer had been bitten and infected, but not by an animal.

His question drew the medics' attention back to him, and Realene inched backward.

The women snarled and said, "I tested to be on the force, but you wouldn't hire me. Said you'd already hit your quota."

"Who are you? Did you do this to me?" he asked.

"Help. I need help," a voice called from the ditch. A man crawled over the small ridge and stumbled into the street in front of the van. Yellow caution tape, likely from the crater, wrapped his ankle and trailed behind him. He wore a white hazmat suit—a bloody gash on the forearm—and an oxygen mask that hung loose below his chin. One of those scientists from the crater.

Realene put her finger to her lips in a shushing gesture.

The medics lunged at the officer again, who fired his gun. The crack of the shot ripped through the dry air, and the male medic fell to the ground, clutching his stomach.

Realene swayed in place, dizziness overwhelming her as the gunshot echoed through her skull. She'd seen people shot in movies and on TV, but never in real life. The scene before her came into hyperfocus, and a metallic smell assaulted her nose. Gritting her teeth, she forced her trembling body to still, no longer wanting the officer to notice her.

The officer had subdued the woman medic and was now fastening cuffs on her wrists while the wounded man writhed on the ground, groaning.

Realene crept back until she was hidden by the ambulance. Walt's legs twitched, and she yelped before covering her mouth with one hand.

The scientist rushed toward her. "You have to help me."

"Be quiet." She pulled him further behind the vehicle, praying the officer wouldn't notice them. A car door slammed, and she froze. Inside the van, Ma leaned forward in her seat to peer out the window.

"What am I doing here? Can you help me?" the scientist whispered.

"What's your name?"

"Hen—Henry."

"Okay, Henry. Are you hurt?" Out of the corner of her eye, she noticed Ma unbuckle her seatbelt.

"I think so, I don't know." He brandished his arm, clearly marked by a tiny set of tooth marks at the wrist.

"That's a prairie dog bite." She made sure to keep him at arm's length, made sure not to touch him in case that simple act could spread the alien worms to her. "Where are the others you were with?"

"What are you talking about?" he asked, his voice breaking. "Where am I?"

Henry reminded her too much of Ma, of that bone-deep fear that comes from searching inside your own mind and finding it a blurred jumble. Realene softened, reached out to him.

"Hey," a voice called, and the officer appeared behind the ambulance, his savaged cheek dripping blood. He grimaced and gave a slight shake of his head, then raised his gun and aimed the weapon first at the scientist, then at her.

Realene raised her hands over her head, her stomach twisted in a hard knot. She thought of Brooke shoving her and knew confusion and short-term memory loss weren't the only symptoms of this infection. Victims of the bite could become increasingly aggressive, like the prairie dogs.

Adrenaline sent a surge of energy through her body, and her hands shook despite her efforts to remain still. The single, black eye of the gun's barrel pinned her in place, threatening to pierce straight through her.

A series of short barks sounded behind her, and the officer lowered his weapon and pushed past Realene and Henry. She glanced back to see a pack of the animals, faces smeared red, galloping across the snowy field like a herd of antelope in a nature documentary.

Henry clutched at her hand. "I didn't want to shoot 'em, but Jenny said they were makin' burrows in the garden and eatin' her lettuce."

"Please be quiet." The officer's attention had shifted, and Realene wanted it to stay that way.

Something grabbed her ankle, and she yelped. The wounded paramedic had crawled his way over and now clawed at the hem of her pants. She pulled her leg from his grip and tripped over the defibrillator, landing on her back and forcing the air from her lungs in a whoosh. Groaning, she wondered how much more abuse her body could take.

The medic continued to crawl toward her, his midsection leaking a trail of gore across the icy asphalt. He took another swipe at her, and she grabbed for the defibrillator's handle. She swung the heavy device with as much force as she could muster, nailing him in the skull with a crack. He rolled sideways, his hands clutching his head.

"Realene, honey? Is everything okay?" Ma called, her door open.

"Get back in the car!" Realene scrabbled to her feet, swinging the machine in a wide arc in front of her to stave off any more of Henry's advances. "I'm sorry. Get away. Just get away."

Realene felt behind her to wrench open her door and jumped in the running van, lugging the defibrillator across her lap and plunking it in the gap between the two front seats.

"Stop right there," the officer said. "You can't leave the scene of an accident."

"Hold on," Realene said to Ma, then slammed her door and hit the gas, sending the back end fishtailing before finding traction. A shot rang out behind them, and Ma looked back, her face deathly pale.

"Is that man okay? Does he need help?" she asked.

"We gotta help ourselves right now." Realene's shoulders tightened in anticipation of a bullet shattering the back window or piercing a tire, and she pressed harder on the gas, sending them speeding up the overpass, swerving from side to side.

Ma screamed and covered her face. The passenger door scraped the railing with a metallic screech before Realene regained control of the van and guided it over the ridge.

"Everything's fine. We're fine," she said, panting. If they could get out of town, away from whatever this infestation was, they'd be okay. She tapped the brakes, slowing their descent as she took in the scene that had been hidden by the crest of the overpass.

Twelve

A MULTIPLE CAR crash clogged the intersection by the Snack Station, forcing Realene to pull over. Several people climbed from their vehicles, and one man threw another on the hood of a car and punched him repeatedly in the face. A woman ran from the site of the crash, screaming and waving her arms at the hawk that dive-bombed her from above, pecking at her face and hair. She swiped at the blood on her face and turned in a circle, as if unsure where her injury had come from.

A truck sat parked on the other side of the road, headed up the overpass. Several guys hung out in the truck bed, hollering at the scene as if watching a boxing match on TV. Realene's nose wrinkled in disgust, and she realized Tony was among the group.

He raised a hand in a wave.

She rolled down the window. "What are you doing?" she yelled.

"Isn't this great?" He raised a metal flask as if toasting, then tipped it back to take a swig.

Another car careened through the intersection, skidding around the crash, then regaining control and speeding off. Tony and his friends cheered.

Ma clicked her tongue. "Early for drinking. And in public too."

Realene almost laughed. At least Ma was focused on something other than the pandemonium in front of them. "I'll go talk to them."

She rolled up the window before getting out, and Tony jumped from the truck to jog across the road to meet her.

"What're you doing here? It's not safe," she said.

"We were headed to check out the crash site when this shit started to go down. Awesome, huh?"

"No. Not awesome at all."

Down the block, a duo of prairie dogs ran toward an oncoming car, causing it to swerve and crash into a light pole.

"Whoo!" he yelled, his face flushed.

"Jesus, are you drunk? You need to get out of here."

He swayed on his feet. "It's like someone hit the self-destruct button on this whole town. All the times we talked about wanting it to happen, I never thought it actually would, you know?" He cheered when a deer galloped past the cars, chasing a junior high schooler.

"People are dying."

"Yeah, the fucking dicks in this town are finally getting what they deserve." He glanced at her. "What's your problem? You hate Demise as much as I do."

They had often fantasized about Demise blowing up or getting snatched by a tornado, their common hatred a bond throughout high school. "That was just talk, venting."

"And now it's real. Our prayers have been answered." He gestured toward the truck. "We got liquor and stuff. You should come, we can watch it all burn."

Bile rose in her throat, and she swallowed it back down. "We're leaving. You should too. It's dangerous."

The guys in the truck called out to him.

"You're missing a hell of a party." He rested one hand on the roof of the van. The sweet and sour tang of whiskey wafted from his mouth. "Come on, you need to loosen up. Let me show you a good time."

"Screw you, asshole." She got back in the van and slammed the door.

"Fucking bitch," he yelled.

She pulled away from the curb, leaving him staring after her.

"Who was that?" Ma asked.

"Just some jerk from school." Shame heated her neck and face at the reminder she wasn't much better than Tony and his friends. Even a few days ago, she might've been right there with them, cheering. "You excited for bingo?"

"I'm tired. Do I have to go?"

Realene maneuvered the van around the accident, making a right toward the highway that would lead them to Fargo. A block of apartments, along with the Roadside Motel and Bar, sat on one side of the road. Cars filled the bar lot, which normally wouldn't happen until later in the evening. Lewis & Clark Elementary, Roosevelt Junior High, and the deserted, snow-covered park took up the whole block on the other side of the road. Kids and families normally filled the park during the day, skating, building snowmen, or engaging in epic snowball fights.

She made it less than a block before having to stop for a school bus that angled across both lanes, blocking the route out of town. Visible through the bus windows, children clamored in the aisle and jumped over the backs of seats. A man in a plaid cap with earflaps, but no coat, likely the bus driver, stumbled from the bus and ran past the van. His hand dripped blood, and he kept glancing behind him, as if afraid he'd be chased. Several prairie dogs scampered down the steps and out the open bus door, darting beneath the vehicle and out of sight.

Realene reached for the door handle, then stopped. She would only succeed in getting herself bitten if she tried to help. Eyes burning, she backed up a few feet, then whipped the van around to head the other direction.

Ma rested her head against the window. "I want to go home."

"I know, Ma." Realene drove once more through the intersection, again maneuvering around the accident, to head in the opposite direction out of town.

She passed another wreck on the side of the road at the edge of the cemetery. A compact car had hit a deer, caving in the hood, and the animal was wobbling to a stand. The driver hopped out to flee, and the deer gave a bleating cry and hobbled after him.

Realene thought of Nate. He wouldn't leave a bunch of kids or a stranded guy behind, he'd help them and anyone else who needed it. Like he came to her rescue when she was surrounded by prairie dogs. He'd always been that way. Even as a kid, he stood up to anyone who bullied her in school. He even blocked his dad, taking punches meant for his mother.

Realene grimaced at the memory of their conversation, at how ready she'd been to leave him behind. Of course he'd been angry, but instead of apologizing, she blew him off. She wished she could talk to him, say she was sorry, but she may never get that chance, may never see him again.

He could be dead or infected by now.

"This isn't the way to bingo," Ma blurted. She grabbed the steering wheel and jerked it right, causing the van to careen toward the curb.

"Ma, no!" Realene turned the wheel back, overcorrecting and crossing into oncoming traffic. A horn blared and she swerved back into her own lane, barely missing being hit by a speeding truck.

"I know this isn't the way to bingo, Ma. I'm sorry, but we can't stay here. It's too dangerous."

"I want to go home," Ma said.

Realene cranked up the volume on the radio, partially to distract Ma and partially to keep herself from screaming back. Ahead, a semi-truck had jack-knifed, blocking the intersection. She pulled to the side, intending to go around it, but a roadblock of concrete barricades extended across the width of the road. The repetitive thump of a propeller filled the air and a chopper passed overhead.

"Shit," Realene said, smacking the steering wheel. "State of emergency."

The entrance to the complex next to the Snack Station that housed Toppers and Cinema Twin was enclosed on the far side, with no exit. She could try to plow over a berm through a low spot in the snow, but that would freak Ma out even more, and they would probably just be stopped by more roadblocks.

They should've listened to the colonel and stayed locked inside. Realene began to make a slow U-turn in front of the semi. The revving of an engine drew her focus out the driver's-side window to a red Mustang barreling toward her at full speed.

She hit the gas and the tires spun on the icy road, causing the rear wheels to slip before the treads caught and the van shot forward a few feet. The Mustang plowed into the van's back end, spinning the vehicle until they faced the intersection by the Snack Station.

The carrier tumbled off the back seat, and the cat screeched.

"Pumpkin!" Ma unbuckled her seatbelt.

Realene shifted the van into Park, trying to catch her breath. "Are you okay?"

A trickle of blood slipped down Ma's forehead, but she paid it no attention. "My poor baby." She knelt on the seat, facing backward, and reached for the carrier, which was wedged behind her seat, the cage door facing up.

"Don't take him out." Realene grasped at Ma's coat to stop her, when something smacked into the driver's door.

She turned to see Brooke framed in the window, blonde hair matted with blood and ski jacket torn and leaking white fluff. A gleeful expression split her face as she struck the door with a tire iron.

"Stay here," Realene told Ma. Then she grabbed the golf club and swung her door open fast, bashing it into Brooke's body.

Brooke fell on her ass and dropped her weapon.

"Get the hell away from us!" Realene held the golf club like a bat, ready to drive it right into Brooke's gorgeous face.

Exhaling from her nose like an angry bull, Brooke stood. "You wrecked my car, you trailer trash bitch."

"You hit me!"

Brooke balled her fists at her sides. "As if I would ever hit your beater of a car. You're jealous of me, aren't you?"

"Walk away, alright? I don't want to hurt you, but I will."

She glanced back at her car. "My dad just bought it. He's going to be so mad that I already got in an accident." Tears spilled down her face, leaving black mascara trails.

"Hey, it'll be okay." Realene relaxed her hold on the club, letting it rest on her shoulder. "I promise he won't be mad. But you need to get out of here. Get somewhere inside, somewhere safe."

"You think I'm going to let some little nobody piece of trash tell me what to do? After you wrecked my car?"

"Whoa, calm down. You're sick, you're not yourself." Even as Realene said it, she realized that wasn't really true. Brooke was herself, just cranked up to ten.

"You fucking loser! As if you would know anything about me."

Movement caught Realene's eye. Several prairie dogs were scampering along the sidewalk that ran in front of the cemetery. She expected them to stop, to come after her, but they only glanced in her direction, then continued on toward the jack-knifed semi.

"You're a disgusting piece of trailer trash!" Brooke swiped the tire iron from the ground.

"Stop calling me that!" It'd been years since Brooke used that particular nickname.

Brooke slapped the tire iron onto her open palm. "No wonder the only person who'll hangout with you is that pizza-face friend of yours."

"Shut. Up."

"Don't you ever tell me what to do." She raised the tire iron and charged at Realene, who barely managed to dodge the blow, which landed on the hood of the van.

Ma screamed.

Brooke charged again, but this time Realene swung her golf club, blocking the blow. She swung again, bashing Brooke in the side of the knee.

Brooke screamed and lunged, stabbing with the sharp end of the tire iron and catching Realene in the stomach.

Realene doubled over, pain gripping her midsection. Another blow hit her back, and she fell to her knees, moaning.

Brooke did a little dance, the fur-lined hood of her tattered coat bouncing against her back.

Music spilled from the van, and Realene glanced up to see Ma leaning out the now open driver's-side window.

"Stop that! You leave her alone!" Ma shouted.

"I'm okay, Ma. Stay in the car."

Realene struggled to her feet, pressing one hand to her stomach as "Lovefool" by the Cardigans played from the car's stereo.

"Please. I don't want to hurt you," Realene said. This was the truth, even after all the hurtful things Brooke had said and done over the years. Realene still remembered the night she and Brooke kissed, knew it had been real. Brooke later played the moment off as a prank, said that she'd wanted to vomit, but Realene remembered the desire in Brooke's eyes, the way she deepened the kiss as if never wanting it to end.

"I'm going to kill you, and no one is even going to care because you're a fucking loser!" She gave a maniacal giggle and charged again. Brooke swung at Realene, but she dodged, and the bat struck the van's antenna, snapped it off and silencing the music.

Brooke raised her weapon again, the expression on her face now one of demented glee, and Realene realized Brooke wasn't kidding. She fully intended to kill her.

Behind Brooke, in the van, Ma huddled back against the passenger door with Pumpkin clutched in her arms.

"I'm sorry," Realene said, and swung the golf club as hard as she could, hitting the tire iron and knocking it from Brooke's hands. The metal bar hit the concrete with a loud ping. She swung again, this time aiming for Brooke's face.

Realene closed her eyes before impact—she couldn't bear to watch the club head demolish the girl she'd dreamed about and pined after since the seventh grade—but the momentum of the club stopped mid-swing. Her eyes flew open.

Brooke now gripped the metal shaft and was pulling the weapon toward her.

"Shit," Realene said, unable to hold on. She dropped to the ground and grabbed the tire iron a moment before Brooke leapt on her back like some kind of rampaging chimpanzee. Realene felt Brooke's hot breath on her cheek, and struggled to free herself, suddenly very aware that the girl could bite and infect her at any moment.

"Get off!" she screamed as Brooke pulled the shaft of the golf club against Realene's neck, constricting her throat.

Gasping for air, Realene managed to stand, but Brooke kept her hold, pulling the metal shaft even tighter against Realene's larynx.

Realene swung at Brooke's hands and arms with the tire iron, but nothing worked. Her vision started to go fuzzy at the edges, and she struggled to suck in a full breath. Summoning her last ounce of strength, she flipped the tire iron in her grip and jabbed the pointed end back and over her shoulder in the general direction of Brooke's face.

The pressure on her neck slackened, and the golf club dropped to the street with a clink. The weight of Brooke's body fell away, tearing the tire iron from Realene's hands. She whirled to watch Brooke crumble to the ground, her blonde hair fanned around her head in a bloody halo, her arms thrown to either side as if to make a snow angel. The tire iron stuck straight out of her left eye, having pierced the retina and burrowed into her brain.

Realene turned away from the sight, retching. She stumbled a few feet, then vomited Skittles down the side of the Mustang. "Taste the rainbow." she said, a delirious giggle erupting from her throat.

She slumped against the car, shaking.

Brooke was dead.

Murdered.

By Realene.

A gray bus with metal plates covering the sides, mesh draped over the windows, and spikes protruding from the hubcaps pulled out of the entrance to the Cinema Twin parking lot.

Realene looked down to hide her face.

Brooke's body lay in plain sight, but Realene hoped whoever drove the bus would ignore the scene and keep going. She tensed as the bus snaked around her van and headed toward the intersection, plumes of black exhaust billowing behind it.

Her eyes burned, and she swiped at them with the back of her hand. She couldn't afford to lose it now, not with Ma watching. Exhaling, she got up and walked past Brooke's body toward the van.

"Ma," she croaked, opening the driver's side door.

The passenger seat was empty, and the door hung wide open.

"Ma!" Realene yelled. The effort was agony on her damaged throat. She ran around the front of the van, praying Ma decided to hide during the fight, that she'd be waiting there with Pumpkin. But there was nothing, no sign of her.

Realene turned in a circle, her eyes scanning the crashed semi, Brooke's car, the cemetery, the pack of prairie dogs scampering toward the Snack Station.

"Ma!" she yelled again, unable to control the quiver in her voice.

Footprints marked the crusted snow on the wide, sloping berm that divided the road from the businesses. She bounded down the snowbank and fell hard on her stomach, half burying herself. Snow scraped and stung the bare skin of her neck and face, and she clawed the stuff away. She urged herself to her feet and continued trudging down the berm, finally making it to the flat expanse of the parking lot.

Cars were sprinkled throughout the lot, and near the entrance to the Cinema Twin, several kids ran from a man, maybe their father.

"Ma!" she cried again, shaking from cold, from fear, probably both. She looked in the direction of the Snack Station, thinking Ma would go somewhere familiar. She scanned for the bright-blue of Ma's scarf. Nothing.

Thinking Tony and his friends may have seen where she'd gone from their perch on the overpass, Realene crawled her way back up the berm, tamping down the urge to cry.

Focus and find her, she told herself, standing on weak legs.

She looked in the direction of the overpass and saw the truck still parked there, but the guys were now battling an infected buck. They screamed as the animal ran at the truck, ramming the metal body with its head. Tony threw a small cooler, which bounced off the deer's back before lodging itself in a snowbank.

The guys yelled and waved their arms as one of one of them hopped from the truck bed and got behind the wheel.

"Wait!" Realene screamed. "Don't go!"

The animal stumbled, shaking its head back and forth, then ran at them again, smashing the passenger side window.

The truck did a donut in the center of the road, circling the disoriented deer. The guys yowled from the back, a couple of them exchanging high fives, and the truck shot forward. After swerving all over the road and jumping a curb, they managed to skid around the accident and speed off in the direction of the lake.

A hawk screeched overhead, swooping toward Realene. The bird snipped at her face, its beak coming so close it brushed but didn't penetrate her skin. Channeling Tippi Hedron from *The Birds*, Realene flailed her arms to knock away her attacker and jumped into the passenger side of the van. She closed the door, then stretched to pull the driver's-side door closed, panicked breaths wheezing in and out of her lungs. The hawk landed on the hood and pecked at the windshield, leaving several bloody smears. Finding the glass impenetrable, the animal flew off.

Maybe Ma didn't leave at all. She was tired, had probably laid down to rest.

"Ma, are you in here?" She strained to check the backseat, hoping to find Ma sleeping, with Pumpkin snuggled beside her. But there were only duffel bags, the box of keepsakes, and the empty cat carrier.

The last thing she'd promised her dad was to take care of Ma, and now she was lost out there and all alone. Vulnerable.

Images bombarded Realene's mind: a pack of prairie dogs chasing Ma down the icy road; a deer pummeling her frail body with its hooves; an infected mob pursing her like a zombie horde. Ma couldn't move very fast, wouldn't be able to escape them. The prairie dogs would pounce on her, weigh her down, bite her face and hands, chew through her clothes—

"No. You'll find her. You'll find her," Realene mumbled to herself, climbing over the defibrillator and into the driver's seat.

She needed Nate. He'd know what to do. He'd help her, if he weren't dead by now. Realene's heart thumped so hard she could feel the beat of her pulse behind her eyes.

"Don't panic. He's okay. They're both okay." Ma wanted to go home, must have headed that way. Shifting into Drive, she pulled forward, gripping the wheel so tight her knuckles ached.

Thirteen

A ROCK PROPPED open the police station door even though the floor-to-ceiling glass window beside the door had been shattered to bits and was open to the outside. Still, sunshine only penetrated a few feet into the dark, one-story building. Somewhere a phone rang, again and again, not stopping, not being answered.

Nate called out to the dark. "Hello?"

He glanced back at his truck parked right out front, less than ten feet away. Not a single cop car occupied the reserved diagonal spaces beside his vehicle. He told himself the officers were probably out responding to the rising attacks and other fallout across town. Nate had passed at least a half dozen accidents on the road and seen multiple people being chased by infected prairie dogs and deer. Still, there was no way the cops would leave the station completely unmanned, not with weapons and evidence stored there.

His sensible side screamed at him to get the hell out, to head back to his apartment and barricade himself inside. But he'd said he would try and help, and hiding out was as bad as running away.

Straining to hear past his own wheezing, he moved farther inside, squinting into the dark. He knew the layout, remembered it from when he'd been arrested. A reception area sat to the left and a room of desks to the right, divided from the hallway by a half wall. The intake area where you were fingerprinted was down the hall, and the holding cells—four rooms fronted and divided by metal bars—took up the back of the building.

Sweat slicked his back at the memory of being hauled in barefoot and high as hell, with his hands cuffed behind his back. He reminded himself he wasn't that guy anymore. "Hello? Is anyone here?"

His eyes adjusted slightly to the darkness, and he made out the shadowy humps of desks piled with stacks of paper. There were no watchful, judging officers sitting in the office chairs today.

A barely audible, repetitive buzzing sounded, and he traced it to a phone that had been knocked off the hook, the handset dangling over the side of the desk closest to him. Near it on the floor, a broken coffee cup with a picture of a sombrero above the phrase 'Nacho Average Cop' lay amid a pool of spilled coffee.

The buzzing of the phone wormed into his ear, making it hard to pay attention to any other sounds. He walked over and replaced the handset, then bent to pick up the coffee cup. A growl came from the darkened corner behind the desks, and a figure surged toward him.

Without thinking, he gripped the mug by the handle and swung it at the face of his attacker, feeling bone break upon impact. The figure—a man—slammed into the corner of the desk, face-first, then slid to the floor in a heap.

Nate recognized the man's face. It was the cop from that morning, the one who'd arrested him, who'd ignored what was happening to his mom. The officer kicked and moaned, severely injured, but not dead.

Nate grabbed the phone and yanked the cord from the wall, then used the length of it to hog-tie the officer's wrists and ankles.

"You're a real asshole, you know that?" Nate said.

A shuffling sound came from the back of the building, near the jail cells, and it drew Nate's attention to the hallway. He opened his mouth to call out again, but snapped it closed when he noticed the trail of bloody hoof prints that streaked the industrial tile floor. Eyes fixed on the narrow passage, Nate backed up. Broken glass crunched under his feet, and he froze.

A figure appeared at the end of the hall, but it wasn't a deer; it was a person.

"Hey, hi. Are—are you okay?" he asked.

The person shambled forward and emerged from the deepest shadows. They weren't as tall as Nate had originally imagined. Curly hair, rounded shoulders, a knee-length skirt.

"Nathan Haugen," a voice said.

"Mrs. Jensen?" Nate exhaled in relief. Mrs. Jensen was a receptionist at the station. She'd been the only one to talk to him during his two days in a cell, even snuck him one of her homemade jelly donuts. "Are you alright? What happened?"

She'd lost one shoe, a low heel, and her bare foot left a trail of red as she limped toward him. She surveyed the cluster of desks. "You causin' trouble again? They said you were a lost cause. Didn't wanna believe it."

"Nope. No trouble." The memory of what happened at his parents' house returned, but he hadn't been the one to kill his dad. No way anyone could blame him for that... He hoped. "Seems like you had some trouble here though. You wanna come with me, and we can find some help?"

"Can't help them who don't wanna help themselves." She lurched forward, gripping the half wall, and the sun sliced across her face. A chunk of muscle and was torn from her jaw, exposing the skeletal grin of her teeth.

Nate stumbled backward and bumped into the door frame. "Jesus."

Mrs. Jensen charged at him, moving faster than he would have thought possible, and she reached out with claw-like hands, snatching at his coat.

Fully bathed in sunlight now, Nate saw that one of her eyes was swollen shut, and a wound, not unlike his dad's, bled on one side of her neck.

Nate shoved her away, then kicked her in the stomach. Her legs slipped out from beneath her, and she fell to the floor, face-down and screeching.

"Shit. Just calm down, okay?"

She raised her head and growled, then began scrambling toward him, undisturbed by the broken glass piercing her skin.

Nate bolted out the front doors and stopped short to avoid a frazzled woman running down the sidewalk, a baby clutched in her arms. He glanced the way she'd come to see a group of prairie dogs loping after her.

"Nathan Haugen, you get back here," Mrs. Jensen croaked from behind him, emerging from the building and struggling to her feet.

He dashed across the sidewalk, yelping at the swipe of claws on the hem of his pants, and managed to jump into his truck and close the door. Mrs. Jensen smacked the hood with her palms, leaving bloody smears, then began to climb over the plow blade.

Nate started the truck and threw it in reverse, leaving her sprawled on the concrete. He shifted into drive, swerving around her body, fishtailing, then correcting. The mother who'd passed him screamed as the prairie dogs chased her down the sidewalk in front of the elementary school, and he slowed, thinking he might be able to grab her.

Something crashed into him from behind, and he glanced in the rearview mirror. A yellow school bus filled his vision. The driver pressed the gas, forcing Nate forward. He struggled to gain control of the car, pressed the brakes, but his vehicle was no match for the weight of the bus.

They reached the intersection with Olson Street, and he whipped a hard right, focusing on the Snack Station a block ahead, and his apartment another block past that. The bus matched his route, speeding up behind him. Instead of hitting the brake, this time Nate hit the gas and pulled ahead. In his rearview mirror, the bus veered back and forth, then finally stopped long ways across the road, blocking both lanes.

Nate slammed on the brakes as he approached the stop sign and went into a spin that sent him careening through the intersection. A car veered around him, horn blaring, and he finally came to a stop in front of the cemetery, passenger-side tires burrowed into the snowy berm. He gripped the wheel and tried to slow his hammering pulse.

The screeching of brakes sounded ahead, followed by the crunch of metal, and he looked up to see a jack-knifed semi blocking the route to his apartment.

"Of course," he said.

A crash sounded behind him, and he glanced back to see two cars collide in the middle of the intersection he'd just skated through. Soon, he'd be totally boxed in. He couldn't stay outside. He had to find somewhere safe to hole up. He tried to pull forward, but his tires spun uselessly.

Keeping an eye out for any approaching attackers, he grabbed the Tidy Cat he kept behind the driver's seat. Working quickly with his hands, he dug the snow from around each buried tire and dumped litter in front and back of all four wheels.

A car zoomed toward him, and he barely made it back into the truck before it sped past. His curses died on his tongue when he watched the car smash into the wrecked semi at full speed.

He shifted into drive and pressed the gas a little. The tires caught, and he pulled forward, sending a silent thank you to the makers of kitty litter. He bet they never thought their product would become essential to every North Dakotan's winter survival kit.

Making a U-turn, he pulled around the accident in the intersection and headed up the overpass on autopilot, toward Realene's. He slowed. She wouldn't be there, though, was probably halfway to Fargo, halfway to a clean bed and pay-per-view TV at the Motel 8.

Nate had almost been killed several times, but what did Realene care? She'd let him go, hardly even tried to stop him. She'd said he was stupid, would probably end up hurt, and she was right. Now she was gone. His throat tightened, and he swallowed past the lump threatening to choke him.

"It's fine. You don't need her." He descended the other side of the overpass, knowing of only one place left he could even try to go. Nate hoped his mom would let him in.

He passed several more accidents and abandoned cars, even an overturned ambulance, where two infected paramedics literally chased after his car. Each time he approached another vehicle, he prayed it wasn't the minivan—that Realene and Ma actually made it out.

A car sped around him when he turned into the cul-de-sac, a bloody-faced man at the wheel. Several prairie dogs scampered down the street toward Nate, and he swerved to take them out, feeling much less bad about it than he did at the start of the day. The creatures were infected with something nasty, but not rabies. After the poisoning attempt, they'd all turned and stared as if they were telepathic or something.

Faint screams came from inside Fred's house. He liked the guy, thought about checking on him and his wife, but he reminded himself that his big plan to help people didn't work out so great the first time. And Fred hadn't helped them when they'd been attacked. He needed to take a cue from Realene and watch out for himself and his mom.

Nate pulled into the driveway of his parents' house, shuddering at the sight of the battered garage door shoved half into the garage. Easing from the car, he checked around the side of the house first, but there was no sign of his mom or of his dad's body, only the two dead deer. Scraping a hand through his hair, he walked up the path to the front door and rang the bell. When no one answered, he rang it again.

After a minute, he pulled his keys from his pocket and slid his old house key in the lock, surprised when it worked, since his dad promised to change the locks. Nate stepped inside and closed the door behind him.

The smell of gun oil and peanuts hit him, and he braced one hand on the wall, unprepared for the weight of the memories the place triggered. The front hallway held a posed photo of his mom and dad, the kind you got at Sears. The picture of the three of them that previously hung right below it was gone.

"Mom," he said. "You in here?" He passed the living room on his right and stopped.

The same fake Christmas tree he'd grown up with sat in the corner, decorated with icicle tinsel and topped with his mom's favorite Virgin Mary angel tree topper, but the rest of the room was not how he remembered.

She'd always kept an immaculate home, but now religious pamphlets, survival magazines, and boxes of ammo filled the coffee table, and peanut shells littered the carpet. His dad had a penchant for cracking the nuts himself, but he'd at least thrown the shells in the trash before.

Nate kept going past the kitchen, where several industrial boxes labeled "Survival Crackers" were stacked against the lower cupboards alongside a dozen boxes of Corn Flakes. A soft click sounded, and he jumped as if it were a gunshot, but the sound just signaled the furnace kicking on.

He continued down the hall to his old room and pushed open the door. His bed sat against the far wall, stripped down to the bare mattress. None of the clothes he'd left behind remained in the dresser, none of his posters or artwork adorned the walls, and none of his books filled the bookshelf. No evidence of him remained.

A pair of baled-hay shooting targets, the kind that hang on a tree branch or hook, leaned against the back wall, and shots were clustered around the paper bullseye on both targets. Mom really was a crack shot.

Nate sat on the bed, removing his gloves and slipping off his coat, as if he'd somehow be able to catch a full breath without it. Mom really had let his dad wipe every trace of Nate from their lives. Eyes stinging, he hung his head. Good thing there was no one there to see him cry. He couldn't get to his apartment, couldn't help stop the infection from spreading or help any victims, and he had no idea where his mom or Realene and Mrs. Gustafson were.

They could all be dead.

His eyes strayed to his closet door, which stood open a crack. He pulled it wide, discovering something his dad missed. Nate's UFO poster, labeled 'I Want to Believe,' hung on the inside of the door. He'd been so naive, watching the *X-Files* and fantasizing about something strange happening in Demise. Nate got his wish about something strange, but he was certainly no Agent Mulder.

Mulder would never storm off and leave Scully or his mom.

Nate tore the poster from the door and crumpled it, tossing it on the floor. He hoped his dad missed something else hidden in the closet. Nate un-wedged the clothes bar from the brackets that held it in place and reached into the end of the hollow metal tube. His fingers brushed plastic, and he pulled free his old stash.

The baggie held a couple joints, some bone-dry shake, a pack of ZigZags, and matches. An empty glass vial bearing a hint of white powdery residue reminded Nate of how close he'd come to falling down a hole he could never climb out of. Even Realene didn't know about that.

After leaning the bar against the doorframe, he opened the baggie and took out a joint, rolling it between his forefinger and thumb, feeling the soft crinkle of the rolling paper. He'd told himself he would never touch drugs again. He'd spent three brutal months in juvie after he was busted with enough weed to be charged with "intent to distribute," even though the weed was only for himself. His arrest ruined his chances at getting any financial aid for college and got him cut-off from his mom.

But the world had gone crazy around him. He'd watched his dad die and witnessed animals and people attacking each other all over town. Finding a way to get into college no longer seemed important. His biggest concern now was simply living through the night. Maybe he could try and forget about how he'd failed the ones he loved, about how badly he'd fucked everything up, at least for just a little while.

Fingers trembling, Nate stuck the joint between his lips and lit a match, holding the flame to the tip and watching it eat away the paper as he inhaled. The first puff hit hard, and he coughed, smoke billowing into the room. But the second drag and the third were smooth, his body remembering that pleasant burn. Within a minute, he'd finished as much as he could smoke without burning his fingers and snubbed out the end on the window frame, uncaring of the black burn mark he left on the painted wood, a brand that claimed this space as his own. He almost stuck the bag in his pocket, but that felt too much like a total surrender. Instead, he stuffed it back in the hollow metal tube and placed the bar back into its housing.

A pleasant fuzziness started in his head, behind his eyes, and spread to his tongue, his limbs, right down to his toes and fingertips. His muscles relaxed, the tension easing away. The world around him softened a little, the sharp edges worn smooth. His stomach growled, and he realized it had been a long time since he'd eaten. Wandering into the kitchen, he eyed the survival crackers but quickly abandoned the idea of eating what would surely be the equivalent of edible cardboard.

He still remembered where his dad hid the good snacks and opened the cupboard above the fridge, fishing out a bag of Doritos. Popping one in his mouth, he savored the fake cheese taste on his tongue, the texture of the corn chip sticking to his teeth. The scent of gun oil threatened to spoil his appetite, so he headed down the hall past his room and out the back door, which opened onto a concrete pad that held a snow-covered Weber grill. Not that they'd ever had anything resembling a family barbecue.

He forgot his coat, but the cold was sort of nice, invigorating. Munching on chips, his gaze strayed to the bomb shelter. He wondered how much the thing cost, figured it couldn't have been cheap. Not that he would ever admit it out loud, but the bunker wasn't actually a bad idea considering their current situation. He squinted at the metal door, which bore a long, red streak.

Had that been there before? He replayed the struggle with the deer, his father being gored and smashed into the side of the shelter. Plenty of blood splattered the side wall and pooled in the snow where his dad's body had fallen, but Nate didn't remember any of them grabbing at the door.

Probably from Mom, he thought. After she'd mourned Dad, she'd gotten up, hands bloody, opened that door, and shut herself inside.

Blinking against the harsh whiteness of the snow, Nate wandered closer to the shelter, the bag of chips still clutched in one hand, but forgotten.

The first deer that had attacked them lay in the snow, staring up at him with big, brown eyes. A young doe. He knew that much from the hunting trips his dad forced him into for years, even though he'd missed every shot on purpose. The doe should have been prancing around in the woods somewhere, snacking on berries and shit. He swiped at his eyes, smearing his face with nacho cheese powder.

The doe's mouth cracked open, and it gave a pained bleat.

"Jesus," he said, taking a step back. The deer lay still, not blinking or breathing. Must have been an exhalation of trapped air. Realene had delighted in telling him about all the noises dead bodies could make.

He refocused on the red streak that marred the bunker door. Footprints packed down the snow in front of the entrance, but there were no drag marks. What did Mom do with his dad's body?

"You," a low voice growled.

Startled, he glanced down the path.

At his dad.

Nate blinked several times, tried to focus on the bloody specter. He had seen his dad die, seen that buck gore him and smash his head against the cement bunker, seen him crumple like a rag doll.

What the fuck was in that weed?

"You need to learn, boy."

Nate's body went numb hearing those words from his child-hood, his dad's signal a beating was coming.

The man sneered and ran toward Nate, slipping in the snow, bumping the buck that still lay impaled on the metal shovel and causing the skewered head to wobble from side to side.

Nate lunged behind the bomb shelter, his back pressed to the cold brick exterior. "Not real. Can't be real." A hysterical giggle escaped his throat.

A growl sounded, and his dad lumbered into view, wheeling around to lock eyes with his son. One eye had popped from the socket and hung from the grisly tether of his optic nerve.

Nate screamed and threw the bag of Doritos at his dad, who clawed at the plastic, then tore it in half, causing an explosion of unnaturally orange chips. His dad cocked his head to the side and reached out for the snacks now resting upon the snow. "Favorite," he mumbled, gripping one of the little triangles between bloodied fingers and raising it to his mouth.

Nate ran past him in a wide arc and spotted the bat he'd left behind in the yard. His dad dropped the chip and made a grab for Nate as his fingers closed around the bat's handle. He tried to bash his dad's good wrist, but the blow glanced off his hand and only yielded an annoyed grunt.

"You need to learn." His dad made another grab, but this time Nate struck him in the head and sent him sprawling to the ground.

Nate hopped over his dad's body, dropped the bat, and grabbed the bomb shelter door. He twisted the handle and pulled, but it didn't budge. The weather no longer refreshing, his body shook from the cold. His dad climbed to his feet, and Nate bolted past the shelter and down the path. The buck's head flopped to the side, and he shrieked as he leapt over the bloodied antlers, suddenly sure it had come back to life too.

His dad wasn't dead though—not completely—and he came sprinting after Nate.

Nate went for his keys, intent on jumping into his truck and getting the hell out of there, but realized he didn't have his coat on. He'd left it in the house. His keys were in the coat.

"Shit." Dizziness gripped his head and narrowed his vision. Something struck his back—his own goddamned bat!— and he pitched forward and fell into Fred's ATV hauler. His eyes landed on the snowmobile's ignition, where a Ski-Doo keychain dangled.

The back gate on the hauler lay unlatched, forming a sort of ramp. Nate jumped on the snowmobile and yanked on the pull cord. The engine roared to life, loud as a chainsaw. His dad advanced from a few feet away, and Nate hit the throttle, launching himself forward off the small trailer. He landed hard on the street, whiplashing his neck, and his dad charged, barreling through the bushes with teeth bared and hands out in front of him like a real-life zombie.

Fourteen

STILL RECOVERING FROM the jarring landing of the snowmobile, Nate hit the throttle, but not fast enough. His dad grabbed the bumper, a narrow piece of metal that looped behind the seat, and held on with one hand. The extra weight made it hard to control the vehicle, and Nate skidded back and forth. The roar of the engine vibrated up through Nate's spine and reverberated through the still, winter day.

"Get off!" Nate reached back to smack at his dad's grip.

His dad's body swung back and forth behind the snowmobile, but the man managed to keep hold. He pulled himself closer and grabbed at Nate with his splinted hand, clumsily snatching at Nate's shirt.

Nate cranked the steering wheel, but the vehicle wasn't designed for tight turns, so the front skis made a wide arc that took them up a neighbor's driveway and across their lawn. He glimpsed two young, startled faces peering out from the picture window of the house before the curtains were snapped closed.

Nate thumped off the sidewalk and into the street, looping back toward his parent's house. The weight on the back of the vehicle fell away as his dad let go, and the snowmobile shot forward. Nate lost his grip, tumbling backward off the seat and landing hard on his back.

He groaned and sat up. With no one maintaining a grip on the throttle, the snowmobile drifted to a stop.

A hand grabbed his pants leg, and his dad crawled closer. "Need to learn." His eye dangled from the socket, bouncing against his cheek.

"Why won't you just leave me alone?" Nate kicked at his dad's hand and scrambled backward before standing. He ran around his dad in a wide loop, hoping to jump back on the Ski-Doo, but his dad rose and gave chase, moving faster than he should have been able to, given all the damage he'd taken. Nate moved in a zig-zag pattern, running down the street, onto the sidewalk, through piles of snow on front lawns.

When Nate passed the house of Mr. Jacobson, whose lawn he'd mowed for years, the old guy opened the front door and peered out, the tip of his shotgun poking through the gap.

"Help," Nate said, leaping over the bushes that lined the yard.

Mr. Jacobsen's eyes widened at the sight of Nate's dad, and he said, "Sorry, son, you're on your own," before slamming the door.

"Goddamn assholes, all of you." Nate slowed from exhaustion, loping down the sidewalk, a stitch burning his side. Half the surrounding houses must have people inside, but not one came to help. Sure, they'd mostly ignored the yells that had come from inside the Haugen house for years, but he thought they would at least intervene in his impending murder, in the middle of the street, in broad daylight.

Realene and his mom would've fought for him, he knew that.

Maybe he should let his dad catch him. He'd get bitten, or maybe killed, but at least he wouldn't have to deal with the nightmare any longer. He could just let it happen.

A series of sharp barks sounded in the distance, and a guy on a bicycle sped past along Main, skidding on the ice. He lost control of the bike, the narrow tires no match for the winter roads, and crashed into a utility pole. The guy popped to his feet and took off in a limping jog. A moment later, a pack of prairie dogs appeared, ready to pursue their next kill.

Nate couldn't give up. People—innocent people—were getting hurt, even killed.

He approached the Miller's house, which had a low, wood fence that usually delineated the edge of their yard, but was now completely buried in snow. Invisible. Nate picked up speed, tromping through their front yard toward the snow drift. A few feet away, he launched himself over the hidden fence, legs barely clearing the top. He came down hard on the other side, but got right back up and kept running despite the sharp pain in his ankle. Behind him, he heard a yell, and glanced back to see his dad splayed out on top of the snowbank, face-first, having caught a foot on the buried fence.

Lungs burning from the frigid air, Nate raced for the still-running snowmobile and hopped on. His dad freed himself from the snowbank and stumbled back into the street.

Nate hit the throttle and headed straight for his dad. He had to finish this.

His dad didn't flinch or dodge out of the way, like a sane, living person would do. Instead, he barreled straight toward Nate. The blunt nose of the snowmobile hit his dad at knee level, and the man fell forward onto the hood of the snowmobile, then slid off and rolled onto his back. Nate hit the throttle again, powering the machine over his dad's body. The ski's skated over torso and arms, but the back tread caught and tore at feet and legs. His dad gave a high, whining scream as the weight of the vehicle, probably a good five hundred pounds, crushed his body beneath it.

The snowmobile would go no farther, skis elevated and treads caught, so Nate let off the throttle. His dad's head peeked out from the front of the vehicle, barely visible past the nose. He opened his mouth, letting out a bloody gurgle, and said, "Need to learn, boy..."

"Fuck you." Nate turned off the snowmobile and climbed off the now unsteady mount.

A scream cut through the air, one he recognized. His mom had appeared in the backyard, both hands over her mouth. Behind her, the door to the bomb shelter hung open.

"You killed him!" she screamed.

Nate gaped at her, then looked at his dad beneath the snowmobile, blood spreading in a widening pool beneath the body. His head lolled to the side, and his one intact eye stared blindly at Nate.

Nate's mom ran past him and wilted to the ground beside her husband. "Dear God, you killed him."

"I...didn't have a choice. He attacked me." Nate tried to swallow, but his throat cinched closed.

"You made him sick, brought the evil here. It wasn't his fault."

Nate gritted his teeth and straightened. "He attacked us plenty of times before today, and he would've killed me this time."

She stood, disgust twisting her face. "He was down, and you still came after him. You attacked him."

Nate couldn't meet his mom's eyes. He could have gotten away that last time, could have escaped, but a part of him wanted his dad dead.

"He was right about you." She stalked toward him. "You're evil. A demon that deserves to be wiped out."

"No." He shook his head, reached for her, but she pulled away. "Mom, please. You have to understand."

"Don't you touch me." She backed away, treating him like some kind of monster.

The chug of a diesel engine sounded up the street, and a strange vehicle headed toward them. Glimpses of yellow revealed it had been a school bus once, but someone painted it dark gray and attached metal plates to the sides, hung mesh over the windows. Sharpened spikes jutted out from the hubcaps, and there were strange symbols spray-painted on the metal plates—crosses overlain by the number seven.

The bus pulled into the Haugen's driveway, and the doors opened with a hiss. Reverend Zebediah descended the steps, no longer clad in his typical Canadian tuxedo. Instead, he wore camouflage fatigues and combat boots like some kind of G.I. Joe wannabe. His open parka revealed a gun holstered at each hip.

"Sophia, are you alright?" he asked.

She rushed over to him, letting him wrap her in his arms.

"What the hell are you doing here?" Nate asked.

"Go on, sister. We'll protect you." Zebediah guided Sophia toward the bus.

"Mom, wait," Nate called, moving to go after her.

She stopped on the stairs of the bus, her face the saddest, the most broken he'd ever seen it. "You'll pay for what you've done, demon." She continued inside, leaving him behind.

"No, please—"

"You did this?" Zebediah studied Dick's body, where it lay pinned beneath the snowmobile.

"I had to." Nate didn't sound convincing, even to himself.

"The mantra of the sinner. You'll pay. All of you will pay. God has seen your sin, seen the infection tainting His almighty creation, and He has sent righteous fire and a cleansing plague."

"You're the sinner, convincing these poor people that some sick animals are sent from God." Nate glanced up at the windows of the bus, at the faces of the parishioners staring out at him. He didn't see his mom, but he did recognize someone else. "Mrs. Gustafson?"

Zebediah climbed the steps, and the door hissed closed behind him.

"Hey, open up!" Nate pounded on the doors, which were painted black to prevent people like him from seeing inside. "Where are you taking them?"

The bus backed out of the driveway, and he chased after it. "Stop!" he yelled, banging on the metal-plated beast. The vehicle pulled away, the faces of the congregation members staring out at him with wide, scared eyes. His mom appeared in the back window as the bus approached Main, focused not on Nate, but on her dead husband. They rounded the corner and disappeared.

Wheezing, Nate slowed, then stopped, hunching over to rest his hands on his knees. A violent tremor shook him, adrenaline giving way to intense cold that seeped deep into his bones.

Motion caught his eye from the neighbor's house, those same little faces peeking out the crack in the curtains.

"What the fuck are you looking at?"

The curtains closed. Again.

Shoulders sagging, Nate shuffled back toward his parents' house. He stopped and stared down at the man who made his life a living hell, tried to muster some sadness, some regret. But he felt nothing. Granted, he was still a little high, and a little numb, and probably a lot in shock.

When he looked up at the house, though, and at the open door of the bomb shelter, he thought of his mom, and guilt cinched his chest tight. She'd called him evil, a demon deserving of death. He rubbed his eyes hard with his fingers until he saw stars.

She'd been freed of his dad, but now another controlling asshole had her in his grip. Nate could only hope she'd be safe from infection. Judging from the state of the bus, which could have been a reject from *Tank Girl*, Zebediah had been preparing for an apocalypse. That must also mean he'd prepared a secure location for them all, probably at the church.

But why was Mrs. Gustafson on the bus? She wasn't a member of the church. One thing was certain: Realene would never have left without her ma. Something bad must have happened for Mrs. Gustafson to end up with Zebediah.

Stopping to give his dad's body one last kick for good measure, Nate grabbed the bat from the ground and ran back into the house to get his coat and car keys.

He had to find Realene.

Fifteen

REALENE STOOD IN the road in front of her trailer, frozen, unsure what to do next. Ma wasn't inside. She hadn't made it home. Realene had searched everywhere, screamed for Ma until the bitter air scraped her throat raw, and now the chirps of prairie dogs sounded intermittently, surrounding her from every direction. The creatures could be hiding in the ditch, behind fences, in the field. They could be anywhere. Police and emergency sirens sounded almost constantly from the direction of town, but none were close enough to flag down for help.

The burn and itch of frostbite ate at her cheeks, and she knew she should get out of the cold, but she couldn't make herself go inside. Not without Ma. She wished more than anything she'd gone with Nate and left Ma wrapped up safe and sound in her recliner.

Shivers wracked her body, and she wrapped her arms around herself. She'd been so stubborn, so stupid, and now she had nothing, no one left. The town emergency siren blared to life, far too late to warn anyone in advance. It wailed, the sound cycling high, then low, again and again.

Snowflakes fell lazily from the sky—the big, fluffy kind they rarely got in Demise. Their snow was almost always propelled by wind, tiny daggers of ice that stabbed and stung bare skin. If Ma was home, she'd have been on the deck, catching the flakes in her mittened hands and counting the crystalline points of each one before it melted. They'd done that several times during Realene's childhood. They would then replicate the shapes they'd seen with paper cutouts, and Ma would use their creations to decorate the Christmas tree.

Realene's legs went weak, and she sunk to the cold ground in the middle of the road. She was so incredibly tired of worrying, of fighting, of struggling. Of everything. The prairie dogs started to howl along with the siren, and she silently wished they would come for her, bite her, make her forget. She considered going over to the meteor they still guarded and offering herself up as a willing victim. Hanging her head in her hands, she cried, shoulders shaking and tears spilling from her eyes to freeze on her chapped cheeks.

An engine sounded, and Realene looked up, ready to welcome whoever wanted to run her over. Sun then glinted on the silver blade of a plow, and she struggled to her feet, sure her desperate mind had conjured a mirage.

Nate pulled the truck to the curb, and she realized he was real.

He hopped from the cab, his coat unzipped to display a bloodstained shirt beneath. She met him halfway, throwing her arms around his neck. For a moment, she worried he might not hug her back, that he might still be mad, but his arms tightened around her waist. She buried her face in the crook of his neck and squeezed her eyes shut.

"You okay?" he asked after a full minute of silence, pulling away.

Realene nodded, not meeting his gaze, wishing she'd planned what she might say if he came back. She opened her mouth, trying to piece together her jumble of her thoughts into an apology, but Nate spoke first.

"I killed my dad." His brow knit.

"Yeah, I know. I was there."

"I mean, I killed him again. I guess he was only mostly dead, and also infected. I went back there to uh…" He shook his head. "It doesn't matter. Anyway, I crushed him with a snowmobile."

She gaped at him. "Sounds very…*x-treme*."

His mouth ticked up at the corners, but his eyes conveyed sadness. "Too bad I didn't have a Mountain Dew to chug after. That really would've pushed it over the top."

"Seriously though. Are you okay?"

"Not really. My mom disowned me and left with her psychotic church group in some sort of apocalypse bus." He blinked rapidly, cleared his throat. "And I saw your mom too...on the bus. They had her."

"What?" she screamed, her voice echoing in the still air. She remembered the bus with the metal plates and spikes. "Fucking Irene! That bitch! She must have kidnapped Ma while I was..." She looked down at her hands, at her bloodstained gloves.

"Hey, are *you* okay?"

"Not really. I killed someone too. Brooke, actually."

"Damn." He wrapped his arms around her again, squeezing tight. "I'm sorry. I know you liked her...for some insane reason that I'll never understand."

"Yeah. Thanks." She sniffled and met his gaze. "About earlier, I'm so sorry—"

Tires screeched, and Calvin came barreling down the street straight toward them in his truck, turning at the last minute to whip into his driveway. He hopped out of the cab, rifle in one hand, and a canvas bag in the other.

Realene and Nate took off toward Calvin, who saw them and headed in their direction, stopping on the sidewalk in front of his trailer. The bag in his hand swung, weighted and bulging.

"You okay, Calvin?" she asked.

He grinned. "Little buggers are no match for me. Been driving around picking 'em off all afternoon."

Nate scoffed. "Yeah, with a gun. Try a snowmobile."

"Or a golf club. Oh, and a tire iron," she said.

Nate raised an eyebrow. "Impressive."

Her chest expanded, as if relieved of a heavy weight. Nate had come back, and Ma was alive.

"What're you two goin' on about?" Calvin asked.

"Ran into some people who've been bitten, and it's bad."

"That's an understatement," Nate said. "And we still don't know what's causing this."

"I might have an idea about that. You've got some dead prairie dogs in there?" Realene asked Calvin, eyeing the canvas bag.

"Three of 'em. But I killed way more than that." He made a sweeping gesture with one hand, calling attention to the many prairie dog bodies dead and frozen in the snow. Across the street, the group of prairie dogs that had surrounded the meteor also lay dead in a ring around the trailer. Their numbers now included a dead deer.

"Keeping these guys," Calvin said, holding up his bag. "Gonna stuff 'em, maybe make another hat. Show 'em who's boss."

"Yeah, we're all super impressed," Realene said. "Can I check out one of the dead ones?"

"Why?" Nate asked, the disgust clear in his voice. He'd always been a bit queasy, unable to even help with dissecting their frog in sophomore biology.

"I want to check something, test a theory about what's happening."

"What about your mom?"

"We'll go bust her out after this. Your mom, too, if we can convince her. But first, I need to see one of them."

"Whatever tickles your pickle." Calvin trekked through the snow to his back door and climbed the set of three steps.

Inside, the wail of the emergency siren was muted, and Realene's ears rung with the memory of it. Calvin's trailer had a similar blueprint to her own, and the back door deposited them at the rear of the kitchen.

Realene came to a halt on the cracked linoleum floor, causing Nate to bump into her from behind. Taxidermied animals stared at them from every direction and surface, from the gap between the cupboards and the kitchen ceiling, to the countertops, to the rows of shelves that lined the wood-paneled living room wall. Ducks, squirrels, gophers, a few foxes, and lots and lots of prairie dogs.

"Jeez, no wonder they have it out for you," Nate said, voicing Realene's thoughts exactly.

A large worktable, covered with a blue plastic tarp, took up most of the kitchen, and the room reeked of formaldehyde. Calvin hung his rifle on a pair of hooks fixed to the wall between the living room and kitchen and tugged off his gloves, shoving them in his pockets.

Judging from the knives and sewing supplies arranged on the table, Realene guessed this served as his taxidermy workspace. The image of preparing and eating food in this kitchen soured her stomach.

Calvin moved aside a small bucket of ice melt and unceremoniously dumped the contents of the canvas bag onto the tarp.

Realene felt a pang of sympathy for the three dead creatures that tumbled out, each one's head punctured by a bloody hole. "I'm going to cut one of them open," she said, wincing at the obvious excitement in her voice. She'd always found dissections fun, hence her interest in going pre-med.

"Ummm, maybe I'll wait outside," Nate said.

She couldn't bear to let him out of her sight again. "Can you stay? This is important."

"I guess. But you owe me."

"I know." She owed him for much more than this.

"What're you looking for?" Calvin handed her a scalpel with a blade so much dirtier than the ones she used in anatomy class.

A box of rubber gloves sat at the back of the table, near a bin of random tools, bungee cords, and other junk. She took off her winter gloves and put on a pair of rubber ones before bending over the carcass and slicing open its belly in a careful line. Blood and guts leaked out onto the plastic tarp, and she leaned down to examine the gunk.

"See those?" She pointed at the black wisps present in the pooled blood.

Nate glanced at the gutted animal, paled, and stared at the ceiling. Calvin moved closer.

"Never seen anything like them before. Some kind of worms," he said.

She stripped off the gloves and dropped them next to the animal on the tarp. "You said meteorites carry life from space, right?" she asked Nate.

"Not life like—"

"Not life like we think of, I know, but listen. Something oozed out of that rock last night, some kind of black gunk. Then today, there were worms in Brooke's eye and Walt's too. *After* they were bitten."

"Whoa," Nate said. "You think that's why the prairie dogs are acting so weird? Alien worms?"

"Yeah, and once you're bit, the worms are passed on. Like a parasite or something that affects cognition and memory."

"Like *Night of the Creeps*." Nate narrowed his eyes. "My dad was wrong. Well, not that he was ever *right*, but he wasn't his normal self. He kept repeating the same phrase, something he used to say years ago."

"The infection, parasite infestation, whatever you want to call it, causes confusion and memory loss at first. Right after being bitten, Brooke thought we were still in high school, and Walt didn't remember me at all." She shuddered. "Kind of like Ma, but happening a lot faster."

Nate squeezed her arm.

"But when I saw Brooke later, she'd gotten a lot worse, like it ramped up all her aggressive tendencies."

"Super bitch," Nate said matter-of-factly.

"Totally." She smirked. "It's like, the longer the parasite infests someone, the more aggressive they become, the more dangerous."

"That would explain why the prairie dogs are attacking everyone when they're normally docile," Nate said.

"And I think the worms are keeping animals and people alive somehow when they should be dead."

"Like my dad."

"And Walt." She told them about finding the ambulance and the infected paramedics. "He must've attacked and bitten them."

"Brooke and my dad were assholes, but not Walt. He was cool," Nate said.

"Yeah, he was." Realene shook off the image of Walt's bloodied face, of his body still twitching and kicking, driven by the aliens to attack.

More black worms oozed from the prairie dog carcass and came together to form a rivulet that slithered across the tarp.

Calvin held out a finger, as if to poke the things.

"No." Realene smacked his hand away, knocking over the bucket of ice melt in the process. "Don't touch them."

"Hey, check this out," Nate said, his queasiness apparently forgotten.

Realene turned back to the table, where the white crystals of ice melt had spilled across the surface and onto the floor. A handful of grains had landed on the rivulet of worms, and she watched as their wiggling slowed, the worms appearing to grow lethargic.

"I think it hurt them, slowed them down or something," she said.

"Of course it did. Lotsa critters don't like salt." Calvin grinned. "Use it to kill slugs and cockroaches. And that's why there are no fish or nothin' in Sauer Lake."

"Yeah, right," Nate said. "I remember that year they tried to stock it with some super-hearty breed of trout, but all of them just wound up dead."

"Catfish, actually," Realene mumbled. "I remember." She'd never told Nate about her one and only date with Tony that ended with dozens of fish carcasses washing up on shore and her puking her guts out. She squinted at the rivulet of worms. "I wouldn't risk trying to stuff these guys, Calvin. Not with those worms in there."

"It's a damn waste." Calvin opened the canvas sack and reached for the prairie dog that hadn't been cut open.

Realene saw the thing move a split second before it chomped down on Calvin's finger. She shoved him away, but it was too late.

Blood welled from the bite mark, and Calvin placed the dirty digit in his mouth.

The prairie dog gave a weak mewl and raised its head an inch before going limp on the tarp.

Calvin looked between the two of them. "What are you kids doing in here?"

"Hey, man. It's cool. You let us in, remember?" Nate said.

Realene knew from Ma that the last thing you should do is ask someone with memory issues to remember something. "Uh, you were showing us some of your, uh, trophies, I think." She angled a look toward the shelves in the living room.

"Oh, yeah, got some real good ones," he said.

"Hey, uh, Nate come over here. Aren't they cool?" She strode into the living room and gave Nate a pointed stare. A tattered sofa, bearing stains that she hoped were food, faced the back wall, where a small TV sat on a metal cart beneath an American flag tacked to the wood-paneled wall.

Nate followed her to the shelves of trophies. "I thought you hated taxidermy."

She lowered her voice. "I do, but we can't let him wander around like that. He's got guns. Someone will end up getting hurt." She remembered that cop, how quickly he'd pointed his weapon at her and that poor scientist.

"What do you want to do?"

"I don't know. Grab him and tie him up?"

"Oh, yeah, of course. Easy," he said.

"You were in wrestling. Like, take him down."

"I wrestled in fifth grade, and I never took anyone down. I sucked."

"What're you two whispering about over here?" Calvin sidled up to them.

"Nothing," they said in unison, sounding like a couple kids up to no good.

Calvin narrowed his eyes as he started to back his way across the living room, his eyes darting to the rifle on the wall just beyond the end of the worktable.

"He's going for his gun!" Realene grabbed the closest object, a stuffed duck with wings outspread, and she chucked the bird at Calvin. It sailed through the air, hitting him in the forehead with its blunt beak.

He gasped, raising one hand to his head.

Nate snatched a curly tailed squirrel and hucked it at Calvin. The little thing thumped off the man's shoulder and fell to the floor, its tail bending at an unnatural angle from the impact.

"Hey, that was my favorite," Calvin whined.

Realene grabbed several animals, loading up her arms.

Calvin raised his hands, as if in surrender. "Whoa now. You stop that."

She chucked two prairie dogs in quick succession, saying to Nate, "The bungee cords. On the table."

Nate grabbed a pair of ducks, throwing one and keeping the other, as he rushed past Calvin.

Realene threw another squirrel as she moved closer, but Calvin swatted it away. Face flushed and jaw clenched, he turned and made a grab for his gun on the wall.

One hand in the junk bin, Nate raised the green-striped duck and smacked Calvin in the face with it. One of the duck's glass eyeballs flew out and went rolling across the floor, but the blow didn't stop Calvin from grabbing the rifle by its barrel.

Realene rushed up with the last of her animal weapons—a snarling red fox. She wedged herself between Nate and Calvin and smacked her crazed neighbor with the fox while she grabbed for the butt of the gun with her free hand.

"Got 'em!" Nate confirmed, raising a bundle of yellow bungee cords, their hooked metal ends dangling.

Realene wrenched the rifle from Calvin's grip. "Let's take him down."

They both proceeded to beat at Calvin with their animals, feathers and chunks of fur flying off all around them. Realene hooked her foot behind Calvin's knee and gave him a hard shove, knocking him to the kitchen floor on his back.

"Why are you doing this?" he cried.

Realene held down his legs while Nate grabbed his arms, tying Calvin's hands with a bungee cord.

"Feet too," she said, wrapping her arms around his knees.

Nate took a pretty good kick to the face, but still managed to bind Calvin's ankles.

Calvin stopped struggling and let his head thump back on the linoleum, where he heaved several deep breaths.

"Told ya you shouldn't smoke." Realene slid off Calvin to sit on the floor beside Nate. They were both panting too, but had no excuse for it.

"I don't have any money, if that's what you're after," Calvin said. "And don't think yer dad won't be hearin' about this."

"We're not robbing you," Nate said. "You got bit by an alien-infested prairie dog, and you're going to go rabid soon."

Realene couldn't help smiling at the explanation. "I know it sounds crazy, but it's true. We're not going to let anything happen to you though."

"Aliens, my puckered asshole," Calvin grumbled, struggling to sit up. "Look what you did to my house. My poor critters."

Realene surveyed the animal remnants that littered the living room and kitchen. Feathers and fur and other tattered remains of Calvin's stuffed victims were everywhere. A duck had been parted from its head, and a gopher from its arms. "Revenge of the Taxidermy."

Nate laughed, and Realene couldn't help it, so she started to giggle too.

"I feel like a Thanksgiving turkey. You just gonna leave me here like this?" Calvin asked.

"Nope. You're coming with us. We gotta rescue Ma from a cult," Realene said.

She knew they had a fight ahead of them, but she felt strangely confident with Nate back at her side.

Sixteen

REALENE PULLED THE minivan up to the stop sign at the trailer park entrance. A gray military helicopter passed overhead, hovering above the landing site before continuing toward town. She wondered how many of the scientists and other personnel lay dead in the crater and how many had wandered off, unwittingly urged to spread the alien worms.

"You okay back there, Calvin?" she called, raising her voice to be heard over the siren. They'd bundled him up and put him in the trunk, propping him up on several pillows and covering him in blankets to insulate him from the cold.

"Be better if you'd let me go."

"Can't do it. Sorry, dude," Nate said.

Realene eyed the meteor on its trailer as they passed and noticed that a new group of prairie dogs had shown up to circle the artifact. Standing tall next to their fallen kin, their heads swiveled to track the car as she drove away. "Why do you think they're protecting that thing? I mean, I know it's probably where the worms came from, but aren't they all out by now?"

Nate twisted to look out the back window. "I don't think so. Remember what Kurt Loder said? They found evidence of life *inside* the meteor. There must still be some worms in there."

"The way the animals are acting, it seems more important than that." She pulled around the wrecked ambulance and started up the overpass. "What if there's more of a hierarchy to these creatures than we realize? Like in *Aliens*. Maybe they're protecting their queen."

"I don't like bees. Or wasps," Calvin said from the trunk area.

"What's he talkin' about?" Realene asked.

"Queens. Bees and wasps have queens. It's why they're so protective of their hive," Nate said. "These aliens are telepathic or something, right? That's how they all knew there was poison in the apples after only one of them ate one."

Realene slowed as she reached the intersection near the Snack Station. The accident she'd seen earlier still hadn't been cleared. A souped-up truck barreled toward the school bus that blocked the east route from town and crashed into the rear end, shifting it a few feet. The truck reversed a half block, then sped forward again, ramming the back corner of the bus and widening the gap.

"That's one way to clear the road, I guess," she said. "Maybe they'll have it open by the time we're ready to get out of here."

"Where are we gonna go? Fargo maybe? Is that far enough?" Nate asked.

"We're not running away." She glanced at him, meeting his eyes. "I'm not running away, not anymore."

"Okay." He gave a small smile. "Then what's the plan?"

She maneuvered through the intersection and kept heading straight down Main. Several infected deer chased a guy through the cemetery while a car jumped the curb ahead of them to plow through the snow and crash into the plywood boards of the ice rink. Realene didn't stop, just continued on toward Revelation Evangelical.

"After we save our moms, we need to get out to Steele Air Force Base and talk to the Colonel. We can tell him what we know, about the meteor and the worms, the ice melt. Hopefully he'll have some idea what to do next, how to save everyone."

"Okay, yeah, good idea. We can hide out there, too, in one of those underground bunkers or old missile silos. No way are any prairie dogs getting in there."

The thought of being trapped that far underground sounded worse than getting bit and infected, but Realene kept that to herself.

She braked to avoid a bunch of prairie dogs scampering across the road, heading for Smithy's Auto Repair. One of the bay doors was open and the prairie dogs joined some others who had already circled a car raised up on a lift. A guy in coveralls leaned out the driver's-side window and batted at the creatures with a long wrench as they leapt one after another into the air.

"Everlong" by the Foo Fighters blared from the speakers outside Skateway, and cars scattered its front lot. The door to the roller rink stood open, and screams sounded from inside. Several people spilled out the door, still wearing skates and looking behind them as if pursued.

Nate stared at the building as they passed. "Maybe they're having a really awesome party."

"I'm not dressed for a party," Calvin said.

"We're not goin' in, Calvin. It's okay," Realene said.

The sun had started to set, the day turning gray in preparation for night, as they pulled into the Revelation Evangelical parking lot. The windowless structure would have appeared deserted had it not been for the many vehicles packing the lot.

The apocalypse bus sat parked long ways across spots in the front row, closest to the building. Glow-in-the-dark tape made sure the cross-and-seven symbols were visible in the dying light.

"You gonna be able to stay cool in there?" Nate asked.

"I'm Norwegian, remember?" she said. "Irresistible politeness is our superpower. We get in, find our moms, get out."

Realene pulled into an open handicapped spot behind the bus and turned off the car. Since that morning, someone had erected a barbed-wire fence around the building.

Nate groped for the door handle, but she grabbed his arm. "Wait."

"For what?"

She pointed at a group of prairie dogs scampering through the snow toward the building, as if they knew there were people inside. One of the animals ran up to the fence, perhaps to squeeze through the chain link or climb over the barbs, but as soon as it touched the metal, an electric zap sounded, and the animal fell dead. The other prairie dogs yowled and ran away.

Within the perimeter of the fence, a person appeared from around the side of the building. They were hard to see at first because they were dressed head to toe in black. They also carried a rifle.

All Realene brought was her bat, safely tucked between the two front seats.

"Shit. We brought a bat to gun fight." Her dad had taught her how to shoot, but she didn't like guns, and she and Nate would be no match for an armed congregation.

"I got plenty of guns ya can have." Calvin said. "And I'm cold. Can I go home?"

"Soon, buddy. Hang in there," Nate said, then turned to Realene. "Seriously, what are we gonna do?"

A truck pulled into the loading zone beside them, and Realene slumped down in her seat. Another black-clad man, this one with a handgun holstered at his hip, jumped from the driver's side. He extracted a heavy duffel bag from the space behind the seats and slung it over his shoulder before circling to the passenger side.

After a moment, the man reappeared in front of the truck, now walking alongside an older woman with neatly curled hair, also carrying a duffel bag.

"Irene," Realene whispered. "Come on. Follow my lead."

She slipped from the van, Nate close behind, and jogged toward the couple. "Irene," she called.

The man placed his hand on his weapon and blocked Irene, but she popped out from behind him. Her forehead was smeared with some kind of gunk. "Realene? Is that you? Oh, thank goodness, I thought they'd gotten you."

Realene wanted to punch Irene in her stupid face for kidnapping Ma, but that wouldn't get them inside. "It's so terrible out there. Have you seen? I think you were right about everything, all that's happening." She covered her mouth with one hand. "You tried to tell me, but I wouldn't listen. And now Ma's gone, I don't know where she is. I think the prairie dogs might have gotten her, and I don't know what to do."

"Oh, sweetie, your ma's okay," Irene said. "We found her wandering like a little lost lamb, and now she's here with us."

"She is?" Realene squeezed out a few fake tears, easy with the bitter wind biting at her eyes. "Oh thank you, God. Please, can I see her? I've been so worried."

Nate nudged Realene, and she said, "Oh, this is my friend, Nate. He's been helping me search for Ma. I really thought we'd lost her."

"You're Irene?" Nate took the old woman's hand in both of his. "I've heard so much about you. Mrs. Gustafson is like a mother to me too, I don't know how to thank you enough, ma'am. You're a real live angel."

"Oh, no. I'm no angel. But we may see some soon." Irene gazed up at the sky, and Realene got a better look at the mark on her forehead. It was the same symbol that adorned the bus, but drawn with ash.

The man who'd been standing aside stepped closer to Irene. His forehead bore the same mark.

"Oh, this is Lieutenant Braun," Irene said. "Lieutenant, this is Marion's daughter."

"Lieutenant? Like with the police?" Nate asked.

"No dear, the police are no help to us in these times. He's an officer of the church."

"Your church has officers? Neat." Realene wondered if they also had their own jail. A quick mental calculation put the likelihood of her and Nate ending up there at about ninety-seven percent.

"Reverend Zebediah will wonder what's taken us so long," the Lieutenant said.

"Oh, yes, of course. We've been gathering the last of the supplies for what's to come," Irene explained. She hitched the bag higher up on her shoulder. "It's truly a miracle you came when you did. This is the last of it, and you'd have had no way to reach us once we're locked inside."

"Locked inside?" Nate said, and Realene jabbed him.

"Come. It's not safe out here." Irene hustled up the long sidewalk and stopped when they reached the gate in the electric fence. She reached down to brush the snow from a small box that contained a switch and an indicator light.

She flipped the switch, and the indicator changed from red to green.

Lieutenant Braun opened the gate and ushered them through, then flipped a matching switch on the other side of the gate. The light turned back to red, and the warm sound of electricity hummed through the fence.

The man who'd been circling the building strode to the front door and opened it.

Realene and Nate followed Irene into a high-ceilinged vestibule, with an exposed roof that boasted beams of golden wood. A mass of pendant lights hung from the ceiling, and sconces dotted the walls. Two tables topped with purple flower arrangements sat along the walls to either side of the entry, which led straight toward a set of ornately carved double doors that most likely opened into the Sanctuary. To the right, dozens of winter coats of every variety hung from racks on the walls, the floor beneath them wet with the remnants of melting snow. To the left, a long hallway with doors on both sides serviced a separate wing of the building.

"Pretty," Realene said, gesturing toward the strange flower arrangements.

"Foxglove," Irene replied. "Reverend Zebediah says they symbolize death and rebirth. We have them brought in special from the florist."

"We usually have carnations." It struck Realene that this all resembled an evening meet-up of her own Lutheran church, except that the crosses adorning the walls were all altered into that strange symbol. "What's the seven for?"

Irene set her bag down by the coat rack and whispered something to the Lieutenant while placing one hand on his cheek. He nodded, then disappeared down the side hallway.

Irene came to stand beside Realene, and Nate sidled over to Irene's bag so as to peek into the gap created by the partially open zipper.

"That's the septumnox. It symbolizes the seven plagues of God's wrath." Irene beamed. "We've already had pestilence, infected animals, and fire from the sky. It won't be long now until the rest arrive."

"Oh, well…that's good," Realene said with a strained grin. She very much wanted to get the hell out of there as soon as possible. "So, where's Ma exactly?"

"Marion's resting. It's been a stressful day," Irene said. "Come. She'll be so happy to see you."

She led them a short distance down the side hallway and into a room that appeared stolen from a military boot camp. Four cots lined both walls, with an aisle down the middle and a metal locker at the end of each bed. Paintings decorated the room: three on the two side-walls and one straight ahead. They depicted scenes of fire raining down upon the Earth, dead livestock, swarms of insects, and most of all, lots and lots of people suffering or dead. These were the seven plagues Irene was so excited to see happen.

The cots were empty save for the farthest one, on which a body lay huddled beneath a blanket.

Realene ran to the end of the room, and relief washed over her as she rounded the bed to see Ma's face, her mouth thrown open in a soft snore. Pumpkin, who lay snuggled next to her, noticed Realene first. He gave a meow and jumped into her arms, rubbing his snout against her chin.

"Hey, Punky, I missed you too."

Irene and Nate walked up to join her. "We don't really allow pets, but she wouldn't come without him," Irene said. She wrinkled her nose.

Realene sat down on the edge of the cot and held Pumpkin close. Of course the evil cult didn't like pets.

"You two can take those beds there." Irene pointed to the ones across the aisle. "Don't take too long to get settled. The Reverend Zebediah will be delivering his sermon in a few minutes, and all are expected to attend."

She left the room, singing some hymn Realene had never heard before. Something about dread, agony, and bloodshed.

"Jesus," Nate mumbled.

Still holding a purring Pumpkin, Realene gently shook Ma's shoulder. "Wake up, Ma. It's okay now. I'm here."

Ma sat up, her face clouded with sleep and that same ash mark upon her forehead. She blinked several times and gave a vague smile. "Hello."

"Are you okay? I was so worried when I couldn't find you."

"Oh, I'm fine. Just fine."

"Good, that's good." Realene's stomach twisted at the vacant look on Ma's face. "Do you remember who I am?"

"Of course, dear." Ma smiled, but her eyes cut away.

Dear. Not Sweetie, or Realene, or Realene Marie. Dear, the term Ma used to address waitresses and clerks and other strangers.

Seventeen

MA'S WORDS HUNG in the air of the empty room, and a heavy weight pressed down on Realene's body. Ma had forgotten many things in her life, but never her daughter—not until now.

"I'm Realene. Your daughter."

"Daughter. Of course." Ma blinked rapidly, then she glanced at Pumpkin. "What a pretty tabby cat. Is he yours?"

Realene controlled her face, tamping down the worry that wanted to show. "Um, he's yours actually."

Ma petted Pumpkin, who had raised his head to meet her hand. "Mine? Isn't that nice. What a pretty boy you are. Yes."

Realene knew she shouldn't ask, that any direct questions would only aggravate things, but she couldn't stop herself from trying. "Ma, do you remember earlier today? What we were doing?"

Nate came up behind Realene and placed a hand on her shoulder. "Hi, Mrs. Gustafson. I'm Nathan. We're actually here to pick you up. Take you somewhere a little safer. You and Pumpkin."

"Take me? Oh no, I don't know. I'm tired."

Realene struggled to regain her composure, reminding herself that the confusion was temporary. Ma always got worse after sundown. After a good night's rest, she'd be okay. "You're missing your shows, aren't you? Don't you want to watch I Dream of Jeannie?"

"Oh yes, that's my favorite. I've got a bit of a crush on Larry Hagman." She giggled and leaned forward. "Don't tell my husband though." Her face furrowed with concern. "Have you seen my Louie? He must be here somewhere."

"He's the one who sent us to pick you up," Realene said.

"Oh, okay." Ma bent to slip on her snow boots, which were stored beneath the cot.

Nate helped her up, gripping one elbow, and grabbed her wool coat from where it lay draped over the metal locker.

Ma slipped her arms into the coat. "You're a very nice young man."

Realene stood, holding Pumpkin in her arms, focusing on his comforting purr. She tried not to think about the possibility that Ma wouldn't remember her tomorrow, or the next day, or the next day after that. Right now, she needed to focus on getting her out of here, getting her somewhere safe.

Nate led Ma across the room and out the door, with Realene trailing close behind. A woman and a young boy of maybe five passed them in the hallway, holding hands.

"Will I get to shoot a gun, momma? Like daddy does?"

"We'll see what Reverend Zebediah says, sweetie." The woman smiled pleasantly at the trio exiting the room. "Blessed be the judgment."

"Blessed be the judgment," Realene and Nate replied.

The woman and her son continued down the hallway toward the sanctuary, and Realene briefly considered rinsing with bleach to cleanse her mouth of the disturbing phrase.

After waiting for the coast to clear, the two of them led Ma down the hall. But just as they reached the last door before the hallway ended, it opened, and Sophia exited carrying a silver bowl, a stack of what looked like pages torn from the Bible, and one of those long barbecue lighters. She'd changed out of her blood-stained coveralls and into a blouse and slacks, looking quite normal except for the ash septumnox adorning her forehead.

At the sight of Nate and company, the bowl and papers slipped from Sophia's hands and fell to the floor. "Nathan? What are you doing here? Where are you taking Marion?"

"Mom, listen, I know you don't want to talk to me." Nate approached her, and she backed up until she hit the wall.

Realene eyed the fallen pages, which were labeled 'Revelations,' and wondered if those were what they burned to obtain ashes.

She pulled Ma to the side, resisting the temptation to rub the disturbing mark from her forehead. "We're going in just a minute, okay?"

"I can't leave without my Louie," Ma said.

"We're taking you to see him. I want you to hold onto Pumpkin, okay? Make sure he stays safe." She placed the cat in Ma's arms. A look of determination settled on Ma's face, and she nestled Pumpkin into the collar of her coat.

Sophia sidled around Nate and backed toward the sanctuary, holding out the lighter as if it were capable of fending him off.

"Listen," Nate said. "We know what's going on with the animals, why they're sick, and maybe how to slow them down."

Sophia pressed her hands over her ears. "I won't believe your lies, demon."

"Mom, you know I'm not a demon. We're just trying to stop this infection, so more people don't end up like Dad."

"You did that," she said. "You brought the evil, and you killed him."

Ma winced at the sound of their raised voices, and Realene put one arm around her. "It's okay. You worry about Pumpkin, okay?"

Ma buried her face in the cat's orange fur.

"If what you're saying is true, then Dad should have been protected, right?" Nate said. "Because he was righteous."

Sophia's lips quivered, and when she spoke, her voice shook. "He *was* righteous, wasn't he?"

"But all the others out there suffering and dying... You think they deserve this? You really believe that?"

"Don't try to confuse me. I see you for what you are." She ran toward the Sanctuary and flung the doors open.

Reverend Zebediah's voice spilled into the vestibule: "And the Lord said to him, pass through the city, through Jerusalem, and put a mark on the foreheads of the men who sigh and groan over all the abominations that are committed in it."

Nate stared after his mom.

"I'm sorry," Realene said. "We have to go."

He didn't speak, just nodded.

They rushed to the front doors, Realene murmuring to Ma that they were going on a car ride, and that she'd be able to watch her shows again soon.

Realene glanced through the open sanctuary doors. The same golden wood beams spanned the long, vaulted ceiling, and a dozen rows of pews lined the room, almost completely filled with people staring straight ahead at the reverend, who preached from a raised dais and was dressed in fatigues. A gun was holstered on each hip and a number of grenades were strung along his belt. A massive painting that depicted the Four Horsemen of the Apocalypse hung behind him, the riders armed with scythes and swords.

The reverend continued, reading from the Bible in his hands. "Your eye shall not spare, and you shall show no pity. Kill old men outright, young men and maidens, little children and women, but touch no one on whom is the mark."

Realene shuddered.

"It won't open, it's locked," Nate whispered, tugging on the door handle.

"We welcome the wrath of God, welcome the cleansing of the wicked. Let them be judged. Blessed be the judgment," the reverend said.

"Blessed be the judgment," the congregation replied in unison.

Sophia, who had been standing at the back of the room, waiting, glanced back one last time at Realene, Nate, and Ma. For a moment, it appeared she might let them get away, but then her eyes narrowed, and she rushed up the center aisle toward the pulpit.

The worshipers whispered to one another, stunned by the sudden intrusion, but Irene, who was sitting on the end of the last pew, looked back to where Sophia had come from and frowned. She got up from her seat and joined Realene, Nate, and Ma at the front exit.

Realene wrenched on the handle again, but it still wouldn't budge.

"You're missing the sermon," Irene said

"Let us out. *Now,*" Realene demanded.

"Only the Reverend Zebediah and his officers have keys. But don't you worry, you're all safe here. Protected."

Inside the sanctuary, Sophia could be seen talking to the reverend and gesturing toward her son and his co-conspirators.

Nate tried the door again, hoping it had miraculously unlocked.

"What's happening?" Ma asked, clutching Pumpkin close.

The reverend was now striding down the sanctuary aisle, Sophia trailing dutifully behind him. When he reached the doors of the sanctuary, he raised one hand to silence the congregation's murmurs. "We have visitors," he proclaimed. He gave something between a smile a sneer. "Sister Irene, join Sister Sophia in leading recitations, please."

Irene rushed to join Sophia, and both of them jogged to the front of the sanctuary.

Reverend Zebediah stepped out into the vestibule and closed the sanctuary doors behind him.

"We just want to leave," Realene said in a rush.

"Join me in my office first." The reverend walked toward the side hallway, not waiting for them to follow, knowing they had no choice.

THE OFFICE WAS the first room in the hall, the one Sophia had been leaving. In stark contrast to the barracks, golden wood panels covered the walls, and a matching desk sat near the back wall, flanked by bookcases.

Realene directed Ma to a comfy chair in the corner nearest the door, and she sunk into the seat, her face etched with deep wrinkles. "Rest here, okay?" Realene said.

Ma closed her eyes and leaned her head against the back of the chair, still cradling Pumpkin to her chest.

Reverend Zebediah took his spot behind the desk, his oversized leather office chair rising behind him like a throne. "Please, have a seat," he said, smiling like some kind of beneficent leader.

Realene and Nate took their seats in the two chairs opposite the reverend, where Realene noticed the absurdity of the reverend's bookcases. Instead of books, the shelves were brimming with collectible action figures and toys, including G.I. Joes, Johnny West cowboys, the Matchbox Military Vehicle set, and various cap guns, all still in their original packaging.

"What's up with the outfit?" Nate asked. "Finally decide to ditch the denim?"

Zebediah narrowed his eyes. "How did you get past my guards?"

"We didn't break in, if that's what you're thinking. Irene invited us in. She's a friend." That last word soured on Realene's tongue.

"She *let* you in,?" the reverend asked.

"Oh, yeah, invited us to stay and everything. Said we could join you, hide out, the whole shebang." Realene almost grinned at the thought of how much trouble Irene was going to be in with her precious leader.

"Outsiders are not welcome here."

"Did you not see us trying to leave?" Nate asked. "Just now, when we kept trying to open the front door?"

Realene wanted to smack Nate. Hadn't he been the one reminding her to be polite? "You've got quite the church, um, facility set up here, reverend, sir."

"We must be prepared for the coming apocalypse. I've seen the signs. War, famine, false prophets, loose morals."

Realene pressed her lips together to keep from laughing, reminded herself they were in real danger while in the company of this nutjob.

"Many have tried to deny that the end days are upon us. Some are still denying it even while fire rains from the heavens and crazed animals roam the streets." He looked to Realene. "But there's still time to repent, to save yourself." He shifted his gaze to Nate. "You, I'm afraid, are beyond saving."

"Because I'm a demon?"

The reverend leaned back, the leather of the chair creaking beneath his weight. "You murdered your father. Joyously, from what I was told."

Nate's grip tightened on the arms of his chair. "It's not that simple."

"What's happening here is not an act of God," Realene said. "There's an infection, and it's spreading from animals to people, turning them rabid and aggressive. That's want happened to Dick, uh, Mr. Haugen. We're just trying to stop it before more people get hurt."

"And how do you intend to do that?"

"We know what's causing the infection, and we have an idea how to slow it down," she said, careful not to mention alien worms. "If we can get to the Air Force base and let Colonel Harmon know, he can contain it, figure out how to kill it for good."

"Even the military cannot stop the wrath of God."

"Are you not listening?" Nate stood up and slammed his hands upon the desk. "This has nothing to do with God!"

Reverend Zebediah got up and placed a hand on the pistol at his right hip. "I have long predicted this day would come, and you will not keep me from claiming my victory."

"So what? You're going to shoot us now?" Nate asked, apparently trying to get them all killed.

"Listen, we're just gonna get out of your hair," Realene said. She grabbed Nate's arm and yanked him away from the desk. "We only came to pick up my mom, and who knows, maybe you're right?" They moved to the door, eyes still on the reverend. "Maybe the end times really are upon us, and we'll get burned up or tortured or whatever. Serves us right, I guess."

Realene shook Ma's shoulder to wake her. "Come on, we're going."

Ma blinked herself awake and stood with Realene's help. "Louie?"

"We're going to see him now. He's waiting for us, knows exactly where we are actually," she said. Just a few more steps, and they'd be out of the office. She had no idea how they would talk themselves out the front door, but they'd cross that bridge when they got to it.

"You're not leaving here." The reverend strode out from behind his desk, hands resting on both guns now, like a villain in a John Wayne western, waiting to draw.

Eighteen

A KNOCK SOUNDED on the door, and Realene grabbed the knob and opened it before the reverend could stop her. Maybe he'd be less likely to shoot them in front of other people.

Irene stood in the hall, fist raised to knock again.

"What?" the reverend demanded, marching up beside Realene.

"Oh, I—I'm so sorry to interrupt, Reverend Zebediah. It's just that there's someone at the gate, and we thought—"

"I'm surprised you didn't let them inside."

Irene just shook her head, terrified and confused. "I'm not sure I understand."

"Did you not invite these demons into our holy sanctuary?" He gestured toward Realene and Nate.

Blotches of red bloomed up Irene's neck. "Demons? No, I would never—"

"Did you know of their plans to stop the blessed cleansing? To keep us from our rightful place?"

Eyes so wide they might pop from her skull, Irene looked from the reverend to Realene. "You, you tricked me. You're not a believer at all."

"You kidnapped my mom," Realene said. She pulled Ma closer, and Nate moved to flank her on the other side.

"I don't like it here. I want my Louie," Ma said.

Lieutenant Braun strode up behind Irene. "She says she won't leave without speaking to the reverend."

"Who?" Zebediah asked the Lieutenant.

"Some reporter lady. Shelley something. Says she met you this morning and wants to interview you."

Zebediah smoothed one hand over his stiff helmet of hair, another shameless abuser of Aqua Net. "Hmm. Alright, let her in."

"Sir, I'm not sure that's a good idea," the Lieutenant said.

"I decide what is and what is not a good idea." He shoved his way past Nate and continued down the hall.

"Please forgive me," Irene begged. She clutched at the reverend's sleeve, but he quickly shook her off. "They tricked me with their lies."

"Come on. This could be our chance to slip out," Realene whispered. She wasted no time leading Ma after the others.

"We can tell that reporter about what's happening here, expose Zebediah for the psycho he is," Nate said. He strode ahead of Realene, and she reached out to snag his jacket collar and stop him.

"Dude, are you trying to get us killed?"

Nate's nostrils flared. "No."

"Then stop starting shit. Our only priority is getting the hell out of here alive, got it?" She didn't wait for him to respond, instead steering Ma into the vestibule.

The reverend and the lieutenant stood near the front door, and Irene lingered a few feet away, looking like a puppy who'd been kicked. The doors of the sanctuary were closed, but Sophia's voice was still somewhat audible from within.

Nate stared at the doors, his hands clenched at his sides.

Realene prayed he wouldn't try to go back for his mom, that he wouldn't force Realene to leave him behind.

But then he turned away, anger seething from every pore.

"Are you alright, dear?" Ma asked him. She leaned into Nate in a sort of hug, and Pumpkin stretched to nuzzle his chin.

The lock clicked on the front door, and it swung open to reveal the reporter Realene had seen at the landing site that morning, though she now looked much less polished. Her previously perfect curls were ratty and windblown, her earmuffs were gone, and streaks of something foul stained her pink pea coat.

"Shelley Schraeder, WDIZ News," she said, reintroducing herself to the reverend. "We met this morning."

Realene guided Ma and Nate toward the wall closest to the door, off to the side of the group.

"Ms. Schraeder, it's so nice to see you again. Come in out of the cold." The reverend smiled wide and ushered her inside.

Mouth pinched in a way that was most definitely not camera-ready, Shelley stomped into the vestibule, leaving a trail of snow behind her.

Zebediah looked outside, frowning. "Your cameraman?"

"The idiot got bit by some rodent, freaked out, and ran off." She pulled a notebook and pen from her pocket.

"I see." The reverend's smile disappeared. "Continue your patrols," he said to the guard before closing the door. There was no telltale click, and neither the reverend nor the lieutenant made a move to lock the door. They were focused instead on Shelley.

She stepped farther into the room, surveying the space. "This is all quite...lovely."

The reverend followed her, trailed by the lieutenant and Irene. "You're surprised?" Zebediah asked.

"After all your talk about the world ending, I have to admit, I was expecting something a bit more sensational." She exhaled and smoothed a hand over her hair, donning her television persona. "Those symbols you have on your foreheads are interesting. Tell me, what do they mean?"

The reverend and his flunkies had their backs to Realene now. She held a finger to her lips and crept closer to the door, Ma and Nate following.

"I assumed this would be a proper interview, a live broadcast," the reverend said.

"Oh, believe me, I would much prefer that as well. Sadly, even if I did have a cameraman, they're blocking all broadcasts and phone calls into and out of Demise."

"*They?*" he asked.

"The military. They're not letting anyone in or out either, which means the national stations are all stuck on the outskirts, can't even get a single shot of the crash site." She smirked, then her expression soured. "They say there's some sort of outbreak among the wildlife, but I don't buy it."

The door was just a few feet away now, and Realene took another step.

Shelley noticed her and said, "Hey, you're that girl from the trailer park."

Realene froze. The others turned to face her, and the reverend scowled.

"You were getting all buddy-buddy with the colonel this morning. I bet you know what's going on." Shelley's eyes shone bright with excitement.

"Nope. I have no idea," Realene said.

"Come on. Just give me the scoop, and once this is all over and we're back in the studio, I'll have you on air for an exclusive interview, just like you wanted."

Realene avoided looking at Nate, an overwhelming sense of embarrassment making her want to curl up into a ball. "Sorry, I really can't help you. Besides, we were just leaving."

Shelley pushed past the reverend. "Are you members of the cult—oh, uh, pardon me—I mean of the church? I'd love to hear about your experiences. And if you want to share anything about what you've heard from the colonel, we can talk about that too."

"This is *not* a cult," Irene protested.

"Of course not," Shelley said. "I simply misspoke. Please, forgive me."

One of the doors to the sanctuary opened, and a worshiper, a middle-aged man, stepped out, leaving the door propped open behind him. "Blessed be the judgment," he said, before walking past them and heading down the side hallway.

Sophia's voice now carried out from the inside the sanctuary. "With pestilence and with blood, I will enter into judgment with him. I will rain on him and on his troops, and on the many peoples who are with him, a torrential rain, with hailstones, fire, and brimstone."

Shelley craned her neck to peer into the sanctuary, scribbling something in her notebook. "Fire and brimstone—I believe you mentioned that this morning. You feel the meteor is a sign of the coming apocalypse. Is that right?

"The end times are upon us, and only the true believers will be spared." Irene said. "Reverend Zebediah has foreseen—"

The reverend clamped a hand on her shoulder to silence her. "What do you plan to report exactly?" he asked Shelley.

"I just want to tell your story. Who you are, how you got here, what Revelation Evangelical believes." She gave a smile that was almost flirtatious. "For example, Zebediah can't be your real name. Who were you before? Where do you come from? What's your story?"

"I have always been who I am; a man of God."

Realene caught Nate's eye and angled her head toward the door. They had to make a run for it before the reporter got herself kicked out. Realene grabbed the doorknob, then waited for the right moment to use it.

"Ah, knowing your calling from a young age is a rare gift. But those that do are often misunderstood, underestimated, even ostracized." Shelley raised the pen to her mouth, as if in thought. "Is that why Faith Church officially exiled this branch after you took over? They didn't understand?"

"It sounds to me like you've been snooping where you shouldn't be. Digging into me, into the church." The reverend opened his camouflage jacket and placed his right hand on his gun. "I don't think you want to tell my story at all, do you Ms. Schraeder?"

"A good reporter researches her subject." Shelley lowered her notebook. "But if you're not interested in being featured, that's fine."

"We are not a cult, and I will not allow you to insult our holy mission." The reverend drew his gun from its holster and brandished it at his side.

"My boss knows I'm here," said Shelley. Her voice turned shrill, no longer polished. "He's actually expecting a report back from me any minute."

"I thought the phones were down." He raised his gun, pointed it at the young woman's chest. "You know, I could shoot you right now, and no one would ever find out."

Realene's pulse pounded, filling her ears, and she ordered herself to stay perfectly still. She felt Ma trembling beside her.

"You won't shoot me. Not in front of all these people."

The sanctuary had gone silent, the congregation having turned in their pews. Sophia walked down the center aisle, slowing when she saw the gun. Her gaze shifted to Realene, to the girl's hand on the exit, and she frowned.

Realene shook her head. *Please, don't say anything. Don't call attention to us.*

Zebediah's voice rose, as if he were back behind the pulpit. "My followers are completely loyal to me." He raised his weapon to aim at Shelley's head, and she flinched. "This woman, this heathen, is a reporter. She's come here to insult us and our beliefs, intends to publicly tarnish our reputation, to stop our righteous work."

Those in the sanctuary had crowded to one side to see out the open doors. Men, women, and children, parents and grandparents, strangers and neighbors and former classmates. Righteous hatred twisted their faces with its ugliness.

Realene trembled, knowing they also saw her and Ma and Nate about to run.

Sophia edged to the front of the group, but didn't enter the vestibule, just watched.

The reverend chuckled and pointed his gun at the ceiling. "Come on now. Did you think I was really going to shoot you?"

Shelley opened her mouth, closed it again, shook her head, but didn't dare speak.

"No. These bullets are holy, reserved for delivering divine justice against only the greatest of evils." He slipped his gun back in the holster, and Realene struggled to slow her racing heart.

Shelley's hands shook as she tried and finally succeeded in slipping her notebook back in her pocket. A small, relieved sob slipped from her throat.

The reverend turned to the lieutenant. "Kill her."

"No!" Realene reached out in instinct as the lieutenant drew his gun and fired point blank into the middle of Shelley Schraeder's forehead.

The crack of the bullet left deafening silence in its wake. Time stopped, and a frozen Realene stared helplessly at her own outstretched hand, at Shelley's falling body just hanging there, puppet-like, her eyes wide and mouth agape.

Screams tore through the quiet, and the world moved again.

Shelley's body dropped to the floor, and the crowd of worshipers pushed through the sanctuary doors to surround her.

Sophia dropped to her knees beside the woman, as if to help, but the reverend yanked her away.

"This demon aimed to stop our divine plan, but I will not allow anyone to interfere with our salvation. Blessed be the judgment!"

"Blessed be the judgment," the crowd half-heartedly replied, some full-voiced, some quiet, some mute. No one, however, uttered a single word of protest.

Ma clutched Realene's arm, still holding Pumpkin, though he'd stopped purring. Nate reached behind her and grasped the doorknob, his eyes locked on the surreal scene before them.

They had to get out now, or they'd be next. The walls and ceiling seemed to move, to close in, and Realene inhaled a deep breath, willing herself not to pass out.

The crowd now encased the reverend, unwittingly blocked him from the exit, which provided a perfect but fleeting opportunity for escape. They had to go. Now.

"Satan has sent his minions to stop this cleansing, to interfere with the will of God and halt the rise of the righteous," Zebediah said.

Realene put her arm around Ma as Nate turned the knob and cracked the door. She met his gaze, then pointed to herself and then to the light switches on the wall beside the door. He gave a slight nod.

Realene swiped her hand over the switches in two fast movements, flipping off all the lights in the room and plunging them into darkness. Nate flung the door wide and shoved Realene and Ma through, as the cries of the congregation erupted behind them. He followed, slamming the door behind him, and the three of them ran toward the gate.

The town's emergency siren still wailed, rising and falling.

"Stop right there!" A figure emerged from the darkness. It was the guard.

They froze, just a few feet from the gate.

"Please, you've got to help him," Realene said, not having to fake the panic shaking her voice. "That reporter, she had a gun."

The guard dropped his aggressive posture and raced toward the church, leaving them behind.

Bitter wind bit at her face as she crouched to press the disarming switch on the fence. She did, and the hum of electricity went silent. She pushed Ma through the gate first, but Nate lagged behind. He'd stopped to pull something from his pocket.

Just then, the front door of the church was flung open, lights back on and members of the congregation spilling out.

"Stay back!" Nate shouted, raising the item in his hand. It was a grenade. Before anyone could even react, he pulled the pin, lobbed it toward the crowd, and sprinted to catch up.

Realene grabbed Ma by the arm and hustled her toward the van. A shot rang out, hitting the cement at their feet, and Ma shrieked. Pumpkin squirmed, but Ma managed to keep hold of him.

A deafening boom filled the air as the grenade exploded, and a whoosh of hot air hit their backs. Thankfully, they all managed to remain standing as they stumbled to the vehicle. Realene shoved Ma through the sliding door, then ran around to the driver's side as Nate hopped in the passenger seat.

Realene cranked the key and peeled out, yelling, "Buckle up!"

"I can't buckle up!" Calvin shouted from the back. "Let me the hell outta here!"

"Who's that?" Ma cried.

Fire and smoke billowed into the air and blotted out the front of the church.

"Whoa. They're not messing around with those grenades," Nate said. "You think everyone's okay?"

Realene knew he was thinking of his mom. "They would have sent out the officers first, those who were armed," she said, even though she had no idea how true that was. She looked in the rearview mirror to see several parishioners charge through the smoke and jump into their cars. "Shit, they're coming after us." She sped through the parking lot and back onto Main.

She wondered, not for the first time, but with much more uncertainty than before: Could they really make it out of this town alive?

THE SUN HAD set, and Realene intended to use the early dark of winter to her advantage. She pulled off on a side street and killed her headlights, then turned randomly for several blocks and parked in front of a house that was dark except for the Christmas lights framing the front windows. The remnants of their display of reindeer pulling a sleigh lay were scattered across the snowy yard, Santa nowhere to be found.

"Take me home right now," Calvin demanded, thumping and kicking.

"Soon, buddy," Nate said.

"We're going to lay low for a few minutes, okay?" Realene turned off the car so their exhaust wouldn't give them away.

"You sure we're okay here?" Nate asked.

"I don't know, but I need a minute. And I think they'll look for us at our houses, places we'd know." Her hands shook, and she clasped them in her lap. "He just…killed her. And no one cared."

He exhaled a shaky breath. "Yeah."

She glanced in the rearview at Ma, who cradled Pumpkin to her chest.

"I did it, I took care of him," Ma bent to press her cheek to his back, and he gave a soft meow.

"You did so great, Ma. I'm sorry for all that, I know it was pretty scary."

"I don't like that church, or those people. They said crazy, terrible things." She leaned forward, her face emerging from the shadows. "Plus, they didn't have one single TV."

Nate gave a startled laugh. "Now that *is* crazy."

There was no mention of them shooting an innocent woman, as if Ma had already blocked that out entirely. *Good.* Despite the siren still cutting through air, she rested her head against the side window and closed her eyes, dozing.

"That grenade move was pretty dope," Realene said.

"Thanks. Stole it from Irene's boyfriend."

"Nice." She stared at the Christmas lights on the darkened house, regretted that she hadn't hung any outdoor lights on their trailer. Her dad had always been the one to do that.

"I shouldn't have talked to my mom." Nate's words were quiet, barely audible. "I thought, hoped, I don't know."

Realene grasped his hand. "You had to try."

"They were really going to kill us, huh?"

"Yeah."

"I knew she was angry, but I didn't know she would do that. Give us up to her psycho cult leader. That's pretty fucked up."

Ma cracked one eye open. "Language."

"Sorry, Mrs. Gustafson," Nate said.

"It's not her fault. It's his, that Zebediah. He's brainwashed them."

Nate shrugged, as if not ready to let his mom off the hook. Realene didn't blame him.

Calvin's grating snores and Ma's baby ones filled the air. Exhaustion infused every inch of Realene's body, but there would be no sleep for her anytime soon.

She restarted the car and flipped the heat on full blast. After waiting for the defrosters to edge back the thin layer of ice crystals that had grown on the windshield, she pulled away from the curb. They drove in silence across town, winding through residential streets filled with accidents, neighbors in fist fights, and the slinking shadows of prairie dogs creeping across snowy yards—just much fewer than what they'd seen on the main roads. Mostly, they drove by darkened houses, and Realene wondered how many of them contained residents not yet infected, hiding, waiting for someone to tell them what to do.

Someone had activated the emergency siren. Had they updated the emergency notifications too? She flipped on the radio and twisted the dial, but all she heard was static. Of course. Brooke broke the antenna. Realene turned the dial off.

They emerged back onto Main right before the park, and she checked in the direction of Nate's apartment. That would be the fastest route to the air base, but the streetlights illuminating the intersection revealed that the roadblock was still in place. A compact car with a couple people inside sat parked in the shadows before the stop sign, its engine running, and Realene pulled around it to ease through the intersection.

A hatchback shot past at twice the speed limit, barely avoiding a collision with them, and barreled through the opening on the other side of the school bus, the hole now big enough for a small car to fit through.

Bright lights blazed in the direction of the fleeing car's brake lights, and Realene envisioned an alien spaceship landing a la *Fire in the Sky* and sucking the vehicle up with its tractor beam. But the aliens were already there, and they had not come via ship.

Realene slowed and came to a stop behind the car that had zoomed past her, finally able to make out the shapes behind the floodlights. Several vehicles parked nose to tail formed a barricade across the only other major road out of town. A shadowy figure holding a gun stood atop each vehicle.

"The city of Demise is under quarantine," a voice called out, amplified by a bullhorn. "Return to your homes. I repeat, return to your homes."

The car ahead of Realene gunned its engine and cut sharply to the side, speeding toward the snowy berm beside the road. Several shots rang out, and the car whipped back and forth, slowed, then stopped. Smoke poured from the hood.

"What was that?" Ma asked, her voice soft and scared.

"You will not be permitted to leave. Return to your homes," the man with the bullhorn announced.

Realene shifted into reverse and backed up several car lengths before flipping a U-turn and heading back the way they came.

A growl came from the trunk, the vehicle shaking as Calvin threw himself back and forth. "Let me out of here!" he screamed.

Ma yelped, and Realene glanced in the rearview mirror to see her lying on the seat, curled up in a ball.

"Shit. He's getting worse," Realene said. It made sense. It had been over an hour since Calvin had been bitten. "We can't go home, not to mine or yours. Those psychos will still be gunning for us."

She pulled around the bus and approached the intersection.

"Holy cow," Nate said as they approached the brightly lit Snack Station lot. A gas pump spurted the noxious liquid onto the pavement in a steady flow, and a car sat parked nearby, its engine running.

"Guess I'm not getting that promotion to manager." Realene watched as a trio in ski masks fled the store by leaping through the smashed front door, their arms full of whatever they could carry. They yelled and high-fived, then threw their spoils into the backseat of the parked car and returned to the store for more.

"They're looting the place." Realene wanted to speed down there and make them stop. Sure, she hated the job, but her boss was nice. Plus, she'd met Walt there.

"You okay?" Nate asked.

She shook herself. "Uh, yeah."

Pounding sounded in the back as Calvin bashed at the door. Ma whimpered.

"So, what do we do? Where can we go?"

"We can't stay in this car all night." She scanned the road ahead of them, caught sight of the movie theater in the distance. "Hey, you still got your keys to the Cinema Twin?"

Maybe it was finally time they snuck into the theater.

Nineteen

REALENE CRINGED AT the sight of Brooke's body still lying in the road. She no longer resembled a bloodied angel with blonde hair fanned out in a halo. Likely a victim of panicked drivers, her body lay mangled, with limbs twisted and head wrenched fully around to glower sightlessly behind her. Nate winced, but didn't comment. Realene edged the van around the corpse and pulled into the entrance to the restaurant and movie complex.

The fluffy snowflakes of the afternoon were gone, replaced by icy pellets propelled sideways by the gusting winds. A car sped past in the parking lot, fishtailing as it whipped between the spattering of parked cars, clipping one before jumping a median and continuing past the theater.

Realene drove passed Toppers, where a shadow moved inside the darkened building. A motorcycle with a Misfits logo on the tank lay on the front sidewalk, tipped on its side. She stopped in front of the restaurant and grabbed the baseball bat.

"Wait here." She opened her door.

"Whoa, hang on," Nate said.

"I think it's Tony." She got out and closed the door. He'd been an asshole earlier, and he wasn't generally someone she wanted to hang out with anymore, but he got her through some rough times in high school. She had to see if he could still be helped.

Realene passed the motorcycle, which didn't appear damaged, and stepped through the broken glass of the front window. "Tony? Is that you?"

A hostess stand stood unmanned, and empty tables filled the checkered tile floor. A retro jukebox sat against the back wall, the kind with neon tubes that framed the window where the records would play, and red numbered buttons to make your selection. "Mr. Sandman" and "Sixteen Candles" were Realene's favorites.

Footsteps sounded, and a figure emerged from the entrance to the kitchen in the back.

"Tony, is that you?" She went farther inside, holding her bat out in from of her.

"Realene, hi." Tony walked into the dining room, carrying a cylindrical tub under one arm. His coat was stained and torn in several places.

"Whatcha got there?" She lowered her bat, holding it loosely at her side.

Tony set the tub down on the closest table and raised a spoon. "Ice cream. Rocky Road." Sticky chocolate rimmed his mouth. "Want some? They've got other flavors too."

"I *would* go for mint chip, but it's a little cold for ice cream."

"Oh, yeah, maybe."

"I saw your bike out front, wanted to make sure you were okay."

"Isn't it the coolest? I always dreamed of having a bike like that." He stuck his spoon in the ice cream. "I can't remember getting it though."

Realene bit her tongue. "There's some kind of disease going around with the animals. Did you get bit? By a deer maybe?"

"Deer don't bite." He laughed and shoved his hands in his pockets. "Hey, listen, would you ever wanna go out sometime?"

Her eyes stung at the sincerity in his voice, as if he'd shed his teen angst and gone back to being the sweet kid she'd first met when he moved to town in junior high. Before they'd both become jaded. "Yeah, that'd be fun."

"Really? Cool. I guess I'll call you when..." His brow furrowed. "Hey, what's going on out there? People are acting strange, right?"

"Yeah." She thought about taking Tony with them, but she already had Ma and Calvin to worry about, and Tony was clearly infected. "Might be best for you to hunker down in here, okay? Hide out for a while. I'll come back and check on you later."

"Okay. I'll save you some mint chip." He picked up the tub of Rocky Road. "Bye, Realene."

"Bye, Tony," she said, her voice tight with guilt, or maybe regret. She reminded herself that the most important thing was to make it safely through the night and try again to reach the Air Force base in the morning. Saving Tony—saving anyone—depended on it.

Realene returned to the van and hopped in the driver's seat, passing the bat to Nate. At least she didn't have to use it on Tony.

"Everything okay?" he asked.

"Could be worse." She cranked up the windshield wipers, attempting to keep up with blowing snow, and drove to the Cinema Twin.

The glass entrance doors were intact, protecting the vestibule that held the ticket booth. A security cage had been lowered on either side of the booth, and the lobby beyond was mostly dark, except for a few small accent lights inside. The marquee overhead advertised *Alien: Resurrection* and *Titanic*, a combination fitting the disaster of a situation they found themselves in.

Nate directed her around the building to an alley that separated the theater from the Liquor Depot next door. The narrow space housed the employee entrance and led to an employee parking lot and a line of dumpsters in the back of the building. She reversed into the alley, facing the parking lot, so they could watch for anyone who might approach.

Nate hopped out and unlocked the 'Employees Only' door, then propped it open with a large rock probably used by those who took smoke breaks during their shifts.

Realene opened the van's sliding door, ignoring Calvin's angry screams, and grabbed the two duffel bags and the box of mementos first, then passed them to Nate, who would take them inside the building. Noticing the defibrillator still wedged between the front seats, Realene handed him that too, and then put Pumpkin back inside his carrier.

Pumpkin yowled unhappily as she latched the door. "I know, Punky. It's just for a few minutes."

"Come on, Ma. We're going inside, where it's warm." Realene grabbed the cat carrier by the handle and held out her free hand to Ma. She helped her step down from the van and onto the icy sidewalk. A frigid wind still blew, but here in the alley, the buildings shielded them from the biting snow.

"I want my shows," Ma said, her tone that of a grumpy child.

"They've got lots of shows here," Realene said, though she knew they weren't the kind Ma liked.

They walked past Nate, who came back out of the theater holding a large, empty popcorn bucket.

Realene gave him a quizzical look.

"For Calvin. In case he gets bitey." He headed back toward the van. "Maybe if he can't tell where we are, the worms inside him won't be able to telepath our location."

"Good idea." They couldn't leave Calvin in the car with how cold it was. "What're you going to do with him?"

"I don't know, broom closet?" Nate shrugged.

"Be careful." She rounded the open door and urged Ma inside.

Realene set Pumpkin down next to the duffel bags and other items Nate had lined up along the wall, and led Ma down the short hallway past a darkened storeroom and the employee-only stairwell that led to the projector rooms. Unwinding film spools and glow-in-the-dark stars decorated the purple carpet that led into the lobby, where paper snowflakes hung from the ceiling.

They passed the snack bar—one long, glass case with tile at either end—and walked in front of the velvet-roped stanchions. The smell of butter flavoring filled the air, and Realene's stomach grumbled at the sight of the candy array displayed behind the glass in neat rows. Luckily, the latching half-doors at either end of the snack bar offered easy access for later. A life-sized cardboard cutout advertising the upcoming release of *Spice World* stood before the counter, and she was tempted to knock it over. The Spice Girls were intolerable, except maybe Posh.

Realene guided Ma to one of two padded benches that sat against the side wall on either side of a Christmas tree that had been strung with popcorn and gummy worms instead of garland.

"Rest here. I'll be right back." She turned toward the hallway, faltering at the sight of a woman silhouetted in the open alleyway door. "Irene?"

Irene held the door open with her hip and bent to pick up the rock that had been propping the door open before her. "You reap what you sow," she said, then backed away to let the door slam shut.

Realene strode across the lobby, stopping when she caught sight of something moving in her peripheral.

A man in a ski mask smashed one of the theater's floor-to-ceiling windows with a pipe, sending a spray of glass into the vestibule.

Ma screamed and ran to Realene, clutching at her arm.

"Shhh, it's okay," Realene said, extremely thankful for the metal security gate that divided the vestibule from the lobby.

Lugging an animal carrier easily three times the size of Pumpkin's, the masked man strode through the vacated window frame and set the carrier down facing Realene and Ma. He then pulled up the ski mask to reveal his face.

Reverend Zebediah.

NATE WATCHED REALENE and her mom enter the theater, then peered through the back window of the minivan. Calvin pushed the pile of blankets off and pounded on the door with his head.

"Listen up," Nate shouted, using his most stern voice. "I'm going to let you out of there, but only if you calm down."

Calvin growled, displaying his tobacco-stained teeth, but stopped his thrashing.

Leaning the bat against the bumper, Nate held the popcorn bucket in one hand and unlatched the trunk, backing up as it rose. Calvin kicked and squirmed. "When I get ahold'a you, I'm gonna gut and stuff you."

Nate wasn't in immediate danger. They'd strapped Calvin in place by looping bungee cords through his wrist and ankle restraints and hooking the ends to the van's metal frame. He only wished they'd thought of gagging and blindfolding Calvin when he'd been a bit calmer.

"Hey, isn't that your girlfriend?" Nate pointed toward the front seat.

Calvin craned his neck to look over the back of the bench seat, and Nate lunged forward to stuff the red-and-white striped popcorn bucket over his head, fur hat and all. Calvin yowled, shaking his head back and forth, the tail of the hat sticking out from beneath the bucket. Nate couldn't help but laugh.

A door slammed behind him, and he whirled to see Irene standing there, the image of a kindly middle-aged woman except for the sneer twisting her face. She raised the rock in her hands and smashed the door handle off the Cinema Twin's employee entrance.

"What are you doing?" Nate strode toward her.

She raised the rock over her head again. "Stay back, demon."

"I don't want to hurt you. And I know you don't want to hurt us. Marion is your friend, right?"

"That doesn't matter now." She raised her chin defiantly. "I must make up for my betrayal, prove I'm worthy of salvation."

The shatter of glass sounded, drawing Nate's attention that direction, his back now turned to Irene.

Lieutenant Braun had accompanied Irene, and he lurked at the rear of the van, a large hunting knife gripped in one hand. He bent to cut through the bungee cord binding Calvin's wrists.

Nate took a step toward the lieutenant and pain exploded in the back of his skull. He fell to the ground. Irene hustled past him, dropping the rock, which was now stained red. Nate touched the back of his throbbing head, wincing at the slight pressure. His fingers came away bloody. Nausea hit him and he exhaled, willing himself not to puke.

The lieutenant dropped the knife at Calvin's feet before grabbing Irene's hand and leading her from the alley.

Calvin's hands now freed, he unhooked the tether at his feet and unwrapped the bungee cord that secured his ankles.

Crawling across the icy asphalt, Nate managed to grab hold of the business end of the bat. A cry sounded behind him, and he rolled to his back. Calvin had pushed the popcorn bucket up off his face, leaving it to balance on his fur hat, and leapt from the trunk, straight at Nate.

Nate jabbed upward with the handle end of the bat, catching Calvin in the mouth as he descended.

Calvin's teeth flew from his mouth in several large chunks, gums and all. Calvin howled and clutched his face as Nate skittered backward. Nate's hand landed on one of the chunks of teeth, revealing them to be made of ceramic. Dentures.

He flipped the bat around to hold it by the handle.

"You messed up my teeth," Calvin said, teeth coming out as *teef*.

"We'll get you new ones, dude." Nate got up, leaning on the bat as a wave of dizziness hit him.

Calvin's eyes landed on the hunting knife Lieutenant Braun had dropped before he fled.

"Oh shit." Nate gripped the bat in both hands.

Calvin swiped the blade from the trunk and stalked toward Nate, giving him a toothless grin. "I'm gonna take your teeth out. One by one." His words were muddled, but Nate got the gist.

Looking like Michael Meyers crossed with Buckethead from the band Limp Bizkit, Calvin swiped at Nate with the blade, but he blocked the blow with the bat.

"Seriously, I don't want to hurt you."

"I *do* wanna hurt you." Calvin lashed out with the blade again, and Nate backed up to avoid it, then extended the bat to tap the popcorn bucket back down over Calvin's face.

Calvin reached up with both hands, stabbing the tip of the blade through the cardboard and crying out.

"Careful, dude! That thing is sharp."

Shaking his head back and forth, Calvin flailed, swiping the air with the knife and catching Nate on the back of the hand.

Nate hissed in pain, but managed to swing the bat and connect with Calvin's wrist. The knife fell from his hand, clattering on the icy asphalt.

Calvin screamed and clawed at the popcorn bucket with his good hand, tearing it off along with his fur hat. He wheeled around in search of his fallen knife.

Nate quickly grabbed one of the bungee cords from the van and rushed Calvin, tackling him face-first to the ground. Sitting on his back, Nate managed to loop the bungee cord around one wrist then the other, tying the man's hands tight behind him.

"Get off! Let me go!" Calvin squirmed and struggled.

"I thought you had me there for a minute." Nate panted, pain throbbing in the back of his head. The sooner he could get Calvin totally restrained and tucked away inside, the sooner he could rest. Nate gripped Calvin's shoulder to flip him over and sit him up.

Calvin twisted his head, chomping down on Nate's wounded hand with his toothless bite.

"Hey!" Nate snatched his hand away. Even with no teeth, it felt unpleasant to have a fresh knife wound gnawed on.

His head went a bit fuzzy, and he sat back down to gather himself. He recognized the Cinema Twin and Realene's mom's van, but what were they all doing here in the middle of the night?

Twenty

REVEREND ZEBEDIAH STOOD on the other side of the gate, now dressed in a heavy, camouflage coat and leather gloves. His pale face stood in stark contrast to the black ski mask pulled back over his forehead and ears. "God has made me an extension of His hand, an enforcer of His will."

"Leave us alone, you psycho!" Realene said, holding Ma close.

Snow gusted through the gate, peppering the carpet, and Zebediah spit at her through the bars. "Your names do not hurt me, servant of Satan."

"Servant of Satan?" She scoffed. "The satanic panic is over, man. Didn't you see Geraldo's big apology?"

"Geraldo?" He smacked his forehead with the heel of his hand. "Do not try to confuse and distract me, demon. I will not allow you to interfere with God's righteous cleansing."

"Righteous? Innocent people are dying. That has nothing to do with God."

He bent to unlatch the door of the carrier. "Those who are infected are deserving of God's wrath." He backed out the way he came, disappearing into the snowy night.

Her breath echoing in her ears, Realene stared into the black depth of the carrier. Something moved within the shadows, and she squinted, edging closer. A tiny, clawed paw shot out from the darkness to grip the metal grate of the door, and Realene stumbled backward, knocking over one of the stanchions.

The carrier door creaked open, and a prairie-dog face emerged from the shadows.

Realene grabbed Ma's hand and led her around the far side of the snack bar, reaching behind the waist-high door to undo the latch. She glanced back at the carrier. Four prairie dogs had emerged and approached the security gate.

Realene closed the door behind she and Ma, and huddled close to watch the animals. The spaces between the metal rungs of the security gate were very narrow, hopefully too narrow for the creatures to fit through.

"It's going to be okay," she whispered, not sure if she was trying to convince Ma or herself.

The lead prairie dog stuck its head through the gate's bars and gave a short chirp before slithering through. The others followed.

"Dammit." Realene scanned the snack bar for a weapon. The counter in front of her held two cash registers, and below the registers, the windowed candy display was shut behind a set of flimsy sliding doors, but Realene doubted chucking Milk Duds at the animals would do any good at all. Behind her, on the back counter, a fountain soda machine hummed beside a dormant popcorn maker.

Seeing no better option, she opened the plastic door of the popcorn machine and grabbed the metal scoop sticking out of the prior day's stale batch.

The prairie dogs had all squeezed their way through the gate and were now advancing across the lobby. Realene turned to face them.

"Stay back, okay," she said to Ma.

"*I Love Lucy* is on. You said I could watch *I Love Lucy*."

"I know. We will."

The animals stopped before the counter. One ran up to paw at the glass, then gave a little jump that only lifted it a few inches in the air. The others behind it joined in, jumping and yipping.

"Prairie dogs can't jump." Realene giggled, a bit maniacally, hearing her own words in Wesley Snipes's voice.

The creatures dropped to the ground, chattering at one another as if having a conversation, then one of them ran over to the Spice Girls cutout. The animal pressed on the display, making it wobble slightly. The prairie dog then ran around the display and began chewing on one of the cardboard supports in back. Another joined in, nibbling on the other support.

"Stop it," Realene said. "Don't do that."

The display began to tip, then fell, Baby Spice's pigtails landing against the edge of the counter. The two prairie dogs who had been standing aside raced up the cardboard ramp, their claws tearing at the glossy surface as they ran.

Realene swung her popcorn scooper at the first one that made it to the top, smacking it in the head and sending it flying through the air. It hit the wall and slid to the ground, twitching. She swung again, but missed the second animal, who launched itself in the air like a flying squirrel.

She ducked and the thing went through the open doors of the popcorn machine, landing in the pile of popped kernels. Dropping the scooper, Realene slammed the doors to the popcorn maker closed and pulled the hairband from her wrist, winding it around the knobs to keep the doors shut. The prairie dog screeched and threw itself against the sides of the machine, throwing around popcorn as if trapped in some kind of demented snow globe. It bashed its head against the plastic wall several times before keeling over.

"Look out!" Ma cried.

Realene turned to see another prairie dog leap off the counter and sail straight for her face.

She managed to catch the thing by both front legs, holding it away from her, her face barely out of reach of its snapping teeth. Realene held the thing down at the base of the butter dispenser beside the popcorn machine. It thrashed and shrieked, almost tugging its paws from her grip.

"Ma, extra butter," she said.

Ma hit the button on the front of the dispenser, and a stream of the hot, yellow, butter-like goo poured from the spout onto the prairie dog's face. The animal sputtered as the liquid filled its nose and mouth, but it didn't stop thrashing.

Realene's eyes landed on the row of salt shakers lined up on the counter. "Now extra salt."

Ma grabbed the shaker, removed the cap, and dumped it out over the prairie dog's face. The salt quickly piled up into a mound that covered the animal's entire head.

The thing finally stopped struggling.

Realene caught movement in the corner of her eye as the last prairie dog launched itself at Ma and latched onto her gray curls.

Ma screamed and shook her head back and forth, spinning in a circle and banging first into the front counter, then into the back one. Realene grabbed her abandoned scooper. "Hold still!" she yelled. But Ma didn't listen, instead careening around and knocking over a tower of paper cups.

The prairie dog worked its way around the side of Ma's head and tried to chomp on her ear, but she jerked at the last second, and the thing bit down on her clip-on earring, screeching when the sharp metal tip of one petal pierced its jaw.

Realene grabbed the creature by its plump body and tore it free, taking Ma's earring with it. She slammed the critter on the tile floor, pinned its body in place with her foot, and stabbed the metal scoop in its neck again and again, until its little head was severed from its body.

Panting, she said, "Good thing you wore clip-ons today." Her laughter dissolved into whimpers.

"Oh, no. Oh, dear, it's okay." Ma opened her arms for a hug.

Realene slumped against Ma, her chest heaving.

The embrace felt comforting for a moment, until she noticed Ma was patting her back uncomfortably, as if hugging a stranger rather than her own daughter.

Realene pulled away. "Sorry. It's been a really long day. Come on, let's go get Pumpkin and find you somewhere to rest."

"Pumpkin?" Ma trailed Realene through the half-door, out of the snack bar and into the lobby.

"That's the name of the cat you did such a great job protecting. He's yours."

Ma's face lit up. "Really? I can keep him?"

Something smacked against the security gate, rattling the metal, and Realene turned, instinctively moving in front of Ma to shield her. Reverend Zebediah gripped the metal rungs, his face red and eyes blazing with anger.

Realene pulled Ma close and scowled at the reverend. How many times did she have to defeat him? "Would you just leave us the hell alone?" The wind howled outside, gusting through the broken window and chilling the once warm lobby.

He shook the metal grate, as if testing the strength. "You may have survived the prairie dogs, but you will get what's coming to you."

"Don't you get it? This isn't some righteous plan from God. It's a disease, an infestation. And you're fucking crazy."

His eyes widened at that last word, and she wondered how many times he's been called that before finding a group of vulnerable people to believe his ranting. "I'm immune to your lies, demon," he said.

"If we're demons, and this is all God's plan, then we should be dead already, right? Your little attack dogs should have killed us."

"No, that's not true. This is a test," he said to himself. "I have to prove my worthiness."

Realene nudged Ma toward the hallway. They both crept across the lobby, watching the reverend, the end of the snack bar just a few feet away. Another few seconds of him talking to himself, and they'd be safe in the shelter of the hallway.

"I am the Hand of God!" His voice boomed through the lobby, and his eyes blazed, as if he were back on the pulpit, preaching to his congregation.

He drew his gun from its holster.

Time seemed to slow, just like it did back at the church, and Realene grabbed Ma in a full-body hold and launched them both into the snack bar door, snapping the latch with their combined weight and sending them barreling through the barricade.

The crack of the gunshot echoed through the space as they slammed to the floor.

The bullet hit the carpet where Realene had just been, releasing a puff of dust and fabric into the air. She sat up, pulling Ma with her. They pressed their backs to the display case. The thin, sliding door that closed off the back of the candy display, and a single pane of glass at the front, the only things protecting them from the reverend.

"Are you okay? Are you hurt?" She examined Ma, patted the front of her coat.

"You can't escape divine justice," the reverend said. Another shot ripped through the space, shattering the glass and stopping somewhere within the boxes of M&M's and Swedish Fish.

"What's happening?" Ma rocked in place.

Realene grabbed her hands, which felt frail and thin in her own. "It's going to be okay. I'm here."

Two more shots rang out, thumping into and through the sliding door, just missing Realene's arm, to lodge in the rear cabinets. The particle-board door split like a tree struck by lightning and fell from its track to the floor beside the beheaded prairie dog.

Only a haphazard display of candy remained to protect them.

Realene inched over, pressing Ma as far as she could into the corner, knowing her own back was completely unprotected.

"I'm scared." Ma gripped Realene's trembling hands tighter.

"I know. I am too," she said, her voice breaking.

Ma's brow creased, and she looked down, a small gasp escaping her throat. She caressed the ring on Realene's finger. "I—I gave you this. It was mine, from your father."

Tears stung Realene's eyes. "Yeah, you did. And I love it." She wrapped Ma in a tight hug, held her close. *She remembered.*

"You cannot escape me, demon," the reverend yelled, and fired two more shots.

Pain sliced across Realene's shoulder, and she cried out. She clutched at what was obviously a bullet wound. The smell of sulfur and metal singed Realene's nose.

Ma's face hardened, and she shoved past Realene to stand. "You leave my daughter alone!" she yelled, but her voice was muffled by the crack of another bullet.

"Ma, no!" Realene reached out to pull Ma back, but her fingers brushed the hem of her coat and clutched only air.

Ma gasped, and her face contorted in pain, before her legs wilted beneath her.

Realene lunged, catching her under the arms as went down to the floor with her. She propped Ma up on her lap, struggling to breathe while red bloomed in the center of Ma's chest and spread, soaking the tan wool of her coat.

"What have you done?" Realene screamed. They were in full view behind the destroyed section of the snack bar.

"You will die, demon." The reverend aimed and fired again, but the gun only clicked. Empty.

Irene's horrified shrieks filled the vestibule as she stumbled in, slipping on the shattered glass. "Marion!" She gripped the metal gate, hysterical.

"Please, she needs help," Realene said, hands pressed to Ma's wound to stem the flow of blood.

An engine revved outside, and a black SUV pulled up. Lieutenant Braun called out through the open window. "Come on. We've got to go."

The reverend grabbed a sobbing Irene and pulled her away.

Warm blood pumped against Realene's palm, coating her fingers. The wound was serious, and she couldn't call anyone for help. No ambulance. No police.

"Why? Why did you do that?" she asked Ma, voice trembling.

"My job…to protect you." Ma coughed, spraying Realene's face with a red mist.

Realene searched the darkness for any sign of help, but found only the flurry of blowing snow that blotted out everything beyond the doors.

"Nate!" she screamed. "Nate, where are you?"

No answer.

Ma groaned, tensing.

"Stay still. I've got you." Biting her lip to keep from blubbering, Realene slid Ma to the grimy tile floor, keeping her hand pressed to the wound. One-handed, she unbuttoned Ma's coat, then removed her other hand to quickly tug the garment off before continuing to put pressure on the wound. Ma's shirt was dyed red with blood, soaked through. Realene pressed harder.

"It's okay. You're doing great." Her voice shook, though she tried to stop it, tried to stop the fear seeping in.

Ma's mouth ticked up on one side. "I think I've"—a cough racked her chest, and Realene again felt the pump of blood against her palm—"been shot."

"I need to get a closer look, okay?" Realene grabbed Ma's shirt collar with both hands and tore it open, popping the buttons in the process.

Ma flinched as the fabric separated from the wet wound in her chest. Blood gushed from the bullet hole just below her sternum.

Realene pulled a glove from her coat pocket and pressed it to the wound with one hand, panic clouding her mind. She'd only seen one injury this bad in her time interning at the hospital—a man shot in a hunting accident. He died within minutes.

"Hang in there," she whispered, brushing Ma's hair from her sweat-slicked face. She was white as ghost, except for the fresh blood staining her lips.

Pumpkin howled from his carrier down the hall, as if he knew Ma was hurt.

"I'm so lucky...to be your mom... So proud of you." Ma clutched Realene's hand. "Your father...here?"

Realene pressed her lips together, hot tears rolling down her cheeks. "You're going to see him real soon. He's been waiting for you."

"I love you so much." Ma's grip loosened, and her face went slack, head lolling to the side.

"Please, don't leave me," Realene pleaded. "I love you too." She pressed harder on the wound, but Ma had lost so much blood already. "Ma, wake up. Please. Wake up."

Blood soaked the carpet and seeped into the knees of Realene's pants. "Come on. You're gonna make it. Come on." She pressed two fingers to Ma's neck, feeling for a pulse.

"No, no, no. You can't leave me. I need you." She kept probing Ma's neck.

Nothing. No sign of life.

Realene slumped back against the cabinets, her hand falling away from the wound. She pulled Ma's coat up to her neck, as if to keep her warm, then tugged it farther to cover her face. Pain wrenched at Realene's chest, threatened to crack her rib cage wide open and spill out her broken heart. She lay down on the tile and curled up beside Ma's body.

Twenty-One

SHUFFLING FOOTSTEPS SOUNDED, a scrape of feet on shattered glass, and Realene sat up, her mouth twisted in a snarl. If Reverend Zebediah had returned, she would kill him with her bare hands. But the figure who came wandering through the busted doorway wasn't the reverend, it was Nate.

"Where were you?" Sniffling, Realene stumbled out from behind the snack bar and rushed to the gate, where snow had accumulated in small drifts.

Nate grabbed the gate and shook it. "What are you doing in there?"

"It's Ma—" Her throat tightened. "You should have been here. I needed you." She noticed his hand, skin split and seeping blood. "What happened?"

He raised his hand to examine the wound. "Oh, I'm not sure."

All the air left her lungs. "You don't remember?"

"Don't worry." He grinned. "It's just a flesh wound."

Her vision grayed, and she eased out a slow breath. They'd gotten Nate.

"Hey, are you okay?" he asked. "Are you sick?"

She shook her head in a jerky movement. "No, I'm okay." She was definitely not okay, but she couldn't afford to lose it now. The aliens had infected Nate, and he needed her help. "We have to get you inside. Do you have your keys?"

He patted his pockets, pulled out a set of keys, and passed them to her through the gate. "How did you get in there?"

"Does one of these work for the gate?" she asked.

"What? I don't think so." He cocked his head to the side.

Of course he wouldn't remember working at the theater. The job was too recent.

She knelt by the lock at the bottom of the gate and tried each key. The fourth one opened the lock. Raising the gate, she grabbed Nate's arm and pulled him inside.

"Whoa, this is cool. Are we sneaking in?"

"Uh-huh." She lowered the gate and relocked it, in case the reverend came back. "Okay, you're inside. That's good."

"I'm not sure about this, Rea. We could get in real trouble breaking in here... Like arrested kind of trouble. My dad... Well, he'd freak out." Red tinged his cheeks.

A painful lump lodged in her throat. She had no idea what to do, how to save him. Even if she tied him up like Calvin, that wouldn't solve anything. If she could only talk with him, work together to figure out a plan. But that wasn't an option.

He bent to pick up the salt shaker she'd ineffectively lobbed at the attacking prairie dogs. "What happened in here? This place is trashed," he said.

Realene snatched the salt shaker from his hand. "That's it," she whispered. They knew ice melt slowed down the worms, saw it firsthand at Calvin's, and table salt was basically the same thing. If she fed some to Nate, maybe it would kill the worms inside him, or at least slow their effects.

She grabbed his uninjured hand and pulled him toward the snack bar, shoving him through the half-door at the opposite end of where Ma still laid.

His eyes widened as he caught sight of the dead animal in the popcorn machine, then the decapitated prairie dog on the floor. "I don't like this. We need to get out of here."

"Just wait a minute."

"Is that...a body?" He took a step closer to Ma.

Realene couldn't afford to grieve right now, had to focus on Nate, on saving him. She grabbed his face in both hands. "I'll explain everything soon. But right now, I need you to trust me. Please?"

"Of course, I trust you. But this is seriously fucked up, right?"

"Yeah. It is." She grabbed a cup and pressed it to the lever on the pop machine beneath the Pepsi spout, filling it about halfway full. After setting the cup on the counter, she dumped in a couple tablespoons of salt and used a straw to stir the concoction.

She hesitated, worried that salting the worms could harm Nate too. But if she did nothing, he'd be lost, like Tony or Calvin. Or Brooke. "Okay, drink this. All of it."

"Dude, are you pranking me? Am I on *Candid Camera* right now?"

"You said you trusted me." Her voice shook. She couldn't stop it. "I can't lose you too. Please. Drink it."

She pressed the cup into his hand.

He grimaced while staring at the cup for a moment. "If this is a prank, I will never forgive you." He brought the cup to his lips and tipped it back, gulping down the whole thing like a kid taking cough medicine.

Her shoulders slumped with relief, and she drew him into her arms, holding him close. Once the salt hit Nate's stomach, it should absorb into his blood stream and do the trick.

"That was super gross. I think I'm going to puke."

She released him, putting her hands on his shoulders. "Try not to, okay? You need to keep as much of that down as you can."

He pulled away, gagging and coughing. Saliva and bile dribbled down his chin to stain his coat. "Yuck."

Realene led him to the closest bench. She glanced at the other bench, the one she'd led Ma to before, and fought back a whimper. "Sit here for a minute."

He winced, pressing his hands to his stomach.

"You're going to be okay."

Of course he was sick. Chugging that much salt and soda would give anyone a stomach ache.

Nate coughed up another mouthful of bile and spit it onto the carpet. "I don't feel good at all."

"I know. But I think that means it's working." She rubbed his shoulder.

His mouth twisted, and he struggled to his feet, knocking into the Christmas tree and still clutching his stomach.

"Whoa, where are you going?" She followed, one hand resting lightly on his back. They just had to wait this out, wait for the salt to work.

His legs buckled beneath him, and he fell to the carpet, curling into the fetal position, his arms wrapped around his midsection.

Realene dropped to her knees beside him. "You're going to be okay." She braced herself on one hand and felt a sharp sting of pain. Snatching it back, she plucked a shard of glass from her palm.

Nate moaned, then began to convulse, his body twitching uncontrollably.

"You're going to be fine. We need to kill the worms, that's all. This is going to work. It has to."

A black spec floated through the white of his eye, not wiggling and squirming like the ones she'd seen in Brooke and Walt. This one barely moved at all.

"It's working," she whispered.

He was going to be okay. She'd done it; she'd saved him.

Nate coughed again, spitting up a mouthful of salty liquid, and then he went limp. His head thumped against the floor.

Just like Ma,

"You have to stay awake. Come on, Nate, wake up." She rolled him onto his back. "Stay with me."

His arm flopped down beside him, a dead weight, and he stared sightlessly up at her, little black worms twitching in the whites of his eyes.

"No, I will not let you die too." She raised herself up and pressed her linked hands over his sternum, using her full body weight to deliver compressions in a count of fifteen.

She tipped his head back, pinched his nose, and blew into his mouth, tasting sugary Pepsi, salt, and sour bile. She couldn't have saved Ma, not with that bullet wound, but she could still save Nate. She *would* save him. An icy gust of wind blew through the gate, and she shivered but kept going.

"Stay with me, Nate, stay with me," she chanted as she continued CPR.

He didn't respond, the only movement caused by her continued compressions. She kept going, blowing into his mouth and watching his chest rise with her breath.

"Wake up. Please, wake up," she whispered.

More compressions, more breaths, so many she lost count.

He was dead, like Ma. She hadn't been able to save either one of them.

"Lemme in there!" a voice screamed.

Startled, Realene jumped and looked toward the gate.

A bloodied and beaten Calvin snarled and clawed at the metal rungs of the security gate. "I'm gonna kill you."

Realene ignored him and continued chest compressions, her arms now trembling from the effort. She knew she should stop, that he was gone. The worms took everything from her, and they'd do the same to so many others. They would spread, consuming countless more lives, maybe until they'd taken everyone in Demise, and eventually beyond.

Part of her wished one of those prairie dogs had succeeded in biting her before Ma, before Nate. But something or someone would come for her soon enough. Calvin would get in, the reverend would come back, or more prairie dogs would squeeze through the bars to tear into her with their teeth. She hoped they'd hurry up so she didn't have to feel this pain anymore.

"Wait 'til I get in there." Calvin rattled the gate. "I'm gonna skin you alive."

She stopped compressions, finally giving up. Exhaustion weighed down her limbs. Her hand throbbed, and she glanced at her palm, where fresh blood wet her old scar. The same scar Nate had. If only she could've gotten him to a hospital, they'd have a crash cart, epinephrine.

Pumpkin yowled again.

"It's okay, Punky," she lied, looking down the short hallway at the leftovers of her life piled beside his carrier. Ma's favorite clothes, her treasured jewelry, their most precious mementos. And the defibrillator.

Realene climbed unsteadily to her feet and rushed down the hallway. Pumpkin stuck a paw through the door of his carrier, but she ignored him and grabbed the heavy-duty defibrillator. She lugged the machine into the lobby and set it down beside Nate's limp body. Most of the device was covered in a red case with zippered pouches. Only the screen, handle, and connection points were visible.

After delivering several more chest compressions and breathing into his mouth, she tore open Nate's shirt. Panting as if she'd just run a mile, she opened the zippered compartment on the side of the machine, pulled out a pack of adhesive pads, and tore it open. She froze for a moment, panic threatening to push all the training from her mind.

"You got this, you know how to do this," she whispered to herself. She had practiced this exact scenario on a dummy for her CPR and AED class.

Calvin yelled a stream of curse words and shook the gate.

"Shut. Up." She forced herself to ignore his ranting and focus on Nate. She stuck one pad in the center of his chest, another to the side. Grabbing the cords from the top pocket, she connected them to the machine and switched it on, then attached the electrode ends to the pads on his chest.

"Please let this work," she whispered, pressing the charge button on the display screen.

A rising whine issued from the machine as the wind gusted through the lobby, pelting her face with icy needles. She stared at the two-inch screen, willing it to hurry. The machine showed Nate's heart was still beating, but too fast, in V-Tach. Soon he'd have no heartbeat at all. The screen finally flashed the words 'Stand Clear.'

"Please, God, let this work." She pressed 'Push to shock' and a faint pop sounded. Nate's body bowed slightly, then relaxed.

The heart rhythm display blipped once, then returned to V-Tach.

"It's okay. Try again." She knew from her classes that patients didn't always respond to the first shock, or even the second.

Realene charged the machine again, delivered another shock. Back to V-Tach. "It could still work, keep trying," she said to herself, willing the words to be true.

She pushed the button to recharge the machine, ignoring the shudder of cold that wracked her body.

Calvin gave a frustrated scream and kicked the metal barrier, then ran full speed at the ticket booth that stood between the two gates. He smacked into the solid structure headfirst and sank to the ground.

Realene felt only relief that he'd been quieted.

The wail of the emergency siren rose outside, cutting through the blustering wind, and she wanted to wail along with it. "I don't know what else to do. Please, wake up."

She cranked up the voltage and shocked Nate again. His body tensed as electricity coursed through him, then slumped once the charge stopped.

"Wake up!" she screamed, bending to hold her head in her hands. "Please. I need you. You're my biff."

The last word came out on a sob, strangled by the reality that she'd never be able to tell him what he really meant to her, how lucky she was to have him.

The machine's screen flashed 'Normal Rhythm,' and a wheeze escaped Nate's mouth. He coughed, then spewed frothy vomit.

"Fuck yes!" She rolled him on his side so he wouldn't choke, breathed slowly in and out to stop herself from passing out. "Oh, thank God you're alive. Jesus Christ, you scared me."

He pushed himself up to a slumped but sitting position, and winced. "Ow."

A giggle escaped her mouth before she could stop it. "You're alive."

He wiped his mouth with the back of his hand, leaving a smear of bile and saliva. "Gross, dude."

"Let me see," she said, grabbing his hand.

"Ew, but okay."

She examined the mixture that coated the back of his hand, black bits of worm dotting the slimy mucus. They didn't wiggle even a little. "It worked."

Realene hugged him too tight, and he hugged her back so hard it squeezed the air from her lungs in the best possible way.

"I thought you were dead."

He pulled away, peeling the sticky pads from his chest. "What the hell happened?"

"I almost killed you by giving you too much salt, then I shocked you back to life. Basically."

His eyes traced the cords from his chest to the defibrillator. "You brought me back Julia Roberts-style?"

She turned off the defibrillator. It took her several attempts to stuff the cords back in their compartment, her hands were trembling so badly. "Guess that makes you Kiefer Sutherland."

"Obviously." He grabbed her hands in his. "Seriously, thank you for saving me."

"Thank you for coming back, biff." She rested her forehead against his.

"Biff?"

"Well, you are." Heat flooded her cheeks.

"You haven't called me that in years, not since junior high."

"I know." The term had been their nickname for each other as kids, but somewhere along the way she'd decided it was kind of dumb. She squeezed her eyes closed against the burning there. "I'm so sorry. For being such a jerk about leaving town. I was selfish and spoiled, and I don't know what I'd do without you."

"It's okay. I was kind of an asshole too. I never should have left you today."

"Today? You remember?"

"I remember everything." He frowned, then looked away and noticed Ma. "Oh God. Is that—"

Realene pressed her lips together, and the tears she'd been holding back finally spilled down her cheeks.

Nate pulled her into his arms and held her while she cried.

A moan sounded from the foyer, and they separated to see Calvin coming to. He wasn't dead, after all.

"Come on. Let's tie him back up." Nate got up, grimacing, and helped Realene to her feet.

"Let's blindfold him too. I mean, maybe it's too late, but if he's transmitted some kind of message, more could come."

She raised the gate, and Nate dragged Calvin inside.

The cries of prairie dogs sounded faintly in the distance, barking and yipping.

"They might already be on their way. We've got to get somewhere more secure." She relocked the gate, even though it wouldn't keep the animals out.

"Feel like catching a movie?" Nate asked.

Twenty-Two

REALENE KNELT BY Ma, her body laid out on a ratty sofa in the movie theater's second-floor break room. A serene expression was on her face. She could easily have been sleeping, dreaming happy dreams. Realene had cleaned Ma's face and slipped her favorite holiday sweatshirt, the one with the happy family of penguins on the front, over the bloody tatters of her blouse. As a last touch, Realene clipped a pair of earrings on—jeweled snowflakes Dad gifted Ma the last Christmas they were all together before he died.

At least the two of them were finally together again.

Realene bowed her head, clasped her hands, and prayed. Not something she did often outside Sunday service, but it was the closest she could come to giving Ma the church funeral she would have wanted.

"Miss you already," Realene whispered, then kissed Ma's forehead.

She thought back to the day before, to how much she'd resented Ma for keeping her in Demise. She had wished upon a shooting star to be free of Ma, free of care-giving, to not be tied to Demise at all. She had wished for a way—any way—out, not thinking for a second about what she'd leave behind. Somehow, she'd felt absolutely entitled to her perfect future. Now, Ma was gone because of her. If she'd left Ma in the trailer, or even left her at Revelation Evangelical, she'd still be alive.

Pain stinging the back of her throat, Realene got up, walked past the cluster of small tables and chairs, and flipped off the overhead light. She took one last look at Ma, lit by the glow of the vending machines, before closing the door to the break room. The hallway extended in each direction, the door to the employee stairs that led down to the lobby on one end. A thump sounded from the broom closet beside the break room, and she shouted, "Go to sleep, Calvin," before crossing the hall to enter the projection room where she and Nate planned to spend the night. He'd originally thought to camp out in one of the theaters, but they'd decided they'd be safer and warmer on the second floor.

She entered and locked the door behind her, just in case.

Industrial brown carpet covered the floor, and the walls were bare, aside from a water leak that left a brown stain. A single metal folding chair sat in the corner. Nate had piled their things against the wall and spread some blankets out beside the chair. He stood by the centerpiece of the room—a tall, black, rectangular contraption, with a lens protruding from the front into a small square window that was cut into the wall.

He closed a panel on the side of the unit. "Hey. You okay?"

She shrugged, peering through the little window at the movie theater below. Dim running lights barely illuminated the aisles on either side of the rows of empty seats. A tiny, shadowy figure caught her eye, a prairie dog scampering in front of the black screen. She shivered and backed away, distracting herself by examining the projector. "I thought there would be reels of film."

"There are, inside." He pressed a few buttons and the machine whirred to life. "I closed the lens and turned off the theater speakers so we don't draw too much attention. But we can listen up here."

"What're we listening to?" She sat cross-legged on the blankets and opened the door to Pumpkin's carrier. He crept out, eyeing the strange room. She gave his back a scratch.

"Found a copy of *Tremors*."

"For real?" They'd seen the movie in that very theater below a few years back, but it was a strange choice given their current situation.

"I thought it might remind us that it could be worse. At least we don't have to fight giant snake creatures with tentacle-tongues."

Realene laughed. "That's true."

Nate sat beside her and pulled the other half of the blanket over his lap.

"If only we had snacks, this would be perfect." She'd grabbed water and orange juice from the snack bar, forcing Nate to drink them to combat against any damage from the salt, but had neglected to take anything else.

He rifled through the duffel bag beside him, pulling out a Slim Jim and handing it to her. "Not candy or popcorn, but at least it has some nutritional value."

"Pshh. Candy has nutritional value. Take Snickers, that's basically a complete meal." She set the jerky aside and dug out the Tupperware of cat food. "Come here, Punky."

Pumpkin ceased his explorations and trotted over at the rattle of the container, digging in as soon as Realene removed the lid. He chomped down his dinner, arching his back when she petted him.

"We lost Ma today, Punky. I didn't protect her like I promised. But I'm going to make sure nothing happens to you, okay?"

Nate bumped her shoulder with his. "That wasn't your fault."

It was though. Ma took a bullet meant for Realene.

"I convinced myself she was such a burden, you know? Didn't think about how lucky I was to have her. Now she's gone."

He didn't say anything, just draped his arm over her shoulder.

"I acted like an asshole to you too," she continued. "About leaving." She clenched her eyes closed, trying to find the right words to tell him how she felt. She never told Ma how much she appreciated her, but she still had time to tell Nate. "When I thought I'd lost you... I don't know what I'd do without you. You know? I love you."

"Ditto," he said.

She pulled away, gaping at him. "You did not just Swayze me."

"Ugh, I love you, too, okay?" His face turned serious. "And I'm sorry for freaking out earlier. I might've been a little jealous."

"Jealous? About what?"

"You going off to school, starting your great new life." He fiddled with the edge of the bandage on the back of his hand. "I knew I'd always be stuck here."

"But you don't have to be," she said. "You're super smart. You could do anything you want to do. I never understood why you didn't apply anywhere."

He gnawed on his lip. "I did actually. And I got accepted at a few places, including UND, but I can't afford to go, and can't get student loans."

"What're you talking about? You don't make that much money."

"Felony record means no student loans. I guess it's, like, a rule. So, it doesn't matter where I got accepted. I can't pay for it."

The air rushed from her lungs. "I...didn't know. You never told me."

"I guess I was embarrassed."

"That's fucking bullshit. Because of a drug bust, you can't get a loan? The cops couldn't be bothered to help you and your mom, but they sure as hell love busting kids for smoking pot. So messed up."

Nate tried so hard to save his mom, and when he couldn't, he drowned himself in drugs and alcohol. The fact he couldn't get any loans because of some stupid teenage mistake—a fact Realene had been too self-centered to even discover—was completely unfair.

He gave a humorless laugh. "At least my dad's out of the picture. But now my mom thinks I'm a literal demon."

"She just needs time. You'll get her back. I mean, assuming we live through this."

"I don't think so. You saw her at the church. She chose the reverend over me. Didn't care if I died."

"He's a fucking monster, the way he's brainwashed those people." She shook her head. "He even got sweet little Irene to help."

"I know." He touched the back of his head. "She bashed me with a rock before that lieutenant cut Calvin loose. He never would have gotten free if they hadn't shown up."

"That bitch." She grabbed Nate and made him bend to the side so she could examine his head. "Why didn't you tell me about this sooner? Are you okay?"

"I'm fine. I cleaned it up."

She parted his hair near the wound. "Looks pretty minor, and the bleeding's stopped. Any headache or dizziness?"

"I'm fine, really." He sat up.

"How about your bite? Can you tell if there are any side effects?"

"I don't think so, but who knows for sure? I remember everything that's happened today, so that's a good sign." His brow furrowed. "There is something weird though. Most of the time I wasn't aware of the worms, didn't feel like they were controlling me or anything. But when I drank the salt water, I could feel them inside me, like their thoughts were mine. They didn't want to die."

The cold pressed in, and Realene pulled the blanket over her lap.

"I don't think this is a simple parasite," Nate said. "It's more than that."

"Yeah. I've been thinking about that too. The worms seem to have the ability to adapt, and they're using teamwork and strategy." She gripped her hands together in her lap. "They may have landed here by accident, but this is an invasion."

"Invasion of the body snatchers." The corner of his mouth ticked up.

"You always did love that movie."

"Yeah, but it's not that fun when it's your own body being snatched. You brought me back though."

She thought of all the people in Demise who were suffering, just waiting for someone to come and help them. "I don't know if we can try that again. I mean, the salt killed the worms in the end, but you almost died too."

"I'm not sure it was just the salt that killed them." He rubbed his chest where she'd stuck the electrodes. "Remember Mr. Volk's science lab?"

"How could I forget? First period and full participation expected. That's how I got addicted to Mello Yello."

"I definitely carried your ass." He gave her a mock punch in the arm. "Remember that time we made the salt water circuits?"

"Yeah. It showed salt is a good conductor of electricity, right? Even carrying the current through water."

"Exactly. I think it was the electricity from the defibrillator that killed the worms. The salt just helped."

"Huh, yeah, that makes sense. They were still wiggling a little after you drank that soda, didn't die until after I shocked you."

"So, we just need to electrocute all the infected in town," he said, all matter of fact.

"Oh, yeah, right. But without killing them." She exhaled. "Seriously, what are we going to do?"

"Right now, we're going to get some sleep." He got up and switched on the movie. The Universal Pictures introduction sounded. She'd seen it so many times, she could picture the spinning Earth perfectly.

She dragged the duffel bags behind them to use as pillows, then laid back. Nate joined her, close enough for their shoulders to touch. Pumpkin wandered over, stopping to tenderize their bodies before turning in a circle and lying down to sleep on Realene's legs.

Focused on the soothing vibration of Pumpkin's purr, and Kevin Bacon's so-so Southern accent, Realene fell into a fitful sleep.

Twenty-Three

REALENE WOKE FROM a nightmare, which was really just a memory replaying itself in her sleeping brain—Ma getting shot, collapsing, bleeding out onto the floor.

Swiping at her eyes, which were puffy and swollen from all the crying she'd done over the last day, Realene sat up and pushed off the blankets. The glow of lights on the control panel of the projector broke the darkness of the room. Nate snored beside her, and a glance at her watch told her it was almost 6:30 in the morning.

The box of mementos sat a few feet away, all that remained of Ma's life. Realene scooted over to dig through the contents, and Pumpkin jumped up from his spot at her feet, arching his back in a stretch before trotting over to his food bowl.

The top item in the box was a zippered, cloth make-up bag she'd thrown a bunch of Ma's earrings in when packing. Realene hugged the bag to her chest, then set it aside. Next, she pulled out a scrapbook Ma had kept beside her bed on the nightstand. A large peace sign covered the front, and when she picked it up and flipped it open, she was met with a photo of her dad as a young man, shirtless on a beach and wearing dog tags. The page opposite held his draft notice.

Ma showed Realene the scrapbook for the first time after Dad died, and Realene only realized then that he didn't enlist by choice. He had planned to work for a few years before enrolling at the local college in Minnesota, where he and Ma grew up, but then the draft notice came. After the war, Ma said everything felt different to him, like he didn't belong on those college campuses anymore. So, he got a civilian job on the Air Force base as a mechanic and never left.

Dad gave up so much after being drafted and never once complained. He only ever tried to be the best husband and father he could. Nate had been robbed of a college education by a stupid mistake and an abusive dad, but he'd tried to make the best of it and always supported Realene... At least until she started being an asshole. Ma only ever spread kindness to everyone around her, despite the disease that drained her memories.

Sitting there with the Ma's scrapbook, Realene pledged to always remember everything she had to be thankful for, rather than wallow and fret over the things she didn't have.

After setting the book beside the jewelry bag, she came across her petite, pink Barbie boombox, which she'd brought along so they could monitor any emergency broadcasts. Nate gifted her the boombox for her most recent birthday. He claimed it cost half as much as the others, but she'd seen his expression as she opened the package and knew he chose it to be funny.

Other than the barely audible wail of the emergency siren, she had no indication of the state of the world outside. When they did air-raid drills in elementary school, the fear had been of nuclear war with Russia, due to their close proximity to the Air Force base and its missile silos. She'd never expected the siren would someday warn of an alien invasion.

Realene pulled out the radio and pressed the power button.

Nate shifted beside her and propped himself up on his elbows. "Everything alright?"

"Yeah. Thought I'd see what's going on out there." She fiddled with the dial until she found a station that wasn't just static.

"This is a message from the emergency broadcast system. A state of emergency has been declared for Steele, Polk, and Walsh counties due to an outbreak of disease in the animal population. The city of Demise is under quarantine. Residents are ordered to shelter in place and avoid all contact with other people, pets, and wild animals."

The message repeated.

"Outbreak of disease? That's quite an understatement," Nate said.

"Sure is." She turned the dial again, hoping to pick up other news, but there was only static. Even the incessant barrage of holiday music was glaringly absent.

"Hey, want to know what I got you for Christmas?" she asked. "I know it's still a week away, but, you know."

"We might be dead, or worm people."

She turned off the radio and set it aside. "Kind of blunt, but yeah."

"Okay, what'd you get me?" he asked.

"You're not going to believe it." She'd picked the gift before the invasion.

"Come on, tell me."

"Alight. It's a poster of the solar system. Planets, stars, even a few meteors."

"You're kidding me." He fell back on the blankets, laughing.

"Soooo, what did you get me?"

"You know pixie sticks? Well, apparently they make extra-large ones. They're, like, two-feet long and an inch around. I got you three dozen." He grinned.

She gaped at him. "That's amazing, I could totally eat a whole one right now."

"Like you'd stop at one."

"Shut up." She smacked his leg. "You're clearly feeling better today."

"Yeah. My mouth tastes like I ate a spare tire boiled in salt, but otherwise I'm okay."

"Come on then." She got up. "We can't stay holed up in here forever."

"Where we going?"

"I think you're right that the salt plus electricity was enough to kill those things." She grabbed the defibrillator by the handle. "But we need to make sure. Let's go see if we can get Calvin back, huh."

She opened the projector room door and peeked into the hallway. A gust of cold air hit her, and she shivered, but there was no sign of any infected creatures.

"I'll grab the salt." Nate headed down the hall and slipped into the break room.

"Just a teaspoon or two," she whispered after him. She didn't think she could handle accidentally killing someone again.

Realene gripped the doorknob to the broom closet, readying herself to whack Calvin with the defibrillator if he came at her. She whipped open the door and sighed at the sight of Calvin curled up on the floor. A broom and mop had fallen on top of him, as well as several bottles of bleach and half a dozen rags that he'd probably knocked from the shelves above during one of his many fits.

Unable to see his face beneath the rags, her mind conjured a monstrous version, one that was torn and twisted, the alien worms having grown large enough to break free from the burdensome confines of his body. Setting down the defibrillator, Realene picked up the broom with trembling hands and used the bristled end to sweep away the rags on his face.

Normal Calvin. Just with a few more cuts and bruises than usual.

"Hey," she said, tamping down the tremor that shook her voice. "How you doin'?"

He kicked his bound feet and screamed something through his gag.

"I hear ya." Hoping the gag held and this didn't end up being the way she got infected after all they've been through, she took hold of him under one arm. "I'm going to help you sit up, okay? But you gotta work with me."

She pulled him to a sitting position. "Scoot back. You'll be able to lean up against the wall."

Still shouting, he pushed himself backward using his heels.

Realene pulled up the blindfold and rested it on his forehead, then crouched down to examine the whites of his eyes. There were a lot more worms than she'd seen with Walt or Brooke. The wiggling mass was so dense, it had turned his eyes a cloudy gray.

Calvin jerked his head, as if trying to bite her.

She snatched back her hand. "Not cool, dude." True, he didn't have teeth, but she had plenty of cuts on her hands from the previous day's adventures. Realene made herself reach out and tug the blindfold back over his eyes—just in case the aliens could pick up any clues as to where they were.

Nate came in wearing his winter cloves and holding a glass of slightly cloudy water.

"Gloves. Smart." Realene took the concoction from him. "Hold his head."

Nate knelt beside Calvin and pressed the man's head back against the wall.

Realene pulled the gag from Calvin's mouth, let it hang around his neck, then tipped the glass to his lips. "I know you're thirsty, Calvin. So you drink all of this, okay?"

She expected him to struggle, but he truly must have been thirsty, because he took several big gulps before realizing the water was spiked with salt. He shook his head and closed his mouth, but Realene plugged his nose—a trick her dad used to use to get her to take cough medicine—and waited. After too long without a breath, Calvin opened his mouth, and she dumped more of the liquid down his throat. He sputtered and spit, but ended up drinking most of the mixture.

"Good job." She shoved the gag back in his mouth just in time to muffle his tirade. She couldn't discern exactly what he was trying to say, but she did catch several extremely unsavory words. "Language," she said. The word opened a fissure in her chest, and she winced.

Nate let go of Calvin's head and unbuttoned his shirt to reveal the man's bony chest.

"Give it a minute." Realene silently counted to one hundred to give the liquid time to make it down Calvin's esophagus and into his stomach. Seemed like there was a better chance of the salt conducting the charge through his body if it were at least partially absorbed into his system.

"Okay, let's do this." She placed the adhesive pads on his chest and flipped on the defibrillator, setting it to the lowest charge. The machine gave a steady blip, picking up Calvin's heart rhythm. He thrashed around at the rising electrical whine, but Nate held his shoulders to keep him in place while Realene attached the electrodes.

The screen flashed 'Stand Clear,' and Realene met Nate's eyes, her mouth going dry. They needed to kill the worms, but shocking a healthy person could send them into cardiac arrest. As much as Calvin annoyed her, she didn't want to kill him.

Nate let go of Calvin's shoulders. "Do it."

Mouth so dry she could hardly swallow, Realene hit the button to deliver a charge.

Calvin screamed, and his body went rigid as electricity coursed through him.

Realene tensed, too, in some sort of empathic response.

The charge ceased, and the steady blip of his heartbeat returned as Calvin slumped against the wall.

"Heart's still beating." *Thank God.* She leaned against the door frame. "Check his eyes."

Nate pulled up the blindfold. "I think it worked."

She edged toward him on her knees, not sure her legs would hold her up yet. Calvin moaned as she pulled open his eyelid. The white was still tainted gray, but the worms were no longer moving, just floating in broken bits.

"Hell yes, it worked." She gave Nate a high five. They did it. They saved Calvin.

Nate pulled the gag from Calvin's mouth. "Hey, buddy. How do you feel?"

Calvin slumped forward, tugging at the binding on his hands. "What is this?" he asked, lisping due to his lack of dentures. "What am I doing here?"

"You don't remember how you got here?" Realene asked. Nate recovered his memories after being shocked, so Calvin should too.

"I don't even know where *here* is." He struggled and kicked. "What the hell you got me all trussed up for?"

"Hold on. I'll let you loose." Nate removed the binding from Calvin's hands, then moved to the binding at his ankles.

"What's the last thing you remember?" she asked, hopeful his confusion would pass, that his memories were fine.

"Why are you asking me that?" He edged away from her. "You a doctor? I got amnesia?"

The triumphant buzz seeped from her body, left her feeling hollow. "No, I... I'm your neighbor, Realene."

"Louie's kid? Nah, she's a lil' string bean."

"Don't worry about that, okay?" Her caregiver training kicked in, and she gave him a calming smile, the one she always used with Ma when she got stressed about not being able to remember. "You've been sick, but you're okay now."

Nate helped him up. "I bet you're hungry, huh?"

Calvin touched his mouth. "My teeth. Where's my teeth?" His voice pitched up.

"We'll find them." She led him out of the closet and into the projection room, sat him in the folding chair.

"This doesn't look like any kind of hospital." Calvin eyed the projector.

Nate came in with a Jell-O Pudding cup and a spoon. "Found it in the fridge."

Realene peeled back the foil top and handed it to Calvin, who immediately scooped the chocolate goop into his mouth with his fingers. She and Nate backed up a few steps.

"It worked. They're dead, right?" Nate said, keeping his voice low.

Realene dropped her chin to her chest. "He doesn't remember. He's lost fucking years."

"But he's alive." Nate squeezed her arm.

She scrubbed one hand over her face. "I should have tried last night instead of listening to a goddamn movie. If I had, he might still be okay, like you."

"I doubt it. He'd been infected for hours. For me it was, what, maybe fifteen minutes?"

"I screwed up. First Ma—".

"You figured out the cure." He grabbed her by the shoulders, gave her a gentle shake. "And there are a lot more people out there that need help. Right?"

Realene swallowed past the lump in her throat. "Right."

"So, how do we spread the word? We can't go to the cops, can't call anyone."

"We need to talk to those soldiers blocking the way out of town. Try to get through to the colonel." She straightened and shoved the black ball of guilt deep down, where she knew it would be waiting. "We could get shot, but it's our only option to stop these things. I mean, other than blowing up the entire town."

"Like in *The Thing*?" He raised his eyebrows. "Come on, you don't hate Demise that much."

"I guess not. Plus, we don't have access to that many explosives."

NATE HELPED CALVIN into the backseat, then took shotgun. He'd offered to drive, but Realene felt oddly protective of the minivan she'd always hated. She pulled from the alley beside the Cinema Twin, relieved to see minimal snow accumulation, the drifts in the parking lot low enough, she could drive through them without getting stuck.

A loud woosh sounded overhead, and two fighter jets thundered past. It was fairly common to see military aircraft in the distance, considering their close proximity to the Air Force base, but the planes never flew over Demise.

She eyed the Toppers entrance, hoping to see Tony's motorcycle still parked there, but it was gone. Guilt twinged in her gut. Another person she didn't protect.

The storm had passed, leaving a clear, cloudless sky in its wake. A heavy silence settled over them.

"No siren," Nate said. "Guess everything's okay now."

Pumpkin gave a low yowl from his carrier, situated on the seat beside Calvin, as if to say that was highly unlikely.

"The prairie dogs probably chewed through the power lines," Realene said, remembering what they'd done at The Snack Station less than twenty-four hours prior.

"Still think yer pullin' my leg," Calvin said.

Realene watched in the rearview mirror as a truck sped across the lot and slammed into the front of the movie theater. The vehicle crashed through the remaining undamaged glass and jerked to a stop at the gate. Pieces of the brick façade crumbled to the ground behind the vehicle. The person in the driver's seat hopped out and started hacking at the ticket booth with an axe.

"I knew we shouldn't have left Ma."

"They're probably looking for money, and she's better off there than with us," Nate said.

"Ma?" Calvin asked. "You talkin' about Marion?"

She ignored his question. If they were going to make it through the day, she had to put Ma, and how she'd died, out of her mind.

A screaming woman ran past, chased by a little boy in a winter coat with mittens dangling from strings at his wrists. He tackled her, and she rolled over, so the child straddled her.

Nate reached for his door handle, as if to get out and help, but stopped when the woman shrieked and shoved the little boy away, clutching her face. The little boy grinned, blood coating his mouth, and ran off, giggling.

Nate pulled his hand from the handle and balled it into a fist.

"Jesus H. Christ." Calvin leaned forward from his spot in the back seat. "You weren't jokin'."

Realene maneuvered around the cars in the lot and pulled onto the road, her eyes drawn to the spot where she left Brooke's body. But it was gone. Realene didn't want to consider who might have taken the corpse and why.

The semi still blocked the intersection beyond Brooke's car, and several people in ski masks stood on top of the over-turned cargo trailer, brandishing shot guns. Septumnox symbols plastered the trailer's once white surface.

"Oh, there's also a crazy apocalypse cult in the mix," Nate said to Calvin. "If you see that symbol, run the other way."

Slumping in her seat, Realene headed toward the opposite intersection, hoping these particular church members wouldn't recognize her or the van. After no gunshots sounded, she straightened and surveyed the destruction all around them.

The Snack Station gas pump that had previously been spouting gas had since caught fire, and it now spit flames and black smoke into the sky. The inside of the store was picked clean. Across the street, several crashed cars had downed headstones inside the cemetery, and more totaled vehicles had joined the twisted-metal heap that clogged the intersection.

Realene hopped the curb to make it around the mess.

A car careened down the overpass, heading straight for them, and Realene floored it, but the tires spun on the ice, and they stalled. She gripped the wheel, urging the van forward, as she braced for impact to the passenger side.

But before any impact came, a loud bang sounded from the direction of the approaching vehicle, followed by the shrill squealing of tires and the sound of violent crash.

Realene looked to see that the car had been rammed from the side and hurtled into a snowbank by a gigantic moose. The moose snorted, then charged the car again, bashed it with its massive horned head, its relentless attacks eliciting terrified screams from the couple trapped inside.

Realene pressed the gas pedal again, and the van fishtailed, caught traction, then shot forward. She barely missed taking out the stop sign as she hopped the curb and ended up back in the road on the other side of the intersection. She came to a slow stop, her heart pounding.

Nate gripped the handle above his door as Realene eased the van forward, her eyes darting every direction for human or animal attackers.

Calvin gaped from the back seat, apparently stunned into silence.

They passed the school bus and caught sight of movement inside. The doors opened with a hiss, and a little girl in a puffy white coat and matching moon boots splattered with blood came down the steps. A shot rang out, hitting the ground near the bus's door, and Realene flinched. The little girl growled before turning and going back inside. The door hissed closed behind her.

"Who the hell is shooting?" Calvin asked.

"They are." Realene pointed ahead of them, toward the line of military vehicles. Several soldiers in olive parkas and balaclavas were perched atop the cars, guns aimed in the direction of town. Behind the vehicles, a line of concrete barriers formed a second line of defense. "Demise is under quarantine."

Realene stopped the van while they were still a good thirty feet away. She shifted the car into Park, but kept the engine running.

"Goddamn government bastards think they can keep us here?" Calvin unbuckled his seatbelt.

"Stay," Realene said.

"The hell I will. I'm gonna give them bastards what for."

Another gunshot rang out, again aimed at the school bus, and he flinched.

"We're outgunned, Calvin. Now you stay here, or you're gonna get us shot. Got it?" She fixed him with a glare.

"Fine. Guess I owe you for saving me from them worms." He crossed his arms like a pouting toddler.

Realene stepped from the van and raised her hands above her head. Nate followed.

"Get back in your vehicle! Demise is under quarantine," the man with the bullhorn commanded.

"We need to reach Colonel Harmon," Realene shouted.

One of the other soldiers pulled down his mask and cocked his head to the side, lowering his weapon. She recognized him from the prior morning as the one who'd been with the colonel at the landing site.

"Sir, remember me? From the trailer park."

He said something to the man standing beside him, then hopped down from the vehicle and strode toward her, his gun lowered. "Ma'am, you need to return to your home."

"It's urgent we talk to the colonel. We have an idea how to stop the infestation."

"Infestation?" he asked.

"The worms. The aliens. The ones causing all this." Nate gestured all around.

The soldier scowled. "Return to your homes."

"He's joking, of course, about the aliens," Realene said. "But we do really need to talk to the colonel about this, uh, outbreak—infection. We have an idea how to stop it."

"Listen, kid, we got plenty of experts working on this. Leave it to us."

"You don't even know what's happening." Nate approached the soldier, who raised his gun.

The sound of the van door sliding open sounded behind them, and Calvin yelled, "That boy is a United States citizen. You cease pointing that weapon at him."

Realene and Nate turned and said in unison, "Get back in the car!"

Calvin grumbled, but stomped back over to the van and slid the door closed.

She faced the soldier, whose expression was no longer amused. "Please, sir, we need to speak to Colonel Harmon."

He glared at her. "Return to your vehicle."

An engine sounded behind them, and Realene gave a silent prayer Calvin hadn't climbed into the driver's seat, with the intent to come to their rescue. Hands still raised, she glanced back to see a baby-blue Ford Escort speeding toward them.

Goddamn Irene.

A warning shot rang out, and the car screeched to a stop. Irene burst from the passenger side of the car, and Lieutenant Braun exited the driver's side, both leaving their doors wide open to sprint toward the roadblock.

Realene dropped her hands and lunged for Irene as she approached, but Irene simply veered around Realene and ran toward the soldier. "Do not listen to these devils and their lies!" she exclaimed, gripping the soldier's sleeve.

"Back up, ma'am," the solider commanded. He tugged his arm from her grip and turned his weapon on her and the lieutenant, both of whom bore a freshly drawn septumnox on their foreheads.

Another vehicle, a truck, approached the roadblock and stopped. Several men with shotguns got out and marched toward the military Jeeps, yelling at the soldiers.

"These two infiltrated our church last evening, absconded with one of our parishioners," the lieutenant said to the soldier, who now had one eye on the new arrivals with the shotguns.

"You kidnapped a helpless woman with dementia," Realene said. "My ma would never have willingly gone with you psychos." She balled her fists at her sides. "Then you cowards ambushed us, and Reverend Zebediah killed her. You know he did."

"This is a war for our very souls." Irene clutched her chest, her voice hitching. "And in war, there are casualties."

"My ma, your supposed best friend, is dead because of you." Realene lunged again for Irene, this time tackling her to the ground.

Irene's head smacked the concrete, and she moaned.

"I hope that hurts, you bitch." Realene smiled at the thought of blood staining Irene's perfectly styled curls.

A hand grabbed Realene's hat and the hair beneath. "Let go, devil," the lieutenant said.

Nate shoved the lieutenant, and the lieutenant tore off Realene's hat, taking a clump of hair in the process. Realene screamed at the pain singing her scalp, but stayed atop Irene, grabbing the old women's wrists to subdue her ineffective blows.

The soldier moved to break up the fight between Nate and the lieutenant, apparently assuming they were more dangerous than two women. Realene took that opportunity to punch Irene in the face, dark satisfaction filling her at the snap of the woman's nose beneath her fist.

"He killed that reporter, Shelley Schraeder! We saw it," Nate shouted.

The lieutenant cocked his arm to punch Nate, but ended up jabbing the soldier in the windpipe with his elbow. The solider stumbled backward into the kneeling Realene, and fell head over heels onto the asphalt. His radio had come unhooked from his belt, but he kept hold of his gun and raised it, firing a warning shot into the air.

Scowling, Realene rolled off of Irene and landed by coincidence atop the dropped radio.

The other group that had approached the roadblock had already been stripped of their shotguns and were now being herded back into their truck by the other soldiers. Upon hearing the warning shot, one of the soldiers broke off to approach the fight between Nate and the lieutenant.

"Break it up," he called, drawing his rifle.

Nate raised his hands and moved away from the lieutenant, who took Irene's hand and helped her up.

Realene hunched over, as if bracing herself to stand, but used the act as cover to slip the radio up her coat sleeve.

"You see! That demon tried to kill me!" Irene shrieked. She wiped at the blood coating her lips and chin, and winced when touching her broken nose.

"We're leaving," Realene said, swiping her hat off the ground. She walked away, her back itching from the invisible threat of the soldier's drawn weapon.

Nate got back into the passenger side of the van, and Realene hopped into the driver's seat. She would have liked to take another run at Irene, smash her face into a pulp, but there were bigger things at stake. If they could manage to get ahold of the colonel and stop the invasion, at least Ma's death wouldn't have been in vain.

Twenty-Four

REALENE MADE A U-turn and headed back the way they'd come, keeping an eye on the rearview mirror. The soldiers at the roadblock were occupied with Irene and Lieutenant Braun, which could work in Realene's favor. She hoped to be long gone before the soldier noticed his radio was missing.

"You think they were watching the theater? Waiting for us to try something?" Nate asked.

"No doubt." Realene seethed at the thought that Irene had been camped outside, probably all snuggled up with her boyfriend, while Ma died. "In their minds, we're the only people standing in the way of their precious Armageddon."

"Never did trust that woman," Calvin said. "You know she steals the Sweet & Lows from Gramma Butterwicks? She dropped her purse once when I was payin' my bill, and a whole flood of those pink packets came floodin' out."

Nate kicked the underside of the dashboard. "And now she's ruined any chance of us getting through to the colonel."

"Maybe not." Realene pulled up to the intersection and stopped, fishing the radio from her sleeve and passing it to Nate. They had their own set of long-distance walkie-talkies as kids, and she figured the basics of operation would be the same.

He held it aloft, like some sort of trophy. "Fucking A. How did you get this?"

"Luck. Fell off that soldier's belt during the fight, and I snagged it." She jumped the curb again and navigated around the pile-up to head back up the overpass. The bashed-up car that had been attacked by the moose sat empty, and the creature was gone.

"I wondered why you didn't try to get one last punch in on that bitch."

"If we get through this alive, I plan to get several more hits in." She held onto the memory of Irene blubbering and bloody faced. "So, can we get through on that thing?" Realene gestured to the radio.

Nate examined the device, turned up the volume.

"This is Delta One, multiple altercations at checkpoint seventeen, all have been contained. Over," a voice said, followed by the reply. "Roger, Delta One. Out."

Nate nodded. "Looks standard, just need to keep it on this channel, and we're set."

"Where we goin' now?" Calvin asked.

"I'm taking you home," Realene said, descending the overpass. Abandoned vehicles clogged the road ahead, but there were no animal or human attackers visible. The lack of activity was eerie, as if they sat in the eye of the alien invasion storm.

"Oh, yeah, makes sense. We need firepower." He gave a double thumbs up.

"Dude, you're definitely in the penalty box," Nate replied.

"For what happened back there with those fascist shitheads? I was trying to help."

"Quiet." Nate pressed the side button on the radio and said, "This is an emergency. We need to speak with Colonel Harmon. Over."

"Identify yourself. Over."

He stated their full names, then said, "We're calling from inside Demise, and it's urgent we speak with the colonel. Over."

"Civilian use of this channel is restricted. Cease communications immediately. Over and Out."

"This is an emergency, I repeat, this is an emergency. Over," Nate said.

Silence greeted him.

Keeping one hand on the wheel to maneuver around the various obstacles in the road, Realene grabbed the radio and pressed the button. If Harmon was listening in on the other end, he might hear her voice and respond. "Tell the colonel this is a matter of life and death. We know how to stop this... infection. Over."

No response.

"Guess my radio plan wasn't so brilliant after all." Realene handed the radio back to Nate. She really thought it would work, that they'd be able to get through to Harmon. "What the hell are we supposed to do now?"

Nate sighed. "I don't know."

"I'll tell ya what we do: We get the hell outta here," Calvin said. "Show those government goons they can't keep us penned in. They can't have all the back roads covered."

"We're not running away," she said. They slid on the ice, and she eased off the gas, guiding the van around the downed ambulance. Pumpkin gave a grumpy meow from his carrier to protest the jostling.

"Maybe we should think about it," Nate said. "Once we get somewhere safe, we could go to the police, send help from outside."

"If those soldiers didn't believe us, with all the crazy stuff I'm sure they've seen, there's no way anyone else will."

Silence pressed down on them, hopelessness threatening to drive her to hunker down and wait for someone else to save them. But she'd made a promise to herself not to think like that. That was how Old Realene would think. New Realene needed to channel Nate, her mom, her dad.

What would her dad do if he were still alive and in the same situation? He wouldn't give up, he wouldn't hide, and he definitely wouldn't run. Louie Gustafson would round up his Army buddies and go after the aliens himself. She didn't have Army buddies, but she had Nate. That would have to be good enough.

"We do it. Ourselves. We stop the invasion," she said, proud her voice sounded so determined.

"What?" Nate's eyes widened. "How? We can't very well get every person in town to drink salt water and zap them one at a time."

"Well, we have to do something. The longer this goes on, the more people die. Or forget." *Like Calvin,* she thought, but didn't say. *Or like Ma.* "And not just in Demise. All it'll take is one prairie dog making it out of town for this to spread to the next city, the next county, the next state. Soon, the whole country is infected. Then the world."

"What about Lake Sauer?" Calvin asked.

"Pretty sure Lake Sauer is part of the world, dude," Nate said.

"Very funny, smart-ass. You need salt water. Lots of it, right? Why not use the lake?"

"Huh," Realene said. "That's not a bad idea, Calvin." Several deer galloped across the field in the distance. She watched to ensure they didn't change direction to attack.

"Does that mean I get to come with?"

"Sorry, still no." She didn't need his death on her conscience too. "So, we use the lake, but what do we do about electricity?"

Nate snapped his fingers. "Easy! We can knock a utility pole into the lake to create a salt water circuit. We'll use my plow."

"That's a big circuit." She slowed as she approached the entrance of the trailer park. "And we'd still have to get everyone there. All the animals and people. We'd have to zap them at the same time."

"You're right." He slumped back in his seat. "How the hell are we supposed to do that?"

"What you need is bait," Calvin said.

"Dude, we're not going fishing," Nate replied.

While Calvin and Nate bickered, Realene stared silently out the van's front window to think. In the distance, she spotted the same group of prairie dogs still guarding the downed meteor with their lives. Her eyes narrowed, then grew wide.

"I have an idea."

REALENE AND NATE sat in his idling truck at the trailer park entrance with Pumpkin seat-belted between them in his carrier. Calvin agreed to stay locked in his trailer, but only after Realene had told him he was the final hope for Demise if their plan didn't work—the only one who'd be able to get word out about how to stop the worms.

Pumpkin, however, had not been as cooperative. He'd yowled and whined, refusing to exit the carrier when Realene tried to return him home. She wondered if he knew Ma had died, that there was nothing left for him in the trailer.

The post-storm weather held at a reasonable, borderline toasty, fifteen degrees, and the accumulated snow blanketing the field behind the trailer park sparkled beneath the shining sun. The beauty of the scene, something Realene rarely appreciated in the frigid winter months, struck her. She took it as a sign that they would squash those alien worms into goo.

"You're sure this is going to work?" Nate asked. They'd already drawn the attention of the prairie dog guards, which stared menacingly at the truck.

"Absolutely not."

Realene's plan was this: The meteor was important enough to guard, which meant all hell would break loose if it were stolen. So, they would steal it. Then, using its alien telepathy or whatever, the thing inside the meteor would send out a distress signal to every infected animal and person in town and command them to give chase. Realene and Nate would then lead their pursuers straight to Lake Sauer. The perfect bait.

"Better give the colonel one last try." Realene pressed the button on the side of the radio and said, "This is an urgent message for Colonel Harmon. We know how to stop the outbreak. Over."

"This channel is prohibited. Cease civilian use. Over."

"Listen, asshole. This is a matter of life or death. You tell the colonel that this is an infestation, and Realene Gustafson knows how to stop it. We're leading the infected to Lake Sauer. Send back-up. Today, we celebrate our Independence Day. Over and out." She placed the radio on the seat beside her.

Nate snorted. "Bill Pullman would be proud."

"Gotta motivate the troops, right?"

"Think they'll show?"

"Maybe to pick up our dead bodies." She grinned.

"You sicko. You're enjoying this." He opened his CD case and flipped through the plastic sleeves. "In which case, we might as well rock some tunes."

"You're such a dork." She opened her door.

"You love it."

"I do. Take care of Pumpkin." Realene got out and climbed into the bed of the truck.

During their brief respite, she'd added a double-layer of top and bottom long johns beneath her clothes so she could keep her coat unzipped for easy access to the guns now holstered at her hips. Not real guns, of course, but her childhood squirt guns filled with salt water. The double-holster was courtesy of Calvin. A Super Soaker filled with the same salt concoction hung across her back via a long shoulder strap.

Realene had also snagged her trusty pocketknife—the same one she and Nate used to become blood siblings so many years before—more for luck than anything else. If it came down to her having to use a three-inch blade to defend herself, she'd be prairie dog food for sure.

A spray nozzle attached to a long rubber hose waited for her inside the truck bed. The hose was connected to the two-hundred-gallon deicing tank secured to the truck beneath the cab's back window. They'd dumped all the bags of road salt Nate had—over twenty pounds—into the tank to ensure a high enough salinity to slow down any pursuers on contact.

Realene grabbed the spray nozzle with her gloved hands and readied herself for battle.

Nate craned his head out the driver's-side window. "You ready?"

"I was born ready." She figured a little bravado couldn't hurt.

He cranked up the radio, and "Sabotage" by the Beastie Boys blared from his open windows. He pulled into the road, then backed toward the pull-behind trailer that held the meteor.

The closest prairie dog gave a sharp yip, and the others lined up to block the truck's path to the trailer. The once adorable animals were now grotesque versions of themselves, their fur clumped and their teeth bared and bloody.

Realene moved to the end of the truck bed and raised the sprayer. "Let's see how you like a salt bath." She pressed the trigger on the sprayer and made a sweeping motion with the nozzle to douse the creatures with the salty fluid.

One by one, they fell to the ground, wiggling and crying.

"It's working!" she yelled, triumph pulsing through her veins. "Keep going."

Nate backed the truck closer to the meteor, and Realene shivered at the crunch of prairie dog bones beneath the tires. Sure, they'd become the enemy, but she still mourned their unfortunate deaths. The only thing she could do for them now was make sure the alien worms died too.

Nate slowed as he closed in on the small, two-wheeled, pull-behind trailer.

"Almost there," Realene said. The truck's hitch inched closer to the trailer's coupler. "Stop."

"I'm coming out. Cover me." He hopped from the truck, and she snickered at the sight of him in Calvin's fishing waders. They'd figured the rubber overalls with attached boots would give an extra layer of protection from claws and teeth.

A wounded prairie dog lurched toward Nate as he ran for the trailer, so Realene hit the creature with another spray from the deicer of death. It whimpered and stopped to paw at its face, but it didn't fall. Another prairie dog got up and shook itself like a dog with wet fur before lumbering toward Nate. Realene sprayed again, earning a shriek from the little creature.

"Hurry it up," she said. "They're down but not out."

Nate kicked the parking blocks from the trailer's wheels and hauled the heavy load the final inch to the truck's hitch, snapping it into place. "Got it!"

Several creatures stumbled out from beneath the truck and wobbled toward Nate like the last remaining drunks at the bar. Realene gave them another spray.

Nate leapt over the crying animals and got back in the truck. "Here we go!" he shouted.

Bobbing her head to the sick beat that thumped from the stereo, Realene braced herself between the tank and wheel well as they set off down the road.

Seeing the meteor pull away must have given the prairie dogs one last burst of strength, because they loped along behind the vehicle. They weren't moving as fast as before, which resulted in a much-needed buffer between them and the truck. She eyed the meteor with a mix of curiosity and contempt.

Breath misting in the air, Realene scanned the neighborhoods on one side and the fields on the other. Tiny tracks crisscrossed the snow in every direction, but there was no sign of more furry attackers. Given the pandemonium they'd seen in town, she suspected they'd headed toward more populated areas.

A speck appeared on the horizon, grew bigger. She squinted, realized the shape was a deer galloping at full speed across the snow-covered field. The animal jumped the ditch and ran into the road, merging with the lagging prairie dogs before passing them to charge at the trailer.

"We've got company," Realene yelled.

The deer raced past the trailer until it was even with the truck, then threw itself sideways into the vehicle.

Realene watched in horror as the deer rammed its face against the truck bed. A chunk of skin and fur had been torn from the face to expose white skull, and one eye leaked worm-ridden slime. The animal gave an unnatural shriek that sent chills up Realene's spine.

"Get away," she screamed, spraying the thing directly in its open mouth.

The deer's legs buckled, and the animal fell to the ground.

"Stay down, dammit," she said, before remembering they *wanted* the animals to chase them. All the infected had to make it to the lake for their plan to work.

Thankfully, the deer stood back up on four wobbly legs, took a few uneasy steps, and trotted unsteadily after them.

They approached the overpass, and a van crested the ridge, headed straight toward them. A string of Christmas lights had gotten snagged on the vehicle's luggage rack and trailed behind the rear bumper like a psychotic snake.

Nate whipped to the side, and Realene held on tight to the tank's handle to avoid being thrown from the truck.

The van barely missed hitting them, and Nate banged into the guardrail that blocked their descent to the train tracks below. Metal scraped against metal, but the rail held.

The van did a one-eighty to follow them.

They descended the overpass, having to slow as they approached the blocked intersection, and the van came up fast behind them.

The pursuing vehicle bore a crumpled hood, and the windshield was missing entirely. The van whipped around the trailer, and Realene managed to shoot a stream of deicer at the driver, a woman with cropped hair matted down with blood. She wailed, as if in agony, then sped past them. A boom sounded as she smashed into the abandoned cluster of cars. Smoke poured from the totaled engine.

Nate jumped the curb by the downed stop sign and carefully guided them around the wreck. The trailer creaked and bumped over the curbs, but the meteor stayed in place.

The passenger door to the crashed van swung open, and the woman spilled out. She climbed to her feet and stumbled after them, her peach coat streaked with gore, and one arm hanging limp at her side.

The prairie dog guards and several deer crested the overpass.

Motion caught Realene's eye in the direction of the bus, where several children were now running down the steps and into the street, their eyes locked on Realene.

A little girl with white-blonde hair raced toward the truck, her mouth twisting in a growl as she led her crazed classmates toward the meteor.

Several shots rang out from the direction of the military roadblock, but each bullet pinged off the icy cement. The soldiers clearly didn't want to shoot children, nor did Realene want them to. If everything went to plan, the kids would be cured. She wondered what the soldiers thought of the fleeing truck and the pursuing animal/human horde, and whether or not they'd try to stop them.

Making it past the packed intersection, Nate veered back into the road and picked up speed. They passed the park and ice rink, and half a dozen kids in green and white hockey uniforms loped across the snow and into the road, surprisingly adept at running on ice skates. As if executing a play, they fanned out in a "V" formation behind the trailer and raised their hockey sticks. Behind the team, more children and animals pursued.

"I don't know if we're gonna make it," Realene yelled.

Nate turned down the music slowed. "You okay?"

"Just get us to the lake." She started to question the wisdom of putting themselves squarely in the crosshairs of every alien-infested creature in town.

The hockey players closed in and began to hack at the straps that secured the meteor to the trailer.

"Stop that right now," Realene said in her best mad-adult voice, but it had absolutely no effect.

She stumbled to the end of the truck bed and grabbed the gate with one hand to steady herself. Extending the sprayer as far as she could, she aimed the nozzle at the kids and pressed the trigger. One by one, the hockey players fell back, shaking their heads and wiping at their eyes with their bulky hockey gloves.

Cars now filled the street, some occupied, some not, forcing Nate to slow. Panting, Realene prayed their pursuers would give her a goddamn minute to rest.

A car sped toward them from the opposite direction, but lost control and went skidding off the road, first hitting the pole for the McDonald's sign before barreling straight into the glass-enclosed PlayPlace. The pole snapped, and the giant golden arches flipped upside down and crashed in spectacular fashion to the ground. Meanwhile, multi-colored balls from the PlayPlace ball pit poured out of the broken windows, bounced across the parking lot, and rolled into the street ahead of Nate's truck.

The hollow balls gave a dry pop when crushed beneath the tires, but many made it unscathed, and now littered the road behind them in a rainbow of colors.

As if compelled by some deep-seated instinct even the alien worms couldn't override, the children from the bus stopped to snatch up all the balls. They stuffed them in their pockets or piled as many as they could carry into their little arms before continuing their pursuit.

Near the center of town now, more people dotted the road and sidewalks, some wandering as if lost, others attacking one another, driven by the random aggression the worms seemed to inspire. Many more people were likely holed up and hiding from the mob. Everyone outside looked up as the truck shot passed, eyes locking onto the their precious meteor and their alien overlord inside. They pursued without hesitation.

Two men fought on the sidewalk that ran along the road. One sported two black eyes and the other struggled with a broken nose that gushed blood down the front of his dress shirt. They stopped fighting and charged the truck.

"Mr. Klein?" Realene said. The one in the dress clothes was her old high school principal, a jerk who told her the incessant bullying she faced would build character. She took great pleasure in spraying him and his buddy with the salty liquid, watching as they fell back in a fit of coughs and spits.

A tangle of cars clogged the road, pinning them in on either side, and Nate slowed to squeeze through a tight spot. A man wearing a flannel shirt and no coat grabbed the tailgate, but Realene kicked him in the face. He scrambled to find something to hold onto, but only managed to unlatch the tailgate. She sprayed him in the face, and he let go, slipping out of sight beneath the trailer. She gagged at the sound of a scream and the thump of the tires as they rolled over his body.

Bowie's "I'm Afraid of Americans" blasted from a speaker out front of Skateway, and people streamed from the roller rink's entrance, most still wearing their skates. Several wiped out on the icy asphalt and went sprawling, but plenty more made it into the road and powered toward the trailer.

Two people in matching lime-green jumpsuits and Martian masks—likely costumes donned for 'Space Skate'—moved in unison toward Realene. She pressed the sprayer's trigger, but nothing happened. Panic seized her lungs, until she noticed she'd stepped on the tube that delivered water for the tank.

She moved her foot and raised the sprayer only to remember that it would do no good against this particular twosome since both their faces were hidden behind masks. Gripping the handle, she prepared to whack the skaters away, but they smashed into a little boy with an armful of balls before reaching her. The three went down in a tangle of balls, skates, and limbs.

Two pig-tailed little girls in matching purple, puffy snowsuits grabbed onto the side of the truck and began to climb over, but Realene sprayed them in their adorable, snarling faces and shoved them off the vehicle. Others continued to attack from both sides of the truck, so Realene sprayed in a wide arc, but struggled to keep them all at bay. The truck lurched forward as Nate revved the engine, and he plowed into a car that was angled across the road, pushing it aside. Upon impact, Realene was thrown backward onto her butt. She dropped the sprayer and barely managed to stay inside the truck.

She reclaimed her weapon as they cleared the biggest knot of cars and sped up. Yips filled the air in a strange harmony, like a group of neighborhood dogs all howling in unison at a passing fire engine. A mass of prairie dogs blocked the road ahead, all standing on hind legs with their eyes locked on the approaching truck. Nate lowered the plow blade and picked up speed, heading right for the animals.

As they got close, the prairie dogs on either side split off in a formation that would have impressed any high-school football coach and ran around the vehicle to leap at the sides.

Realene sprayed one group, then the other. They howled upon contact with the salty liquid and fell away to roll on the ground and paw at their faces.

She felt the minor impact as Nate plowed through the remaining creatures still blocking the road, but not all of them were pushed aside or sent flying. Several had leapt over the plow blade onto the hood. Nate tried the wipers, but they were useless to stop the animals from scampering up the windshield to the top of the truck's cab. Realene wasn't fast enough with the sprayer, but managed to swat them aside with the tool's long tip. She wished she'd grabbed her bat as a backup, rather than leaving it in the truck's cab.

Behind her, a grunt sounded, and she whirled around to find a woman in a fake fur coat trying to climb into the truck. Frau Berg, her old high school German teacher. She issued a gurgling, zombie-like growl and hooked a leg in a knee-high stocking over the side of the truck bed. Realene sprayed her in the face, and she released her grip. "*Auf wiedersehen*," Realene said. The woman rolled several times before coming to a stop in the middle of the street, coughing, but intact.

Sweat stung Realene's eyes, and she swiped at her face with the back of her glove. Nate honked the horn in two quick taps, and she looked ahead to see they'd reached Revelation Evangelical. The stop light flashed red from all four directions. Nate hadn't planned to slow down, but a little Geo Metro barreled toward them from the cross street. Nate slammed on the brakes, this time causing Realene to smack into the tank and bonk her head on the back of the truck's cab. Pumpkin yowled, and Realene sent him a silent apology for dragging him along on their suicide mission.

The Metro careened out of control and crashed into the Taco John's on the corner, dashing her hopes of rewarding herself with a nice order of Potato Oles and nacho cheese after this was all over. While the horde of people still followed, they were a good block back now, so Realene took the chance to sit on the wheel well and rest.

An engine revved and a postal truck approached from the opposite direction, coming at them head on. Nate swerved to avoid the mail carrier, which tossed Realene from her place of rest and sent her sliding down the open tailgate and onto the trailer. With nothing to stop her momentum, she rolled off the back of the truck bed and landed violently against the asphalt. Somehow, though, she had managed to maintain her hold on the deicing sprayer nozzle and was now being dragged behind the truck like a cowboy in an old Western. She could only pray the hose wouldn't snap.

Twenty-Five

REALENE SKIDDED BACK and forth across the asphalt on her back, hands raised above her head and clutching tight to the sprayer. The pavement shredded the outer layer of her parka and gnawed at the stuffing. Her mouth opened to scream, but she clamped her lips closed before any sound could escape.

She wasn't sure if Nate knew she'd fallen from the truck bed, but if she yelled, and he slammed on the brakes, she'd be road-kill. A car approached from behind, swerving erratically as if trying to pick her off. Or the driver could be confused and panicked. Not that it mattered. Both were equally dangerous while she was in her current predicament.

Realene was swung wide to the left, out into the middle of the road and into the path of an oncoming car, then swung back to the right. Her shoulders screamed from the strain, and her gloved hands began to slip. As soon as she bounced over the curb, she let go and allowed herself to roll off the pavement and onto someone's snowy lawn.

Snow that had hardened to an icy crust cut into her face as she rolled, but she ended up on her back, staring up at the clear blue winter sky. Heart hammering so hard she thought it might burst, she willed her bruised and battered body to get up. Something sounded beside her head, a burrowing beneath the snow, and she popped to her feet seconds before a prairie dog emerged from a tunnel mere inches from where her head had just been. It bared tiny, blood-stained teeth and hissed.

Realene leapt through the snowbank in long strides and made it back into the road, where Nate's truck sat idling twenty feet ahead. The hose trailed behind it, somehow still attached to the tank. He'd opened the door and stepped from the cab.

The pursuing mob was maybe half a block behind them now. "Go! Drive," she yelled, her breath fogging the air.

Nate's eyes widened, likely at the sight of the advancing mass of people gaining on them, and he jumped back into the cab.

Realene stooped to grab the sprayer nozzle and felt the thump of something hitting her back. That damn prairie dog.

"Get. Off." She shook her upper body, expecting to feel the sharp pierce of claws and teeth at any moment.

The weight fell away as she ran up the base of the trailer, hopping over the straps that tied down the meteor and throwing herself into the truck bed. Chest heaving, she closed the truck's tailgate and collapsed in a heap, still gripping the sprayer.

The truck lurched forward.

She peeked over the tailgate to see the prairie dog she'd narrowly avoided standing in the road, down stuffing from her gutted coat wrapping its paws and filling its mouth like cotton candy. She shivered, partly from the cold, partly from the realization of how close she'd come to being bit.

They passed Revelation Evangelical, whose parking lot was still packed full of cars. The congregation had, sadly, not regained its sanity overnight. She wanted to tell every one of them the truth about the reverend, that he shot and killed Ma, an innocent woman trying to protect her daughter, but they wouldn't believe Realene anyway. They'd just convince themselves she was telling the devil's lies.

Several armed guards assembled in front of the church to point at the truck and its horde of pursuers. One of them pounded on the church's front door. A moment later, the door opened, and the guards moved to either side so as to allow Reverend Zebediah to stride out into the cold. His fatigues and camouflage coat were now covered in the septumnox that marked his followers' foreheads.

"God dammit," Realene mumbled. She wouldn't mind a rematch with that evil bastard, but they were already being pursued by hundreds of alien-fueled attackers, and she doubted salt water would be effective against misguided religious zealots.

They passed Blockbuster Video, and she suffered a fleeting pang of guilt after remembering the Total Recall VHS still laying on the floor of her abandoned car. Maybe she could get Tony to wave the late fees. At the Piggly Wiggly, a man in flannel burst from the Christmas Tree lot in the parking lot to join the others in pursuit.

After another block of houses, they hit the city limits and the paved road transitioned to gravel. The lake was only a few minutes away, and the scenery quickly changed from businesses and neighborhoods to open fields. The snowy vista leading to Sauer Lake was normally quite serene, but now the expanse filled her with dread.

Prairie dog colonies inhabited most of the undeveloped land in town, and she wondered how far the alien worms had spread, snaking underground through the vast network of burrows. She shook the thought away, knowing she couldn't let herself get lost in hopelessness.

Sauer Lake shimmered in the distance, its glassy blue-green surface reflecting the sun that hung directly overhead. Several miles wide in each direction, the lake was bigger than Demise and extended beyond its borders. There was plenty of room to fit all the town's residents, and with a salinity ten times higher than the Pacific Ocean, there was very little risk of drowning, thanks to the natural buoyancy.

They bumped along the rutted gravel, and the mob of people and animals trailed behind, their numbers stretching back a quarter mile.

Farther in the distance, parishioners poured from Revelation Evangelical and climbed into the apocalypse bus that still sat parked across several handicapped spots. Exhaust plumed from the tailpipe, and the bus lurched forward, barreling past the parked cars and clipping one as it sped from the lot and into the street.

The reinforced vehicle plowed effortlessly through the swarm of people and animals, mowing them down in a wide swath. A handful of prairie dogs, a woman in a waitress uniform, and the girls in the matching purple snowsuits disappeared beneath the bus, as if swallowed by the blood-thirsty machine.

"No!" Realene screamed, eyes riveted on the broken bodies and smears of blood in the road. It may have been too late for some of them, but she still hoped that many of them could be saved if they only made it to the lake.

The bus sped up, and the mob of people and animals now split up to avoid it. Most, but not all, made it safely out of the way. A growing trail of dead bodies extended behind the vehicle.

Now close enough, Realene could see the face of the reverend behind the wheel, hands gripping the rubber.

She rapped on the back window of the cab and yelled, "Cult incoming," in case Nate somehow missed the reinforced apocalypse bus gaining on them. She held tight to the handle on the tank as Nate accelerated to an unsafe speed, the truck now slipping and sliding along the icy gravel road.

A top hatch on the apocalypse bus flipped open and Lieutenant Braun popped out, a rifle in his hand. The air froze in Realene's lungs. A spray of salt water wouldn't do shit against bullets, and in that moment, she very much regretted declining Calvin's offer of a bulletproof vest.

Eyes searching the truck bed for a weapon, she landed on the only thing handy: a small fire extinguisher secured to the truck bed's inner frame. She grabbed the metal canister and flung it toward the bus as hard as she could, sending up a silent prayer to God almighty as it left her hand. The extinguisher flew through the air in a high arc, spinning end over end and coming down on the lieutenant's head as he bent to line his eye up with the scope.

He cried out and slipped back inside the bus, the rifle sliding from the top of the bus and clattering to the ground to be trampled by the pursuing horde of infested.

"Oh. My. God. Yes!" Realene exclaimed. "Who's the last pick in dodgeball now?" She did a fist pump, but her enthusiasm quickly died at the thought of more parishioners armed with weapons. Even if Lieutenant Braun had been hurt, there were others willing to kill.

A motorcycle emerged from behind the bus and zoomed past it on the narrow gravel road. She wasn't sure whether the erratic arcs of the driver's path were due to the incessant demands of alien worms or icy conditions that were far from ideal for a two-wheeled vehicle.

The driver gained on the truck, and she recognized Tony. For a moment, she felt a sense of relief. He'd made it through the night. Perhaps he intended to come to her rescue, making some grand gesture to secure her affections and help save the town they'd both professed to hate. But he didn't wear a helmet, or even a coat, and his face bore the determined focus of the infected. He was chasing her for the same reason as everyone else—to stop her from taking the meteor.

His irregular driving appeared to throw off the reverend, and the bus veered to the side, the tires digging into the snowbank that bordered the road. The vehicle managed to avoid getting stuck and swerved back into the road, but not before being passed by several infected deer and a man who Realene could only assume was a competitive runner based on his impressive form and speed.

Movement caught her eye to the left, and she turned to see a huge brown animal galloping toward them through the open field.

"Bison!" she screamed. The beast, who was as tall as the top of the truck bed, charged toward them. She'd only ever seen a bison once on an exceedingly boring field trip to Medora, the former home of Teddy Roosevelt. Realene remembered the animals as huge but peaceful creatures, roaming in packs and nibbling on the grassy plains.

The dark scruff around its neck glittered with collected snow and ice. Giving a low bellow, the animal lowered its massive head and charged harder.

Realene sprayed deicing fluid at the beast, but the liquid wouldn't go far enough, wouldn't catch the creature until it was too close, too late. Nate slammed on the brakes as the bison got near enough for the salty spray to hit its unblinking, black eyes, causing it to falter. The beast still thumped into the front end of the truck with enough force to shove it sideways several feet, but that was nothing compared to the damage it could have done. Shaking its giant head, the beast took several stumbling steps back.

"They're coming!" Realene yelled. Their pursuers had gained ground.

The trailer now sat wedged in the ditch, the back end even with the surrounding snow, but the trailer hitch had held. Realene saw Nate lower the plow and heard the engine rev.

"Come on, hurry," she said to herself.

Tony led the pack, and he pulled a wheelie on approach. While raised in the air, his front tire caught the back end of the trailer, and he pulled back on the throttle to power the bike on board. He drove over the first strap holding the meteor down and snapped it. The second strap, however, held as he attempted to do the same, and his front tire slammed into the back of Nate's truck with such force that his body sailed over the handlebars and flew through the air like Superman. He smashed into the deicing tank like a discarded action figure and fell to the truck bed in a crumpled heap, unconscious.

The wrecked motorcycle fell sideways off the trailer and tumbled into the path of the runner, who gracefully leapt over it without breaking stride.

"Whoa," Realene whispered.

The crunch of metal sounded as the apocalypse bus crushed the motorcycle beneath its tires. While the outside of the vehicle was reinforced with tough metal and mesh, the tires were still rubber, and one of them blew. The bus swerved, and she glimpsed the reverend's furious face in the windshield as he struggled to regain control. A blown tire wouldn't put them out of commission completely, but it would slow them down.

Realene had a brief moment of satisfaction—even flipped Zebediah the bird—before something grabbed her ankle and yanked her feet out from under her.

Tony had woken up. He climbed on top of her and wrapped his hands around her throat. He grinned down at her, but it wasn't the good-natured, if slightly over-enthusiastic, expression she remembered. This was something dark.

His lips, still rimmed with the dried crust of Rocky Road ice cream, stretched too wide, bared too many teeth. "You owe me a date," he croaked.

Throat burning, Realene whacked the side of his head as hard as she could with the sprayer.

His grip loosened.

She shoved the spray nozzle into his mouth and pressed the trigger. "I think we're better off just friends."

Coughing a spray of salt water all over her face, Tony released his hold and rolled away. She got up, rubbing her throat, and Tony rose to meet her, so she gave him a firm shove to the chest to send him flying over the edge of the truck. He fell into the path of the runner, who didn't react quick enough this time and got taken down hard.

The road widened ahead into a gravel parking lot that the town kept plowed even in winter. While she'd often heard the older guys, including Calvin, complain about the lack of ice fishing because Lake Sauer wouldn't freeze, it was a popular destination for Polar Bear clubs across the state. She couldn't understand the desire to plunge oneself in ice-cold water, but she owed them for the lake being open.

Barren oak and elm trees circled most of the lake, but the public access area past the parking lot had been cleared of trees to accommodate boaters and swimmers. A short wooden dock jutted out into the water, with a slipway on one side—the ramp was used to load and unload boats. On the other side of the dock was a man-made beach that stayed largely free of snow due to the lapping tide of the heavily salted water.

Nate sped through the lot and down the gravel path in the corner intended for boaters. He pulled in a wide circle ahead of the dock and backed toward the structure. Poking his head out the window to line up the trailer, he reversed the truck until both the trailer's wheels were on the wood surface of the dock.

"Unhook me," he called.

Realene dropped her sprayer and jumped from the truck bed to unfasten the hitch. "Done. Go."

Nate pulled away, leaving Realene to stand on the dock alone. The nearest utility pole stood at the far end of the small beach, and he drove to it. He angled the truck until the pole stood between him and the lake, and he parked.

The armored bus charged into the lake parking lot, flanked by the bison, a ten-point buck, and several deer. Behind them, hundreds more people and animals followed.

Just as the two had predicted, none of their pursuers paid Nate any attention. All of them focused on the meteor and Realene.

Twenty-Six

REALENE SHOVED THE trailer onto the dock using all her weight, her boots slipping on the wet wood surface. The wheels struggled over the cracks between the planks, but she managed to muscle the trailer forward and fully onto the dock. She grabbed the hitched end and turned toward the water, intent on shoving the entire thing, meteor and all, into the frigid water. One of the planks snapped under the weight, and one wheel wedged itself into the hole. She pushed, but it wouldn't budge.

Too short on time to unfasten the straps from beneath the trailer, Realene fished the knife from her pocket, kissed it for luck, and sliced through the one remaining strap on the first chunk of meteor. The blade may have been old and rusty, but it was sharp, and it made quick work of the thick nylon. A screech sounded above her as a hawk dove through the air, beak and claws aimed at her face. She unslung the Super Soaker from her shoulder, calling on years of experience derived from water fights with Nate in her backyard, and sprayed the animal square in its tiny, feathered face. The hawk veered off, tumbling through the air and thumping onto the rocky beach in a way birds should not. Growls and screams sounded from the approaching horde, but she ignored them. Breath wheezing from her cold-singed lungs, she cut through each of the remaining two straps.

The meteor began to ooze that same sludge she'd seen that first night in the crater. Black goop seeped from the rock's surface on both halves and slithered along the bed of the trailer toward her. She had to get the whole trailer in the water to douse all the worms.

A gunshot ripped through the air, and a bullet hit an inch from her foot, releasing a spray of wood splinters. Realene yelped and glanced behind her.

A different gunman had taken the place of the Lieutenant, aiming at her from the hatch in the bus's roof. When the whinny of wild horses sounded, the gunman lowered his weapon, confused.

Four horses galloped through the snow-covered field—one tan, one chestnut, one pale-white, and one a dappled gray. Their manes streamed behind them, and when they whinnied, they displayed blunt, white teeth. Realene was reminded of that atrocious painting in the Revelation sanctuary, where the beasts spit fire on the suffering masses. Cold fingers gripped her spine at the worry the four horses were a sign the reverend would prevail, that he would stop them, that he would foster the alien invasion and forsake all of Demise.

Behind the impressive horses, a fifth came into view, this one a miniature pony struggling to keep up. The animal trudged through the snow on short legs, stopping to give a high, frustrated whinny before trotting after the others. A laugh escaped her throat at the sight of the silly animal, all worry of signs gone.

The apocalypse bus slowed, and the gunman gaped at the horses as they barreled toward the beach. Realene took advantage of the distraction and returned to her task of pushing the meteor into the lake.

The sludge had moved closer, to within inches of where she gripped the end of the trailer to push, and she noticed it wasn't just a gathering of tiny worms. At the center of the sludge was one giant, iridescent worm, roughly a foot long and pulsating in the grossest of ways. The queen.

Realene's coat sleeve rode up, exposing a sliver of skin past her glove.

The queen, surrounded by a pool of worm-laden goop, rose into the air to expose a belly dotted with pores that seeped more baby worms. The creature stretched tall and drew back its head, like a viper ready to strike.

Realene gave a loud war cry and lifted the trailer just enough for the one wheel to clear the splintered hole, and she shoved with all her strength until the trailer tumbled off the side of the dock.

The meteor separated from the wood as it met the lake's surface, and the queen quickly undulated through the water and back into the rock. The trailer sunk while the meteor halves bobbed in the salty water like two disgusting buoys from Hell.

The gently lapping waves carried the meteor halves away from the dock and toward the interior of the lake.

Realene's shoulders slumped, and a shiver shook her tired body. Step one done. Now it was up to Nate.

Screams erupted behind her, and she turned to see the approaching mob veer away from her and toward the water's edge. Animals and humans streaked wildly down the beach like excited tourists on the hottest day of summer. The first wave was the fastest of the adults, who splashed into the water and dove beneath the surface. Next, the Bison plowed into the lake alongside a buck, several deer, and the four horses. A mass of prairie dogs followed and doggie paddled into the lapping waves.

Children of all ages plunged into the lake next, wearing hockey uniforms, roller skates, snowsuits, or pajamas. Some still carried the brightly colored balls from the McDonald's PlayPlace that they had gleefully gathered from the road. The elderly and the injured were the last to enter the water, including Tony and Principal Klein. Mayor Opdahl crawled along the ground, dragging a broken leg behind him. The miniature pony finally made it in, and Realene resisted the urge to cheer the little guy on for making it.

All that entered Sauer Lake did so at an urgent pace, but immediately slowed as the salt water took effect. They didn't turn back, though, continuing their pursuit of the precious meteor that was the source of their infection. The only creatures not in the water were the owls and hawks, who flew helplessly in the sky above, swooping down toward the bobbing meteor only to ascend again empty-clawed, unable to do anything to rescue it.

The apocalypse bus pulled to a stop near the slipway, and two dozen parishioners piled out. Bundled in their winter coats and hats, they seemed like anything but cult members—if you ignored the ash septumnox on their foreheads, that is.

Lieutenant Braun hugged Irene close, and Realene smirked at the bandage on her nose and the dark bruises beneath her eyes.

Reverend Zebediah moved to the front of the group, his face red and nostrils flared at the sight of the grand dunking—of his precious Armageddon coming to an end. Sophia waited behind him, with her arms wrapped around her middle like she might be sick.

A few hundred feet down the beach, Nate hit the gas and sped toward the utility pole, his plow raised. Realene watched from afar, hoping he and Pumpkin were both wearing their seat belts. Nate raced across the icy gravel lot and smashed perfectly into the wooden pole. She opened her mouth to cheer, but fell silent.

The utility pole had only tipped slightly toward the water, but mostly, it remained upright and intact. Realene worried that the congregation would try to stop Nate, but no one did. They didn't know that electricity was the key to killing the worms.

Nate backed his truck up again, farther this time, and took another run at the pole. He smashed into the pole so hard that his head whiplashed forward, and he banged his forehead hard on the steering wheel.

The pole wobbled this time, but still did not fall.

"Shiiiit." Realene looked at the bobbing meteor halves. The runner had already grabbed one half and was swimming it back to shore. Soon, someone would save the other half too.

While the reverend didn't know the full plan, he must have read the fear on Realene's face. "God's will prevails," he said, turning back to his congregation. "You saw for yourself the four horses."

"Five, actually. You missed the little one," she said.

"These demons sought to stop God's righteous destruction, but they have failed. Our holiness and devotion shall be rewarded." He raised his hands toward the sky as if expecting Jesus to swoop down with a high five.

Realene clenched her fists. Against all odds, they had managed to get all the infected into the lake. The plan couldn't fail now. Not after all they'd been through. Not after all they'd lost.

Nate drove the short distance from the utility pole back to the dock parked his truck parallel to the shore, front end facing the bus. He slid across the bench seat and jumped out the passenger side door.

The reverend continued his impromptu sermon, his back to Nate and Realene.

Realene ran up to Nate. "What do we do now?"

"Unless you have a chainsaw on you, we're hosed."

Pumpkin's carrier had been thrown from the seat, and the door hung open. He hopped from his kitty prison and trotted up to rub against her legs.

"Poor Punky." She picked him up, and he rubbed her chin with his nose. "We can't let the reverend win."

"I mean, he's going to find out real quick that there is no rapture coming for him."

"Always finding the silver lining."

"You face one final test," Reverend Zebediah bellowed, facing Realene and Nate, where they stood near the end of the dock, totally unprotected. "Cleanse the world of these demons. Show God—show *me*—that you deserve your place in Heaven. Kill them."

Realene's body flushed with heat as she stared at Reverend Zebediah and his brainwashed parishioners. She set Pumpkin down, and he ran to hide beneath the truck. "Go ahead. Kill us like you did my mom."

A few of his followers had the good manners to look shocked, while most just glared at Realene, suspicious.

"Oh, didn't he tell you? That he attacked us last night at the Cinema Twin? That he shot my ma in cold blood, like a coward?"

Zebediah puffed up his chest and took a step closer to Realene. "She was in league with you, which makes her a servant of the devil too."

"You shot Marion?" Sophia asked.

"He had to," Irene said, meeting Realene's eyes for a moment, then looking away.

"You all knew my ma," Realene said. "If there was ever an angel here on Earth, it was her."

"I did my divine duty." The reverend raised his chin in a way that begged someone to punch him in the face. "Your eye shall not spare, and you shall show no pity. Kill old men outright, young men and maidens, little children and women. It is only those with the mark that are saved."

"But she had the mark," Sophia said. "I did it myself." She backed away from him, eyes wide and scared.

"Look around you. These are your friends, your family, your neighbors. They're good people that are sick," Realene said, gesturing toward the lake and everyone in it. "They don't deserve to die, and neither did Ma, regardless of whether they wear your stupid mark. Ask yourself what would Jesus do. I bet it's not celebrate while everyone dies."

"We're not the devils, not the ones spreading evil," Nate added. "He is." He pointed at the reverend.

Zebediah grabbed Sophia by the shoulders. "He killed his own father, your beloved husband, a good and pious man."

"Bullshit," Nate said.

A van painted with the Carpet Emporium logo sped through the parking lot and onto the beach, swerving to stop parallel to the edge of the lake just ahead of Nate's truck. Vickie got out of the driver's side, her hair matted and mascara smudged in dark swaths beneath her eyes. Oblivious of the yelling match with the reverend, she stumbled toward the water, another of the infected bent on saving the meteor.

Realene almost yelled at her not to bother. The runner was only thirty feet or so from shore, and the buck had found the other half of the meteor and was now nudging it toward the shore with its horns.

"Show me you deserve your place," the reverend ordered, spittle collecting at the corners of his mouth. He drew the gun from one of his holsters and pressed it into Sophia's hand. "Do your duty. Execute him."

Her expression pained, Sophia raised the weapon and pointed it at Nate.

The clouds shifted in the sky, muting the sun.

"No," Realene said, trying to step in front of him, but Nate quickly pushed her away.

"You were right, Mom," he said. "I could've run away today, from dad, and I didn't. Part of me wanted to hurt him after all he did to you, to us. I'm sorry. But that doesn't make me a demon. You know that killing us, killing me, isn't right."

The gun wavered in Sophia's two-handed grip.

"He's a murderer," Realene said of the reverend. "Don't let him make you one too."

Sophia let out a short sob and lowered the gun. "I'm sorry."

Realene wasn't sure which of them she was apologizing to.

The reverend strode up to her and smacked the gun from her hand. The weapon bounced and landed in a pile of snow. He grabbed her head with one hand and scrubbed his sleeve across her forehead until the septumnox was wiped away. He then shoved her to the ground.

Sophia stared up at him not with devotion, but determination.

"Prove your loyalty," he bellowed at his congregation. "Earn your place."

Most of congregation visibly shrank away from him, but Lieutenant Braun straightened and strode forward, pulling a handgun from his belt. Irene clasped her hands before her in barely contained excitement.

"I'm really starting to dislike Irene's new boyfriend," Realene said.

The Carpet Emporium van rocked, and something banged against the back doors, but Realene kept her focus on the Lieutenant. She'd worry about Murray if they lived through this.

With no other weapon to use, Realene pulled the squirt gun from her holster and pointed it at the lieutenant. "Do you feel lucky, punk?" She felt a small measure of satisfaction at quoting her dad's all-time favorite movie and really hoped they weren't the last words out of her mouth. "Well, do ya?"

The lieutenant hesitated, giving Irene a confused look.

"Bet you really wish you were in Arizona now, huh?" Nate said, his earnest face appearing younger, like the kid who'd always defended her against any bully.

"I wouldn't have made it a week without you." Keeping her squirt gun raised, she bit the glove on her free hand and yanked it free with her teeth. She spit the glove to the ground and displayed her scar. "Best friends forever, right?"

Nate pulled off his own glove to reveal his matching scar, then took her hand so their old wounds were pressed together like the day they'd made their pact. "Best friends forever."

Sophia crawled over and clutched the lieutenant's leg. "Don't kill my son. I'm begging you. Please."

He grimaced and lowered his weapon. Whether due to a helpless mother's plea, or the image of Realene and Nate holding hands like a couple of squirt-gun-wielding kids, it appeared he was finally catching on to who the real villains were.

"Useless. All of you." The reverend drew his second gun and stalked toward Realene and Nate. "You escaped me once. It won't happen again."

"Go to Hell," Realene said.

Sophia climbed to her feet and ran at the reverend, leaping onto his back. "Leave my son alone!" She wrapped her arms around his neck in a chokehold, and he spun in a circle, his gun arm pinwheeling.

The parishioners screamed and ducked as the gun arced in their direction. Zebediah fired a shot, which hit the back of the Carpet Emporium van, and a roar sounded from inside.

Sophia bit the reverend's ear, latching on and tearing off a hunk of flesh, Mike Tyson-style.

He shrieked and dropped the gun. Sophia kicked the weapon away, then spit out the chunk of his ear. It landed at his feet. Eyes widening at the sight of his amputated lobe, he grabbed her arms and bent forward to flip her over and onto the ground. She landed hard on her back, the air leaving her lungs in a whoosh.

"You bit me, you stupid bitch!" Blood leaked down the reverend's neck, staining his fatigues, and his face warped into that of a feral animal. "You're all useless! None of you deserve salvation!"

The congregants, including the lieutenant and Irene, backed away from the man they'd worshiped, watching as he screamed and sputtered like a lunatic. They climbed back onto the bus, the door hissing closed behind them.

Realene spared a glance at the lake. The salt water, combined with the cold, were slowing the runner and the buck, but not stopping them. They continued inching the meteors toward shore, the runner having only fifteen feet to go. There must be another way to get the utility pole down before it was too late.

Laughing in a way that made Realene wonder if she'd snapped, Sophia got up and stomped on the masticated chunk of the reverend's ear, grinding it into the rocky sand with the heel of her combat boot.

Zebediah backhanded her, and she fell hard to her hands and knees.

"Don't you touch her!" Nate charged forward, Realene close behind.

A repetitive sound suddenly filled the air. It was the thump of helicopter blades.

Realene searched the sky. A chopper flew toward them, hovering over the lake and sending concentric waves crashing over the animals and people within.

The reverend fled past Nate and Realene and grabbed his gun from the beach. He spun to point the weapon at Nate, the lake and its alien-infested swimmers a macabre backdrop for his dark visage. "Die, demons!"

Realene lunged toward Nate and tackled him to the ground at the same time a shot rang out.

The gun flew from the reverend's hand, and he howled in pain as he clutched his wrist. He raised his hand aloft to stare through the bloody hole at the center of his palm.

"Stay where you are," a loudspeakered voice commanded

from the helicopter. A sniper sat perched in the open side door, his weapon trained on the reverend.

Nate helped Sophia to her feet. Tears streamed down her face. "I'm so sorry," she said, her words muffled as she buried her face in his chest.

A military Jeep sped toward them from down the road. The four passengers wore tan hazmat suits with attached gas masks. The two in the rear were standing and bearing rifles. A man in the front tugged the gas mask up to rest on his forehead. It was Colonel Harmon.

"Wait! Stay back!" Realene shouted, waving her arms and making a stop signal with her hands. "It's not safe!"

Though they were moving slower than the zombies in the *Night of the Living Dead* remake, a wave of animals and people neared the shore and would be free of the water soon, and hazmat suits hadn't been enough to protect the scientists at the landing site.

She turned back to see the reverend reaching into his pocket with his uninjured hand and watched him pull out a grenade. Zebediah raised it to his mouth, and pulled the pin with his teeth. "I am the Hand of God."

A growl sounded from the van, and the back cargo doors flew open. Murray leapt from his prison, landing less than six feet from Nate and Realene. He froze them in place with his golden gaze and opened his mouth to let loose a deafening roar, displaying enormous, white teeth.

Pumpkin emerged from his hiding spot beneath the truck and jumped between them and the tiger. He arched his back and hissed at Murray, who growled but changed direction to pad toward the lake.

The poor guy must be infected too, Realene thought.

The reverend whimpered and backed away from the approaching tiger, but stepped on his own gun and slipped, falling on his ass. The grenade fell from his uninjured hand and rolled toward Murray, who batted it like any cat would an approaching ball and sent it rolling along the beach. The motion must have intrigued a watchful hawk, which dove down to snatch the grenade only to drop it moments later after realizing it wasn't food.

"Get away," the reverend shrieked as the tiger lumbered past him, but his outburst only succeeded in capturing the animal's attention. Murray sniffed the air, then lunged, chomping down on the reverend's bloody hand and dragging the man into the water with him. The reverend punched and kicked at the animal until Murray released his bite on the man's hand. The tiger growled, baring his teeth, then latched on to the reverend's throat and dragged Zebediah's now limp body farther into the lapping waves.

The grenade blew, the explosion reverberating through the ground and erupting in a fireball that sent a shock wave through the air. The helicopter faltered, catching a few of the infected birds in its propeller, then rose higher to escape the blast.

By some miracle, the hawk had dropped the grenade at the base of the utility pole, causing the pole to crack in two and fall, power lines and all, into Sauer Lake.

Every living creature in the lake froze in place as electricity coursed through the salt water and into their bodies. The runner, who was inches from the dry beach, tensed and fell backward, releasing the meteor he'd been carrying.

The transformer at the base of the pole popped and blew, emitting smoke from the gray, metal box. Everyone wilted into the water, limp bodies floating on the undulating waves like those dead catfish from Realene's doomed date years ago.

"Oh, God." Gray tugged at the edges of Realene's vision, and she clutched Nate's arm to keep from collapsing. "They're dead."

She'd been so convinced they were doing the right thing, that the plan would work, but instead, she'd made it so much worse. Realene had murdered hundreds of people.

When a little girl in Powerpuff Girl jammies who'd been lying face down in the water near the shore raised her head and coughed, Realene cried out in relief. Even better, the girl was the first of many to recover. Others stirred, their moans and cries of confusion filling the air.

Wave after wave of people stumbled and crawled out of the lake, sloshing through the water, asking where they were, how they had gotten there. One of the hockey boys called out for his mother, and an older man stopped every person he saw, asking if they'd seen his wife. Realene hoped their loved ones were okay, that they'd just been hiding somewhere and would soon be reunited. That they hadn't ended up like Brooke.

The bison charged from the water, and everyone froze, but it galloped past them all and into the snowy field. The four horses and a few deer followed, stumbling but upright, returning the way they'd come. The animals seemed to fare better than the people.

Men, women, and children of all ages filled the beach, their bodies trembling so hard from the icy water, one could make the honest assumption that electricity still coursed through their frigid veins. They cried and begged, turning to one another for some kind of answer, but finding none.

"What is happening here?" Colonel Harmon asked, jumping from the Jeep where it had stopped at the edge of the parking lot.

"They'll be okay, I think," Realene said to Harmon. She struggled to find the words to explain the situation without mentioning aliens or worms, but she quickly gave up. "Anyone that was in the lake should be cured. Some of them are really hurt though."

Colonel Harmon narrowed his eyes, drawing attention to the scar that extended out from the corner of his eye. "You heard her, soldier." The man beside him pulled out his radio and spoke into it, calling for emergency personnel before grabbing a kit from the back of the Jeep and running toward the survivors on the beach.

The colonel pulled Realene aside until they were out of earshot. "The worms, they're dead?"

She gasped. "You knew?"

"After we get this cleaned up, you and Nathan are coming with me for debriefing."

"What... Why didn't you answer our messages?" She punched his arm. "We could've used your help a lot sooner, you know."

"Seems like you had it pretty well under control."

"Yeah, right." She said a silent thank you to Murray and pledged to buy him the biggest order of burgers he'd ever seen.

She remembered the fighter jets flying over that morning. "What were you going to do? To contain all this?"

"You know I can't tell you that."

She nodded. She wasn't sure she really wanted to know.

They stood in silence, watching the scene before them, which rivaled the worst disaster footage she'd seen on the news. "We tried to get as many as we could, but there are more infected out there."

"Why don't you leave that to me. You've done plenty."

Two more Jeeps pulled up and the hazmat-suited soldiers pulled stacks of blankets from the back. "Well done." Colonel Harmon stuck out his hand and shook hers. "You saved Demise, maybe the world. But you can never tell anyone what happened here."

She rolled her eyes. "Top secret. I get it."

He patted her on the shoulder before pulling his mask back over his face and joining his men in helping the freezing and wounded. She returned to Nate, who held a very freaked-out Pumpkin.

"Your Mom okay?" she asked, giving Pumpkin's head a scratch and earning a glare that said he did not forgive her for bringing him face to face with a tiger.

"She'll be okay. She's stronger than she thinks." He angled his chin toward the shore, where Sophia worked with the soldiers to pull survivors from the lake.

The door to the apocalypse bus opened, and the parishioners filed out carrying blankets, water, and other provisions. They joined in the efforts, fanning out to help as many as they could. Playing the part of real live Christians.

"I hope they don't think that makes up for anything," Realene said.

Irene hurried past, carrying several bottles of water and careful not to meet Realene's gaze.

Realene knew Ma would preach forgiveness if she were there, but she wasn't. Her best friend betrayed her and set her up to die. Realene really hoped Irene got what she deserved.

People crowded the beach and parking lot, many clutching one another for warmth and comfort. Murray padded from the water, people crawling or limping out of his way. He collapsed on the ground, and his tongue lolled out of his red tinged mouth. Vickie stumbled over to the tiger and wrapped her arms around the animal's neck, cooing, "My poor baby."

Tony wandered by, shaking from exposure. Realene went after him, taking off her tattered parka to drape it over his shoulders. He needed it more than she did. "Are you okay?"

"What am I doing here? Do I...know you?" He blinked at her, not even a hint of recognition on his face.

The expression was one she knew well, and pain cinched her chest. "You're going to be okay. Help is coming."

He pulled the coat tighter around him and continued toward the military personnel. Unfortunately for Tony, they wouldn't have answers for him either.

The two halves of the meteor bobbed near the shore, the water licking at the now harmless rocks. A few feet away, the reverend lay on his side, throat mangled and eyes vacant. She felt no sympathy for him.

Not all of the infected made it. Many bodies floated lifelessly atop the water—dozens of people, several deer, and every single prairie dog. Realene suspected they'd been worse-off than the rest, having been infected first, and that their tiny bodies couldn't hold up to the force of the electric shock.

Nate walked up, Pumpkin still cradled in his arms. "You okay?" he asked.

"Not yet, but I will be." She hoped that was true.

He pulled a Caramello from his pocket and handed it to her. "Probably need some sugar. I'm surprised you haven't gone into shock yet."

"You're my hero." She tore open the wrapper and took a bite, reveling in the explosion of sugary caramel and chocolate on her tongue.

The pony trotted from the lake, one of the last out of the water, and the little girl in the jammies squealed in delight. She threw her arms around the pony's neck and hugged it close.

"What are best friend's for?" He winked. "Is it me, or did we just defeat an alien invasion?"

"Goddamn right we did. And took down a psycho cult leader too."

"Taught those aliens not to mess with a North Dakotan, huh?"

They watched as a fleet of military trucks barreled down the gravel road toward them.

"Damn straight. If we can survive the winters here, we can survive anything." She laid her head on his shoulder and took another bite of her candy bar.

Epilogue

REALENE STEERED THE minivan from the hospital parking lot. Elizabeth Blackwell had been relegated to the junkyard, but that was okay. She'd actually started to like the van and christened it Barbara Eden. The colonel even fixed the antenna, and "All the Small Things" by Blink 182 played from the radio.

The box of Nerds she'd promised herself as a reward for good work sat in the cup holder, and she dumped half the strawberry flavored sugar nuggets into her mouth, savoring the sweet sting on her tongue. Exhaustion weighed her down, but not the same kind she'd experienced as an intern, where her body got worn out from doing menial tasks for the doctors and nurses.

Mental exhaustion plagued her from leading back-to-back dementia support groups. So many families and friends needed help with how to handle their loved ones, many of whom lost huge chunks of their lives in the span of a day. While the victims were able to create new memories, they'd been robbed of years they would never get back. Children and parents alike no longer remembered birthdays and holidays and first days of school. Lovers and friends lost countless experiences that defined their relationships, made them who they were to one another. Demise was full of traumatized strangers forced into proximity and trying to cope.

Realene drove past the elementary school, where a construction crew worked to enclose the back wall that had been busted through by a garbage truck whose driver had been bitten. The junior high had been destroyed by a fire, but Bethel Lutheran offered its building for the remainder of the school year. Realene thought Ma would've been proud of that—that her church stepped up to help. They were even hosting a charity bake sale the following Sunday to raise money for school supplies. Realene never learned to make homemade lefsa, but she planned to contribute a giant batch of Puppy Chow.

She smiled at the sight of several kids zooming around the ice, hitting the puck around. Nothing kept Northerners from their hockey, not even a supposed mass-poisoning. It had been three weeks since the invasion, and while they all needed time to mourn and nurse their wounds, the time had come to reclaim what they could of their lives. She'd certainly learned the importance of appreciating what you had, rather than lamenting what you didn't. If only that happened sooner, while Ma was still alive.

Realene approached the intersection that led to the overpass, her gaze catching on the bouquets and small signs that lined the snowbanks on either side of the cemetery. With the ground too frozen to bury anyone, the memorials became a way to honor the dead. She and Nate made one for Ma and one for Walt. Pumpkin and Trout even contributed their paw prints, which resulted in them painting her kitchen tile with paw prints, as well. Come spring, Demise would have a mass funeral for the three-hundred and twenty-seven people who died.

She'd felt responsible for some of those deaths at first, those who hadn't emerged from the lake. Autopsies had shown those who died had already sustained critical injuries, were merely walking corpses whose hearts still beat, muscles propelled by the alien worms. She and Nate had somehow managed the perfect voltage, enough to kill the worms but not so much that it killed those not already too damaged. It turned out that while salt impaired the worms, it wasn't necessary to kill the creatures, but the use of the salt circuit had been the only way to shock so many at once.

An Army Jeep sat next to a gas pump at the Snack Station, and she pulled into the lot. Police tape roped off the building, which was the case for half the businesses in town. The location had been repurposed as a food and supply station. A boxy, white

Red Cross emergency vehicle was parked on the far side of the lot, and a line of cars led to the pass-through window. As one of four emergency stations set up across town, it provided hot meals, bottled water, and other necessities to residents.

Realene pulled into the food line and gave a short honk to catch the colonel's attention. He stopped at each car, chatting with those inside. The mayor was among the dead at the lake, and half of City Council lost their memories, so Colonel Harmon volunteered to spearhead the recovery effort. He could have done that from the comfort of his office on base, but seeing him in person made people feel better, Realene included.

Colonel Harmon shook the hand of the driver he'd been talking to and made his way over to her.

She rolled down her window, letting in a gust of cold air that sent her teeth chattering. Just three more months of winter, she reminded herself, before a non-existent spring led into the brutally humid summer.

"Hey, kiddo. How you holding up?" he asked.

"Some good days, some bad. You know how it goes."

"You give any more thought to my suggestion?"

She wrinkled her nose. "I don't think I'm cut out for military life." He'd tried to convince her and Nate to enlist after everything that happened, insisting their quick thinking and willingness to risk their lives to save others were the qualities he valued in a soldier. "Plus, I still plan to get to school eventually."

He raised an eyebrow. "Fleeing for Arizona after all?"

"Nah." She'd already told the school to give her scholarship to someone else. "I'm thinking NDSU." The governor had announced that the state would fund some special scholarships for survivors, and she hoped to get one. Plus, Fargo was only a forty-five-minute drive, so she could keep the trailer.

"They have pre-med?"

"Thinking of changing my major, actually, to psychology." With all that happened, the behavior of the Revelation parishioners disturbed her the most. Despite not being infected, they'd acted more irrational than anyone else.

"Head-shrinker, huh?"

She rolled her eyes. "How are things going with the clean up? All clear?"

"Officially, I don't know what you're talking about." He bent closer. "Unofficially, the quarantine worked to keep folks in, and we've completed a full sweep of town to identify the remaining infected. Some animals made it outside the perimeter, but we've successfully treated or euthanized the lot of 'em."

She winced. "Euthanize? You mean kill?"

"The animals that weren't treatable, yeah. It could have been a lot worse, if you hadn't figured out how to kill the creatures without killing the host. You should get a medal, but—"

"I know, I know, top secret." She narrowed her eyes. "So, the worms are gone? You're sure?"

"We'll keep monitoring, but we think so." He squeezed her shoulder. "Your dad would've been so proud of you. Your mom too."

"Thanks." She forced a smile. "See you tomorrow for dinner?"

"I'll be there."

"Wear jeans this time, huh? It's weird when you show up in your uniform." The cars started moving, so she said goodbye to the Colonel and pulled ahead. Her stomach growled. She heard they were serving tuna mac-n-cheese, which she placed in her top-five favorite hot dishes.

REALENE REACHED FOR the hood of her parka to stave off the frigid wind, before remembering she had no hood. She'd been making do with her dad's old wool coat, and she reminded herself to make a trip to the Super Target in Fargo come the weekend. She knocked on Calvin's back door, stamping her feet to keep her toes from freezing.

He opened the door, flinching as a gust of wind hit him. "It's colder than a witch's tit out here."

She grinned. His colloquialisms were really quite amusing. "Well, ya better take this quick then." She handed him the Styrofoam container.

He gave a toothy smile, showing off his new dentures. "That my supper?"

"Sure is. I even sweet-talked them out of an extra brownie."

"Brownies are my favorite." He frowned. "Did you already know that?"

"Nope, but I do now." She rubbed her gloved hands together. "I'll come by in the morning, and we'll have breakfast, okay?"

"Alright, but I ain't cookin."

"I'll pre-toast the Pop Tarts then, yeah?"

"Guess we'll both find out if I like Pop Tarts." He shrugged and closed the door.

Her shoulders slumped. He reminded her of Ma in the early days, before the Alzheimer's got worse. Hell, half the town reminded her of Ma.

Realene trudged across the yard and inside her trailer, leaving her boots in the draining tray and her coat on the hook by the door. Pumpkin lay in the recliner, curled up on Ma's favorite Afghan. "Hi, Punky." She scratched him on the head and earned a nice purr for the effort.

Though they were halfway into January, the fully lit Christmas tree still sat in the corner, almost no needles remaining on the dry branches. Realene couldn't bring herself to take down the decorations or open the gifts Ma left beneath the tree, even though they were probably just random things she'd found and wrapped, like a jar of pickles or a single slipper.

Realene flipped on the TV, and the spinning MTV satellite dish filled the screen.

"I'm Kurt Loder with an MTV News Brief. The now deceased Jeff Hozak, known to his congregation as Reverend Zebediah—"

Realene gave a surprised laugh. His real name was Jeff Hozak?

"—has been implicated in the deaths of more than three hundred people and the serious illness of hundreds more in Demise, North Dakota." An image of Revelation Evangelical filled the screen, the apocalypse bus parked out front. "Believing the recent meteor landing a sign that the final judgment day referenced in the book of Revelations had arrived, Hozak, possibly with the help of his followers, poisoned the town's water supply with lead. In what is being referred to as the reverse Heaven's Gate, Hozak intended only for his congregation to survive."

"While rumors of aliens and government conspiracy abound, the residents of Demise are simply trying to reclaim their lives in the wake of this disaster. Anyone wishing to help can donate to the Red Cross by calling 1-800-RED-CROSS. That's the news for now, stay tuned for more throughout the day on MTV."

The TV switched to videos, and Will Smith filled the screen, clad in sunglasses and a suit, the chorus singing about the Men in Black. Realene switched the channel to *Nick at Nite*, having had enough aliens to last her a lifetime.

She'd been doubtful anyone would buy Colonel Harmon's explanation, but the story was close enough to the truth to be believable. Lead poisoning did cause confusion, aggression, and memory issues, and Reverend Zebediah—scratch that—Jeff Hozak, certainly deserved plenty of blame.

The Colonel shared that local police had been investigating Hozak, considering him the prime suspect in the death of the church's previous leader, Reverend Miller. Apparently, the reverend's heart attack was caused by digitalis, a poison derived from foxglove.

The members of the church publicly denounced Hozak, insisting they had no knowledge of the poisonings, which was true. But Realene knew they'd been ready to watch their friends and neighbors die, even help them along, in order to guarantee a spot in Heaven. The townspeople needed some-one living to blame, and even though no criminal charges were filed against most of the parishioners, they'd become pariahs. Lieutenant Braun had been arrested for the murder of Shelley Schraeder, with Sophia the star witness for the prosecution. Realene had witnessed Irene get surrounded, taunted, and chased from the Piggly Wiggly, which was extremely gratifying.

Realene did wonder if some of the congregation, particularly those who'd been holed up in the church and didn't witness the events at the lake, might still believe Hozak's teachings.

After turning off the TV, she grabbed a Peach Snapple from the fridge and took it back to her room. Nate and the Colonel had upped their lectures about her diet, so she'd agreed to try and be healthier. Plus, she liked the little facts under the cap. This one said '#94: Lizards communicate by doing push-ups.'

Setting her drink on the nightstand, she opened her curtains and stared out at the field. Snow blanketed the landing site, hiding all evidence of the crash. They planned to dig up the whole field come spring, demolish the prairie dog burrows just in case. She could understand why, but it made her heart ache a little knowing they'd never be back.

She picked up the phone and dialed Nate's mom's house.

"Yellow," he said. Trout barked in the background. "I'll take you out in a minute, okay, buddy?"

"How's he doing?"

"Okay. He still misses Walt, leads me over there just about daily. But my mom really likes having him here. I think the company is good for her."

"You're company." He hadn't moved in, but he'd been spending most of his time there.

"Eh, we're still in that awkward phase where she keeps remembering I killed my dad."

She slipped from the window to sit cross-legged on her bed. "She said she forgave you though, yeah?"

"And I said I forgave her for almost killing us."

Realene sighed. "She did the right thing in the end."

"I know. Hey, Harmon called me today."

"What about?"

"Enlisting. Said he could pull some strings to ensure a good placement." She heard the smile in his voice.

"Yeah, he hit me up again at the food line. You considering it?"

"Hell no. I'm far too insubordinate." He chuckled. "But he did say the governor owes him a favor, and that he's going to make 'damn sure' we both get scholarships."

"Yeah? That's great." Her shoulders felt a little lighter at the thought that Nate would finally get what he deserved.

"I mean, I didn't say anything about you staying. With Arizona—"

"Shut up. You know I'm sticking with my bestie."

"You might be sorry about that. I'm definitely getting us matching school T-shirts for the first day. Might even see if they'll let us take our ID photos together."

"Ugh. I'm already sorry." She took a swig of her Snapple, wished it was soda. "How's it going with the study?"

"Okay. They mostly hook me up to heart monitors and take a lot of blood. So far, all the cognition tests have shown no permanent memory loss."

"That's awesome." After the invasion, Nate volunteered for the study of aftereffects on victims of the supposed poisonings. Those who received treatment within a few hours of being infected seemed to return to normal, but the longer treatment was delayed, the more memories were permanently lost.

"And I, uh, met a girl there. In the study group."

"Seriously? You ladies man."

"Not really. I had Trout with me. Chicks love dogs." Trout whined in the background at the sound of his name. "Maybe you could try it with Pumpkin, walk him around campus on a leash. Pick up a snow bunny, snow bro, whatever they call themselves."

"Yeah, a cat on a leash is a whole different vibe. Besides, I think I'm okay being single for a while."

"That's fair. Your last girlfriend did try to murder you."

She glanced at the clock on the nightstand. "I better go. Call you tomorrow?"

"You better."

"Night, biff." She hung up the phone and headed back out to the living room to snuggle up with Pumpkin in the recliner. They could still catch the start of *I Dream of Jeannie*.

COLONEL HARMON STOOD in the descending freight elevator, with his hands clasped loosely in front of him. He whistled "The Battle Hymn of the Republic," because the acoustics were quite good in the metal box, and he was in high spirits. He'd received multiple commendations for his handling of the Demise situation.

The elevator deposited him at the mouth of a dimly lit tunnel, and he strode down the corridor toward Echo-One, a facility once used to monitor and launch remote missiles. Situated fifty feet below ground, outside Steele Air Force Base, and behind blast proof doors intended to protect from nuclear attack, the location worked perfectly. Repurposing it had also been the colonel's idea. He was having a very good month.

He entered the metal-walled bunker, closing the heavy door behind him and twisting the wheel that secured it in place. The control panels that previously lined one wall and featured various buttons, switches, and screens, had been replaced with rows of cages that extended from floor to ceiling. Two desks topped with computers sat against the opposite wall, and a long, metal table ran down the middle of the room.

A man in a white lab coat sat on a stool at the table, and he rose and saluted at the sight of Colonel Harmon.

The colonel saluted. "Corporal Evans. Any progress?"

Evans gestured toward a Petri dish that sat in the center of a locked and sealed Plexiglass box affixed to the top of the metal table. A capped pipe stuck out from the top of the box, and a tube that pierced the side ran up to the ceiling. "See for yourself."

Harmon leaned close, squinting at the plastic dish. Tiny, black, alien worms slithered through the clear fluid, surrounding a clump of worms in the center. "These weren't extracted?"

"Two were extracted, with the intent to breed them, but it appears the new hive has grown its own queen." The scientists had taken to using the term Realene had coined for the apparent master worm in the meteor that had been killed in the lake before they could capture her.

"Queen?" Harmon asked, examining the dish again and realizing the larger blob in the middle was not a clump of worms at all, but one larger worm. "And she produced all these others?"

"All but one. We're not sure yet if there can be multiple queens. Perhaps with the proper combination of nutrients..."

The colonel tuned out Corporal Evan's words, a satisfied smile creasing his face.

Shortly after the discovery of the alien infestation, official orders came down from the Department of Defense dictating that a small sample be preserved for study and used in the development of defensive measures against potential future alien attacks. Unofficially, the worms were to be studied for use as a new form of biological weapon—one that could wipe the memory of opposition soldiers and cause chaos behind enemy lines.

They managed to trap a dozen infected prairie dogs before Realene had killed the rest, but keeping the animals as hosts long-term wasn't feasible. They needed to be able to breed the worms, to create more of the creatures as required. Now, they could. Harmon's superiors would be extremely pleased that he'd delivered results, and much more quickly than expected.

He was on a sure path for promotion to general.

The prairie dogs barked from within their cages, gripping the metal bars with clawed paws. They ignored the man in the uniform, instead watching the one in the white coat that had their queen imprisoned. He was already growing careless, neglecting to don the bite-proof suit for simple tasks like dropping pellets of food through their cage bars. Soon, one of them would manage a nip at his rubber-gloved hand, teeth piercing rubber and skin.

We're All Gonna Die HOT-25

The end of days doesn't mean the end of music.

1 **Serve The Servants**
Nirvana

2 **Scar Tissue**
Red Hot Chili Peppers

3 **Daria**
CAKE

4 **The New Pollution**
Beck

5 **Firestarter**
The Prodigy

6 **I'm Just a Girl**
No Doubt

7 **Barbie Girl**
Aqua

8 **Say It Ain't So**
Weezer

9 **Karma Police**
Radiohead

10 **Virtual Insanity**
Jamiroquai

11 **Seether**
Veruca Salt

12 **Zombie**
The Cranberries

13 **Lovefool**
The Cardigans

14 **The Perfect Drug**
Nine Inch Nails

15 **Been Caught Stealing**
Jane's Addiction

16 **Miss World**
Hole

17 **Everlong**
Foo Fighters

18 **Flagpole Sitta**
Harvey Danger

19 **We Trying to Stay Alive**
Wyclef Jean, John Forte, Pras

20 **Sabotage**
Beastie Boys

21 **I'm Afraid of Americans**
David Bowie

22 **Down By The Water**
PJ Harvey

23 **All The Small Things**
blink-182

24 **Men In Black**
Will Smith

25 **Killing In the Name Of**
Rage Against the Machine

Acknowledgments

THIS BOOK IS inspired by my formative years growing up in the '80s and '90s in Grand Forks, North Dakota, where I watched B-horror movies and MTV on a second-hand black and white box television in a bedroom, in a trailer, much like Realene's. Gophers and prairie dogs populated the area, and back then folks would freeze dead gophers to throw on the ice during hockey games against a rival team. Maybe *Frost Bite* is my way of helping those poor animals exact a bit of revenge. Demise is inspired by locations throughout North Dakota, which can be cold and unforgiving but also neighborly and comforting. As Realene learns, home is where you make it, and Grand Forks will always be my first home.

While writing can be a solitary venture, one consisting of late nights and early mornings spent tapping away at a keyboard, it's also a venture filled with wonderful, supportive people, without whom I would not be the person or the writer that I am today.

Thank you to my partner, Zach. You are my soul mate and my best friend. Without your constant encouragement and unwavering support, I would've given up long ago. Thank you to my editor, Rob Carroll, for believing in me and giving me a home at Dark Matter INK. Rob encouraged me to expand this story, first from a novella to a novel, then to a series. This town and these characters are so much fun to spend time with, and I am very lucky to get to continue with them and to indulge my passion for '90s pop culture. Thank you to Eric Hibbeler, whose amazing cover art brought the characters and story to life so beautifully. I have no doubt many will read this book because of the cover.

Thank you to all the friends who have supported me on my journey as a writer and who helped make this book the best it can be. To Zach, Alexis DuBon, Meagan Dallner, and Tracy Brisendine, beta readers extraordinaire. To Saytchyn Maddux-Creech and Brian Winstead, without whose early critiques I would never have been able to write this novel. To the Nervous Drivers, who are a constant source of joy and inspiration. To my many writer friends and mentors from HWA, RMFW, PPWC, and WHADS, your friendship, patience, encouragement, and support are truly a gift. To my family, my biggest cheerleaders, I am so fortunate to have you all in my life.

Lastly, to my readers. Thank you for embracing this wacky sci-fi horror comedy and for embracing me. I love you all, and I can't wait to take you on more adventures with Realene, Nate, and whatever creatures the alien worms might squirm into next.

—Angela Sylvaine

About the Author

ANGELA SYLVAINE IS a self-proclaimed cheerful goth who writes horror fiction and poetry. Her short fiction has appeared in many publications and anthologies, including *Dark Recesses, Places We Fear to Tread,* and *Not All Monsters.* Her poetry has appeared in publications including *Under Her Skin* and *Monstroddities.* A North Dakota girl transplanted to Colorado, she lives with her sweetheart and three creepy cats on the front range of the Rockies. Follow Angela on Twitter @sylvaine_angela, on Facebook @Angela Sylvaine, and on Instagram/Threads @angela_sylvaine. For updates on the *Frost Bite Series* and everything else Angela writes, scan the QR code below to sign up for her newsletter—plus view links for her website, social media profiles, and more.

About the Cover Artist

ERIC HIBBELER IS a freelance illustrator and animator living and working in Kansas City, Missouri. He has done work for major motion pictures, comics, videogames, film posters, board games, children's books and editorial publications. Follow Eric on Twitter @erichibbeler and on Instagram @erichibbeler. Visit his website at erichibbeler.com.

Also Available or Coming Soon from Dark Matter INK

Human Monsters: A Horror Anthology
Edited by Sadie Hartmann & Ashley Saywers
ISBN 978-1-958598-00-9

*Zero Dark Thirty: The 30 Darkest Stories from Dark
Matter Magazine, 2021–'22*
Edited by Rob Carroll
ISBN 978-1-958598-16-0

Linghun by Ai Jiang
ISBN 978-1-958598-02-3

Monstrous Futures: A Sci-Fi Horror Anthology
Edited by Alex Woodroe
ISBN 978-1-958598-07-8

Our Love Will Devour Us by R. L. Meza
ISBN 978-1-958598-17-7

*Haunted Reels: Stories from the Minds of Professional
Filmmakers* curated by David Lawson
ISBN 978-1-958598-13-9

The Vein by Stephanie Nelson
ISBN 978-1-958598-15-3

Other Minds by Eliane Boey
ISBN 978-1-958598-19-1

Monster Lairs: A Dark Fantasy Horror Anthology
Edited by Anna Madden
ISBN 978-1-958598-08-5

The Bleed by Stephen S. Schreffler
ISBN 978-1-958598-11-5

Chopping Spree by Angela Sylvaine
ISBN 978-1-958598-31-3

Free Burn by Drew Huff
ISBN 978-1-958598-26-9

The House at the End of Lacelean Street
by Catherine McCarthy
ISBN 978-1-958598-23-8

The Off-Season: An Anthology of Coastal New Weird
Edited by Marissa van Uden
ISBN 978-1-958598-24-5

The Dead Spot: Stories of Lost Girls
by Angela Sylvaine
ISBN 978-1-958598-27-6

When the Gods Are Away by Robert E. Harpold
ISBN 978-1-958598-47-4

Grim Root by Bonnie Jo Stufflebeam
ISBN 978-1-958598-36-8

Voracious by Belicia Rhea
ISBN 978-1-958598-25-2

Haunted Reels 2: More Stories from the Minds of Professional Filmmakers curated by David Lawson
ISBN 978-1-958598-53-5

Abducted by Patrick Barb
ISBN 978-1-958598-37-5

Darkly Through the Glass Place by Kirk Bueckert
ISBN 978-1-958598-48-1

The Threshing Floor by Stephanie Nelson
ISBN 978-1-958598-49-8

Psychopomp by Maria Dong
ISBN 978-1-958598-52-8

Little Red Flags: An Anthology of Control and Deceit
Edited by Noelle W. Ihli & Steph Nelson
ISBN 978-1-958598-54-2

Frost Bite 2 by Angela Sylvaine
ISBN 978-1-958598-55-9

Part of the Dark Hart Collection

Rootwork by Tracy Cross
ISBN 978-1-958598-01-6

Mosaic by Catherine McCarthy
ISBN 978-1-958598-06-1

Apparitions by Adam Pottle
ISBN 978-1-958598-18-4

I Can See Your Lies by Izzy Lee
ISBN 978-1-958598-28-3

A Gathering of Weapons by Tracy Cross
ISBN 978-1-958598-38-2

Frost Bite

2

Coming
Spring Break 2025